C000177582

ABOUT THE AUTHOR

Jeff Dowson began his career working in the theatre as an actor and a director specialising in productions of contemporary British and European playwrights.

From there he moved into television, and after early Channel 4 commissions he became an independent writer/producer/director. Screen credits include arts series, entertainment features, drama documentaries, drama series and TV films.

Turning crime novelist in 2014, he introduced Bristol private eye Jack Shepherd in *Closing the Distance*. The series developed with *Changing the Odds*, *Cloning the Hate* and *Bending the Rules*.

The Ed Grover series, set in Bristol in the years following World War 2, opened in 2018 with *One Fight At A Time*.

Born in northeast England Jeff now lives in Bristol. He is a member of BAFTA and the Crime Writers Association.

Visit: www.jeffdowson.co.uk

Published in Great Britain in 2021
By Diamond Crime

ISBN 978-1-8384026-1-7

Diamond Crime is an imprint of Diamond Books Ltd.

DIAMOND
BOOKS

Thanks to:

John Bone for his help in photographic research

Peter Nash for reading the manuscript

Staff at Bristol Central Library

All at Diamond Crime for their enthusiasm and support

Book and cover design: jacksonbone.co.uk

Cover photograph: King Square in Bristol used under licence
from the Reece Winstone Archive

Also by Jeff Dowson

For information about Diamond Crime authors
and their books, visit:
www.diamondbooks.co.uk

For Mary
Simply the best…

NEW FRIENDS
OLD ENEMIES

JEFF DOWSON

PRELUDE

The banner headline on the front page of the *Bristol Evening Post* roared **Thou Shalt Not Kill**. The copy underneath was lean and chilling…

The Prison Chaplain read the Bible to Ruby Willis at 8.40am. Fifteen minutes later, he watched as Mr Pierrepoint led her into the scaffold cell and closed the door. At noon Ruby was lowered into her grave, while the Prison Governor watched and the Chaplain read the burial service – all present, and indeed all of us not there, complicit in the breaking of the 6th Commandment.

Ruby Willis was hanged at 9 o'clock on the morning of April 1st 1950. There were demonstrators and onlookers in equal measure outside the gaol. The former, supporting the campaign to repeal capital punishment; the latter, determined to be there as the law exacted revenge on the city's notorious 'Goodtime Girl.'

The following Monday, a packed house at the ABC Cinema on Whiteladies Road watched enthralled as Humphrey Bogart and Gloria Grahame lit up the screen, in the tense melodrama *In A Lonely Place*, providing enough electricity to power the whole suburb. Those who turned up for the entire programme, watched the *Movietone News* pictures of the crowd outside the South Gloucester prison four days earlier, listening in cold satisfaction to the narration.

The life of Ruby Willis was the stuff of which headlines were made – 'Exotic and Shameless' according to *The News of the World*. She was a model, executed for the murder of her lover, Bristol club owner Ronald Eaves. Her lawyer implored Ruby to plead temporary insanity. To which she simply responded, "I took Ronnie's life. I don't want you to save mine." Lord Chief Justice Bannerman told the Jury that Ruby's defence was 'essentially non-existent'. He instructed the twelve good men and true to ignore the extreme abuse dealt out by Eaves, the assault which resulted in a miscarriage, and her poor mental health, as 'according to the law of the land this is no defence.'

She was shown no mercy. Petitions signed by thousands of people were ignored by the Home Office. Ruby Willis went to her death alone, save for the presence of half a dozen civil servants. There was no one to grieve for her.

***

The same day, in Aero Shop 1 at Filton, the launch of the latest Marshall Plan scheme was as ritzy as rationed Bristol could manage. With help from a huge chunk of American dollars, Filton boffins were about to start making jet engines for Gloster Javelins. The whole workforce, most of Bristol Chamber of Commerce, local worthies and faces, and a swathe of USAF 3 and 4 Star Generals, were invited to the bash.

There were speeches, toasts, steak, and fruit and cream. Everyone agreed that the future glowed with promise.

CHAPTER ONE

Sam Nicholson was red-faced, heavily built and around five feet eight. Leader of the City Council, business man, fixer and long-time fence; he was sitting alone in the office he shared with the Mayor.

Bristol Council House stood on the corner of what remained of Broad Street and Corn Street. The building was flanked by a series of huge craters, some of them partly filled by the debris they had disgorged when hit by the Luftwaffe. Miraculously, the big, bold Victorian edifice built in the 1830s, had stayed upright, while the buildings around it had crumbled under the onslaught of incendiary bombs, and later, subsidence.

No longer scarred by rubble and bombed out buildings, simply full of gaps and holes where the buildings had been, the city was broke. And the question which now paralysed all council action and stifled debate was – new homes or restored places of business? Pre-fabricated houses were going up at a miserably slow rate. Something close to twenty percent of the city's population was still bivouacking in the spare rooms of relatives, straining even the best of family relationships. The problem was clear as day; people needed homes. But even pre-fabs cost money. And no money was available, because city centre business had no place to work, and the council was earning no revenue.

Sam Nicholson had worked hard to get the red plush upholstery under his arse. He was too old to be called up in 1940. So, he stayed in Bristol and kept his home fire burning, with some advantage to himself. Today however, he was not in the sunniest of moods. He ran the fingers of his left hand through his comb-over and scratched his scalp. He could always smell trouble, and right now, the hair in his nostrils was standing on end. He needed to make some calls, but it was best not to do so from the office.

As if on cue, the phone on his desk rang. He picked up the receiver and immediately panicked.

"Why the fuck did you call me here?" He listened for a second or two. "He's what?... Slowly, slowly..." His eyes popped and his facial muscles began to twitch. Explanation over, he said, "Alright. This is no fucking way to do business." He listened again. "No..." Then yelled into the mouthpiece. "No no no, leave me to deal with this."

He slammed the receiver down and stared across the room. "Fuck. Fuck fuck fuck."

He got up out of his chair, grabbed his jacket from the bentwood coat stand near the door and left the office.

Since the war, a series of one-way traffic systems devised to make journeys across the city smoother, had grown like Topsy. But Bristol traffic had never been speedy before the blitz, and now the Highways Department was baffled and desperate. A smaller lobby than the citizens who had no roofs over their heads, Nicholson mused, but a bunch of irritating fuckers nonetheless. It took him half an hour to get to Albert Vale. And less than a minute to feel his gorge rising. He parked, got out of the Rover and fell to considering, yet again, what the hell Rodney Pride was doing to repay the city council's generosity.

Albert Vale had been a community of tiny terraced houses, bordering narrow streets to the south of Temple Meads Station, until January 3rd 1941. That night, the Luftwaffe launched an eight-hour onslaught on the city. Two bombers overshot their targets and dumped one hundred kilos of high explosive on the citizens of Albert Vale. Now the area was a flattened fifteen acres of rough, stony land, ringed by a chain link fence.

Rodney Pride had persuaded the council to sell him three acres for 'light industrial' use. The fantasy with which he magicked the City Planning Department promised a mini industrial park of warehouses, car workshops and small manufacturing sheds. He must have crooned better than Perry Como during his hour in the council chamber, because he got the three acres for a song. As yet, unsurprisingly, there was no development; save for the newly built headquarters of *Prides Rides*. A garage with offices above it, another alongside, and enough space on the site to park 30 cars.

At the window of his office, Pride grinned as he watched Nicholson muttering to himself. He waved as the Council Leader looked up at him from the tarmac.

Pride was short and wore shoes with lifts. By the most generous of opinions he was no oil painting. Ginger haired, with huge eyebrows, his teeth were uneven and he had a pronounced over-bite. To compensate for all this, he had bullied his way through life. Unmarried and never to be the first choice of any eligible spinster, his sex life consisted of weekly visits to prostitutes who could manage to get through an hour with this embittered, social deviant.

He had hated the war. Conscripted into the army, just one eighth of an inch taller than the minimum height, he came home with his army issue Webley .38 still in his kitbag, raging at the injustice of it all. He ignored the VE Day celebrations. Instead, he proceeded to call in favours he was owed by people terrified of him, and who had fervently hoped he would be killed in the conflict. He extorted a few hundred quid to buy a couple of taxi cabs. Now he had thirty of them and no competitors on the streets of south Bristol.

Prides Rides was a legitimate concern. Squeaky clean. The proprietor made sure of that. The books were done by a highly respected firm of Queen Square accountants, happy to take double fees for dealing with someone they contrived to meet only once a year. And with petrol now off ration, the firm was set to expand yet again.

Nicholson walked into the office, stood in front of Pride's desk and bellowed at him.

"It's not what we agreed. And you're now trying to extort money out of my wife's nephew."

The greengrocery in question, was a shop on a disputed corner in Windmill Hill. An area which had been designated Nicholson territory until Sam decided he no longer had an interest in it. Sam's brother in law had chosen to diversify, handed the shop over to his son, who put the business in his wife's name and changed the sign above the door.

Pride leaned back in his leather swivel chair and spread his arms wide.

"Calm down Sam. It was a mistake. It won't happen again."

"You're fucking right it won't."

"For God's sake man, sit down."

Nicholson burbled into silence. He sat in the armchair facing the desk.

"That's better." Pride waited until Nicholson was settled. "The place changed hands and one of my associates saw an opportunity. He didn't know, hell I didn't know, he was a relative of yours. It's all been ironed out now, so let's forgive and forget eh?"

Nicholson grunted in agreement. Pride beamed at him.

"Good."

He stood up and stepped across the office to a sideboard with a drinks tray on it. He picked up a bottle of malt whisky.

"This is your tipple isn't it?"

Nicholson nodded. "Thanks."

Pride poured a generous double, handed the glass to Nicholson and moved back to his chair.

"Now, as you're here, there's something I'd like you to take a look at."

He pulled out a drawer in his desk, produced a sliver snuff box, and placed it front of Nicholson.

"Georgian. Made around 1786, apparently. The hallmark's underneath."

Nicholson put his glass down, picked the box up and turned it over.

"Where'd you get it from?"

"Nowhere local. Don't worry".

Nicholson looked across the desk.

7

"I got it from a bloke who owed me some money," Pride said.

Nicholson turned the box the right way up and opened the lid.

"Where did he get it?"

"I've no idea."

Nicholson gave him his best 'this is me you're talking to' look. Pride reciprocated.

"Come on Sam... How much?"

Nicholson closed the lid and put the box back on the desk.

"On a good day, given the right circumstances... Thirty quid."

"Bollocks. It's worth three times that."

"So, take it to Clifton Auctions and let them sell it."

Pride grinned across the desk. "Don't be too clever Sam."

Nicholson sucked at his teeth. "I'll give you thirty-five."

"Sixty," Pride suggested.

"Forty-five," Nicholson said.

"Fifty,"

"Forty-five, is as far as I'll go."

"Fucking crook," Pride said.

Nicholson dug his wallet out of the inside pocket of his jacket. Fished around in it, gathered up a fistful of notes, counted out nine fivers and handed them over.

"Meanwhile, I'm working on the scheme of a lifetime," Pride said. "It'll make us a fortune. I just need you to rubber stamp the project."

Nicholson looked alarmed. Pride stared at him. The alarm morphed into mild terror, Pride's stare into a wide smile. Nicholson managed two words.

"What project?"

"I want to buy the old Scarlet Fever Hospital in Brockley Wood."

This was a massive surprise. The news that anybody would want to buy the place was a minor miracle. The fact that it was Rodney Pride however, sucked all potential joy out of the prospect.

"Why?"

"Make yourself available. I'll keep you posted."

Back in the yard, Nicholson looked at his watch. 4.35. He decided he might as well go home. Give himself time to get into the right mood for the evening ahead. His wife had dinner planned for some relatives on the take. Another bunch of idle bastards he was expected to support.

He got into the Rover. Pride watched him from his office window.

CHAPTER TWO

"Help me out with this, Ed."

Lieutenant Stephen Lee Berger was an eight-years in, career soldier. A West Point graduate, nephew of a Colonel sitting behind a desk back in West Virginia. Tall, straight backed and handsome, with the movie star looks of Gregory Peck. He was at the office window, looking out over the runway to the Cotswolds beyond. The late April afternoon was grey, damp and dull. Fairford was silent as the grave.

"You've been here four months now. You're in no hurry to go home. I've conceded that and helped you out with every excuse to stay. Now I want something in return."

The Adjutant's office was a fourteen feet square, brick-built hut, with a corrugated tin roof. The accommodation was basic. A wooden desk with a swivel chair behind it. Two three drawer filing cabinets to the left of it. Bookshelves on the wall each side of the door. And in one corner of the room, a cast iron stove with the chimney reaching up to the roof and on through a hole in it. The stove was burning wood and the office was warm. There were matching battered armchairs each side of it.

Sergeant Major Ed Grover sat in one of them, staring down at his knees. He raised his head and looked at Berger.

"And what would that be Sir?"

The Adjutant turned back into the room.

"I need the benefit of your wisdom," he said.

"In what area?"

"Morale."

Always a problem with a bunch of people in transit. And multiplied tenfold by several battalions of infantry.

Almost to a man, the 21st was bored. Most of the GIs had been in Europe since 1943. With a great adventure and purpose – to rid the continent of the most inglorious regime in five hundred years of history. Two days after Grover's twenty-third birthday, the 21st began the embattled slog across every yard of ground from Omaha Beach to the River Elbe. Grover got his first stripe after Baker Company broke out of Bastogne. Another after his platoon led the charge over the Saar River. As he slogged eastwards, his brother Arnold, building Sherman Tanks in Detroit, wrote to tell him his mother had died of liver cancer. The letter got lost and was eventually pinned to the side of his jeep by a corporal from Div Comms, two weeks after the funeral. He replied to the letter, stitched on his third chevron and kept going.

By June 1945 Baker and Charlie Companies were in the charnel house that was West Berlin. Over the course of eleven months, Grover had morphed from scared rookie into experienced killer. Close up, he had seen the whites of his enemies' eyes. In summer 1945, he looked into the faces of bewildered mothers and children, sick, traumatised and homeless, and tried to help win the peace.

Four and a half years later, on New Year's Eve 1949, the 21st flew from Templehof airport to Fairford in

Gloucestershire. Those waiting to be repatriated home sat around with nothing to do. The weather was foul and all the comforts of home were conspicuous by their absence in the Cotswolds. Boredom morphed into restlessness, which in turn generated night long poker games and eventually, debts and disagreements.

Grover stayed clear and found things to do.

With help from his best buddy, Master Sergeant Henry Whelan, he re-built a Jeep and christened her *Salome*. On leave in Bristol, he re-connected with the family he had met during the blitz in 1941. After a night of ferocious incendiary bombing, Grover had wandered, totally lost, through the ruins of rain-soaked Bedminster. Ellie Morrison, her husband Arthur and young son Harry, took him into their home, dried his clothes, put his shattered wits back together and gave him sanctuary. Grover and Ellie wrote to each other regularly until May 1944, by which time he was camped on the south coast along with another 156,000 GIs waiting for the word 'Go'.

He and Ellie wrote again during his time in Berlin. And on his arrival in Fairford, he pitched up on the Morrison's doorstep as soon as he could scrounge a 48-hour-pass. A now grown up Harry was in trouble. Ellie asked for Grover's help. He owed the Morrisons. It was the thing to do. In the process, he made connections high and low, as well as a lasting impression on the local constabulary.

The USA and Tomah Wisconsin were thousands of miles and light years away.

Grover had nothing to go home to. So, if helping out the Adjutant gave him reason to stay where he wanted to be…

"The men need something to do, Sir," he said.

"Clearly," Berger said.

"Hobby sessions, monthly films and baseball games don't hack it."

"So…?"

"I suggest you lift restrictions regarding fraternisation with the locals."

Berger stared at him. Speechless for a moment or two.

"Let the men loose on the women of three counties?"

"No. Invite the women here."

Berger's eyes widened. Grover moved swiftly on.

"Able Company has a five-piece band. They've been practising out in the emergency hanger on the south western perimeter."

"Have you heard them?"

"Yeah. Turns out, Sergeant Malin's a drummer. He's gathered together a piano player, tenor sax, clarinet and double base. I've offered them Private Ronnie Dean as a vocalist. Do you know him?"

"Yes. Does impressions of Johnnie Ray and Frankie Lane."

Berger moved back to his desk. Reached down, adjusted a bronze paperweight of a rearing horse and stared at it for a moment or two. Then he looked up at Grover.

"Okay Ed. So long as you run the show."

Grover stared at him.

"I'd rather not, if you don't mind, Sir."

"Take it or leave it Sergeant Major."

Grover took it.

***

Master Sergeant Henry Whelan was the boss of the Motor Pool. A black Texan, six feet three inches tall and a tough, muscular, thirteen stones. Big and strong and quietly spoken, he never had to raise his voice to anyone. And he knew about women. In times past, wherever the infantry ended up, the moment there was a break in hostilities Henry had appeared with a girl on his arm. He and Grover first met in Bayeux two weeks after D Day, where Whelan introduced him to twin sisters he had encountered in a newly liberated bakery. The man had magic.

Now he was running the most prestigious poker game on the base. Players were admitted to the bi-weekly events by invitation only; the proceedings conducted with the kind of security that would have outshone Checkpoint Charlie. Whelan even had MPs on the payroll, policing the area within in a hundred yards radius of the Jeep workshop. The 'Snowdrops' received ten percent of the house take.

Grover shared his problem with Whelan, and together the two men set about invigorating every second Saturday night. Grover got on with base organisation. Henry sent out invitations. The first dance was scheduled for Saturday, May 1st.

The band, now calling itself *Fairford Swing*, was excused regular duty and began rehearsing seriously. And gradually, the noise coming out of the emergency hanger, grew smoother and richer. The musicians played swing, Ronnie delivered R&B and a kind of country boogie-woogie. Somehow, it worked.

Fairford got in the mood.

While Private Bradley Parsons applied for his fourth weekend pass since his return from Berlin.

"You're stretching the spirit of the rules Private," Lieutenant Berger said.

"I appreciate that, Sir. But there's a lot to do in the house, Sir."

Parsons stood ramrod straight in front of the Adjutant. The nailed-on picture of a grade A GI. Just under six feet, dark hair, crew cut and wide smile. The sort of guy who would go out of his way to help an old lady cross the road.

He had woven a convincing story since his return from Berlin. His sister-in-law's cousin Margaret, had moved to England in 1938, after accepting a proposal from a Bristol draper on holiday in the US. A whirlwind courtship. She lived in the south of the city, in a small semi at the end of a partially blitzed street. That bit was true. The rest was embellishment. The house, although shaken to its foundations by a bomb blast, was still standing and needed a lot of work to make it safe and habitable once again. That had been accomplished, finally, but the interior was still a mess. The family budget was pushed to the limit, so any work in the house which could be done free was worth its weight in gold. Surely the good old US of A could free him occasionally, to help his sister-in-law's cousin, him being a carpenter back home. That last bit was true also. Berger knew that Parsons was a chancer. But in the interest of Anglo-US relations was prepared to accept his word. And in return, Parsons was happy to make sure he was always checked back into Fairford dead on time.

He accepted the weekend pass with a smile and a razor-sharp salute, and left the Adjutant's office.

CHAPTER THREE

It was high noon. Sam Nicholson's morning had gone to rats. He was at odds with the Mayor, yet again. This time over the proposed development budget he had suggested for a section of Broadmead. The mayor was no pushover and had queried some 'disbursements' in the council leader's proposal. Fuming, Sam had watched a carefully constructed little earner cut from the budget.

His temper was by no means under control. He was in the driving seat of his Rover; on his way down the A370 towards Weston Super Mare, as pissed off as he could remember. He snarled to himself, for the umpteenth time, then leaned forward and bellowed through the windscreen.

"Where the hell is this fucking lane end?"

Brockley Wood, several square miles of glades, combes and cultivated forest lining the road, had not been accessible for years. The Old Scarlet Fever Isolation Hospital, or rather what was left of it, sat in the middle of the wood. Closed since the summer of 1939, it was now a major embarrassment to Bristol City Council, who had taken over the hospital after a fire burned most of it to the ground. With its patients re-housed, North Somerset Hospital Company was strapped for cash and only too pleased to be rid of the place. However, the war had wrecked a succession of half-arsed and hurriedly laid plans for the site - even the brand new NHS had no desire to take it on. And now, eleven years, endless meetings, and four buildings sub-committees later, it had become Sam Nicholson's personal white elephant.

It was this burden, which had driven him to listen to Rodney Pride. Well that, and the prospect of making money.

There was a break in the hedge just ahead on the left.

"This must be it," he said. "At fucking last!!"

He swung the Rover onto a lane with grass growing up the middle. The car bottomed out. A stone on the surface wacked the silencer box on the exhaust. He negotiated the holes and the broken verge for about half a mile, until he saw the old hospital iron gates in front of him. They were open. He drove into the courtyard and pulled up.

Pride was already there, leaning against the bonnet of a cream and brown Pontiac Chieftain Coupé.

"Fucking poser..." Nicholson muttered and got out of the Rover.

Pride stood up straight. Nicholson did a survey. The place looked like the Messines Ridge had in 1917, except the holes in the ground weren't so deep.

"So?..." he began.

Pride picked up his cue.

"You have a Projects Finance meeting tomorrow night. Here's the offer." He handed Nicholson a piece of paper with the figure on it. "The Finance Committee will bite your arm off."

Nicholson stared at the paper. Then looked back at Pride in disbelief.

"Don't be ridiculous. That's bugger all for Christ's sake."

"Anybody else offering anything?"

"No. But that doesn't mean we can give the place away."

"You haven't been able to do that in eleven years."

Nicholson took time to sniff, exhale, look around and think.

"Come on Sam, agree in principle," Pride said. "And I'll tell you the real deal."

Nicholson acquiesced, and ten minutes later he was roped.

Pride give him a conducted tour of the only part of the building to survive the fire – Wards 3 and 4, on opposing sides of a corridor leading to what had been the kitchen, a staff lounge and a couple of store rooms. The beds, five in ward 3 and seven in 4, were as the last patients had left them. Years of dust and cobwebs apart, the place was all but ready to re-open for business.

Pride pointed to the pocket where Nicholson had stored his paper offer.

"That price, buys us all of this. It's what we intend to do with it, that's going to make us a small fortune."

"I didn't realise they'd left so much stuff behind," Nicholson said.

"The water and drains still work," Pride said. "Toilets still flush. No electricity of course, we'll have to get generators in." He pointed through the window to his right. "The phone line can be reconnected from that pole there."

"But it's a hospital for God's sake. I mean, you're not going to run a -"

"Not quite. But the next best thing."

He offered no more, waiting for Nicholson to take the bait. Eventually he did.

"Go on..."

"Babies," Pride said. "We're going to turn this into a maternity hospital."

Nicholson stared at him. Pride waited, in no hurry to elaborate. He watched Sam's face twitch as the idea took hold. Then he went on to explain.

"Let me tell you one of the by-products of the miserable time we now live in. It's this… Regiments of un-married, pregnant women. Thrown out by their families. Living on their own in shithole single rooms. Too terrified to use bottles of gin and the old wire coat hanger, or to visit some backstreet bedroom and hand themselves over to an abortionist. So here we are. The saving grace."

Nicholson found his voice. "The illegal, saving grace."

"Well yes. But the right service, at the right time, in the right place." He opened his arms and spread them wide. "Here..."

"And doctors, and midwives, and nurses?"

"Don't need that many. Twelve beds, twelve clients. We'll turn one of the rooms along the corridor into the staff area. Leave a couple of beds in there for overnighters. One of the store rooms will become an office and we'll convert the old staff lounge into a birthing room. A dozen members of staff will do the trick. Along with somebody else to run the place."

"Erm..."

Nicholson looked at Pride, who grinned in response.

"We're going to make a fortune."

"How?"

Back in the day, Nicholson had been an accountant whose grasp of double entry book keeping was legendary. And so far, while all this sounded acceptably philanthropic – albeit not in an entirely legal sort of way – there was no profit he could see. Pride looked straight into his eyes.

"We're going to sell the babies."

Nicholson sat down on the bed behind him, gobsmacked, unable to say anything. Meanwhile, the man standing next to him was on a roll.

"Staffing is easy," Pride grinned at him. "For a start, we can recruit armfuls of abortionists."

Nicholson stared at him horrified.

"What?..."

"Give them the right conditions to work in," Pride went on. "And pay them well. At least, more than they charge for their potions and tubes and dubious efforts in damp bedsits."

"Nurses and midwives?"

"More of the same," Pride said.

"And doctors?..."

"A struck off GP or two. Plenty of them about as well."

"All of whom cost money," Nicholson said.

"Only a percentage of what we'll sell the babies for. There are more couples desperate for babies than you can shake a stick at. Infertile newlyweds, forty something year olds who lost their sons in Europe after D Day, women who have already had miscarriages and know they can't produce... No shortage of customers Sam. And look at the service we can provide here. Five-star accommodation, clean beds, experienced staff. And no pills, gin bottles, or coat hangers. You couldn't get better in the BRI maternity wing."

"The major difference being Rodney, is that what you propose is against the law."

Pride grinned at his putative partner.

"We have to think big Sam. Like winners. This decade's going to be a belter. And we are in a great position to profit by it. This place is in in the middle of nowhere. Long forgotten. Who's going to come poking around?" He paused for a beat or two, then wound up. "What do you say?"

In spite of feeling horrified by all this, Nicholson heard himself say "How long will it take to set up?"

"We can have the place cleaned up and working in no time at all; including the bathrooms and the kitchen. We don't have to bother the electricity board. There are two generators in the *Pride's Rides* workshop, ready to be moved. Power problem solved. The only other thing we'll need is a phone line. We'll have to get the GPO to pull its finger out and install one. You can exert some pressure there. Tell them the building contractors need to be able to communicate with suppliers?"

"What building contractors?"

"Oh for fuck's sake, Sam. Any fucking pretend labourer..." He walked over to a window. Pointed across the ground. "That can look like a building site in a couple of days. And we'll put a cabin out there, with a couple of desks in it. Add some box files, phoney paperwork, shelves, filing cabinets. The GPO can run a line in, like they do with every other building site. Then we'll turn the place around and have it operating within a month."

Nicholson had downgraded horrified to fearful. Which morphed into nervous, then back into fearful again.

"Well yes erm..."

"Look, I know the phone palaver is a bit of a risk. Unfortunately, we need a line. But once the GPO hook up our phony business, that'll be it. We'll disguise the place."

Nicholson was shaking his head, but Pride was on a roll.

"We'll put an iron gate and some barbed wire across the entrance from the road. With a big sign. *PRIVATE PROPERTY, KEEP OUT. SITE AQUIRED FOR RE-DEVELOPMENT.*"

"Okay," Nicholson said. "But what happens when people start to notice vehicles and staff coming through that gate and begin to wonder?"

"We'll only use it at the beginning, while we're bringing in the generators and the stuff we need to set everything up. Two visits at most."

"Cleaners?"

"Our own blokes. Be a change for them for a few days. After that, once the staff are here, they'll share the chores."

"And then?..."

"Then we'll close the place up tight. At the back of the ward, there's a path through the woods to the road

23

between Cleeve and Wrington. A country lane, with a bus stop about two hundred yards from the end of the path. That's how everybody will get to work. We will have to use the front gate when we do the turnaround. Women out and in. Once every couple of months."

Nicholson was trying to like the idea now, but he was still struggling a bit. He thought of something else to worry about.

"Surely there'll come a point when too many people will know about this scheme," he suggested. "All the once pregnant mothers for a start."

"They'll be footloose and fancy free," Pride said. "Paid off and living miles away. Part of the agreement."

"Not one that you can enforce."

"But a situation we keep an eye on. Alright, it'll end up costing more, but not much." He paused and watched the clockwork ticking in Nicholson's head. "Of course, this is something we won't be able to keep going. Maybe only eighteen months, two years. By which time, we'll have enough money to close the place up and figure out something else to with the site. And while we're here helping to create a new generation of God-fearing citizens, we'll keep the council planning department's head spinning with schemes for workshops, housing, old people's homes... the list is endless." He could sense the clockwork in his partners head winding down. "It's a win win Sam."

Nicholson was getting there. Pride summed up.

"Our clients will never know where the babies come from. The business with them will be done in an office somewhere. Your job to find one. Small and simple, no signs on the door. We'll hand over the kids, complete with birth certificates; the clients will hand over bags full of dosh. Hell Sam, the office could be staffed, occupied and running within days. And within months, we could be counting the money."

Nicholson walked the length of the ward. Turned, paused, then walked back to Pride. Smiling. Now he was hooked.

He drove back into the city, a mounting excitement getting the better of all good sense and earlier misery. In the Council House, he sought out the Finance Director and acquainted him with Rodney Pride's offer.

The following evening, the FD announced he had a last-minute item to place on the agenda and relayed the offer to the committee. Sam, pretending he had no part in this, sat on his velvet cushion his insides in uproar. Nine minutes later, the offer was accepted.

He climbed the stairs to his office, sat down and stared at the phone. Then screwed his courage to the sticking place and phoned *Pride's Rides*. It rang unanswered. Nicholson ended the call, trembling from head to foot. The phone burst into life before he took his hand from the receiver. He breathed in and lifted it.

"Sorry about that," Pride said. "Otherwise engaged... Well, how did it go?"

Nicholson exhaled. "It went through on the nod."

There was a mighty bellow down the line.

"Fan... fucking... tastic."

Pride waited for his partner to say something more. Disappointed by the lack of response he went on.

"I called the GPO earlier. Took your name in vain. Said this development was just what the council wished to support…"

He wasn't able to see the receiver trembling in Nicholson's hand.

"The engineers are putting in a line the day after tomorrow. And the entrance from the main road will be locked as soon as the taxis have delivered our first guests."

"You didn't waste any time."

"At this rate, stage two will take no more than a few days. I've got the head of the unit lined up. Doctor Havers."

"Where did you find him?"

"All you need to know Sam, is he's a proper doctor. And he's going to hire a matron. Bloody brilliant. We've started work on the site. You ought to go up there and have a look."

"No thanks," Nicholson said. "I'll pass. I don't want to be there."

"Oh cheer up, for Christ's sake. And bend your mind to the search for an office."

Nicholson shouted down the line.

"I'll do it Rodney, how many more times?... I'll do it."

He rang off. In Pride's office, the line clicked and buzzed. He took the receiver away from his ear and stared at it.

"Gutless prick," he muttered and put the receiver back in its cradle.

CHAPTER FOUR

May Day at Fairford was as dull and despairing as all the repatriation promises and squad expectations. An early morning mist clamped itself around the Cotswolds and refused to let go. The temperature spent all day struggling to six degrees above freezing. By early evening, it was a couple below.

Not low enough, however, to discourage Henry Whelan's guests. He laid on trucks from the Motor Pool to Malmesbury, Cirencester and Swindon. And to ferry their important cargoes, three privates he could trust not to drink too much.

By 7.30 in the evening, Fairford was ready to go.

Grover and Whelan stepped out of the Sergeant's Mess into persistent rain and walked across the concrete towards Hanger 5. Whelan shivered in the cold. Unlike Grover, who came from one of the coldest states in the union, he had never got used to European weather.

"This damp seeps into your bones like guilt," he said.

Four MPs, the peaks of their white snowdrop caps low over their eyes, sat in a jeep stationed by the wicket gate of the hanger. Grover had persuaded them to remain outside. Nothing more calculated to put a damper on things than a parade of Snowdrops around the dance hall.

Charlie Company had a resident designer in Claude Rattenbury. Claude had been a set dresser in Hollywood before the war and he had taken on the challenge of Hanger 5. He had transformed the place into a night club, building a band stage out of engine pallets in front of a section of hanger wall he painted white. He had managed to assemble a ground row of coloured lights on the floor behind the stage, which lit the wall in red, white and blue. The bar was set up along the wall opposite the band stage, backed by red, white and blue drapes. Claude had raided the Baker Company mess and looted a couple of dozen tables which he arranged in front of the bar in zigzag rows. His team had strung lines of coloured 40-watt bulbs through the roof girders, which hung down in loops like Christmas streamers from a ceiling. The *Coconut Grove* it wasn't. But it came damn close.

Fairford Swing opened with *Bugle Call Rag.* Grover had listened to it in rehearsal and thought it a tad ambitious. But the five-piece made it through the number and the evening got under way. *In the Mood* followed, to substantial applause. Then Private Dean stepped up to the mic and knocked out a version of *Let's Face the Music and Dance.* By which time, the crowd was on the floor and doing just that.

Grover and Whelan began to relax.

"Are we laid back enough to allow ourselves a drink?" Whelan asked.

Grover led the way to the bar.

Two black corporals from Easy Company, Clinton Lee and Walton Mills, were the 6th's lindy hop kings. The real deal. Natural, fluid, their moves connecting seamlessly. Dipping and swinging round the floor instinctively, flowing like a quart of Havoline. Poetry in motion.

By 9.30, there was not much poetry about Private First-Class Harvey Vanderbilt. He had been drinking steadily all night. Recently passed over for promotion again, he loathed his one stripe; like it was an arm tattoo with his ex-wife's name on it. Big, burly and neck-less, miserable, disgruntled and as bored as it was possible to be with England, he wanted to be home – even though home was a grubby trailer park in Canton, Mississippi. He didn't like the British weather either. In fact, just about everything conspired to frustrate the hell out of him. And tonight, he was pissed out of his mind and pissed off at the whole world.

He watched Lee and Mills dancing with the two best looking women in the room. He knew that the lindy hop was merely the preliminary to getting laid. That was the mission and the two men were seventy-five percent of the way there. Exotic, that's what they were to the local broads. Black sweat-backs were all they were at home. They dug ditches and drains and laid cement. They travelled in the back seats of buses. They couldn't eat, drink, sit down or shit anywhere near whites. They used different entrances for shops and bars and toilets. Some they couldn't get into at all. As for black women... Only good for one thing, well three, if you counted cooking and cleaning. And that was how it should be in this fucking country.

The man sitting next to him, Private Larry Toomes, had matched Vanderbilt drink for drink and he was ready to thump anyone who suggested he should not have another.

He was a shorter than his buddy, but considerably wider. He could not take his eyes off the shaking female hips and the thighs exposed as the skirts swirled. He stood up to get a better look. Swayed on his feet.

Out on the dance floor, the crowd had bowed to the brilliance of the two couples and moved back to form a circle which ringed the virtuoso performances. The two girls were now matching the skill of their partners. Moving in close, swinging away and whirling back, to be caught and lifted and swung through the air then down to the floor again, hitting the beat dead centre. The band went through the chorus, then the middle eight and then the chorus again. The audience on the floor clapped and cheered.

From the bar, Grover saw Vanderbilt get to his feet. Watched him kick back the chair he had been sitting on and fall over the table in front of him. He nudged Whelan.

Toomes helped Vanderbilt to his feet again and both began to sway in unison. People sitting at tables around them shifted in their seats. One soldier took his girl by the arm and moved away.

Grover and Whelan knew what was coming. They moved towards the dance floor. Vanderbilt and Toomes staggered and stumbled their way through the tables and chairs of front of them. It took some time, accompanied as it was by a hefty amount of swearing and drinker shoving.

The piano player saw what was happening too. He stood up at the piano, looked across the dance floor, saw Whelan on the move and sat down again. The base player monitored this, swung his base and turned to face the drummer. Sergeant Malin had seen the developing commotion too and nodded at the base player. The rest of the musicians appeared oblivious to the events. Malin thought 'What the hell, the band always plays on.'

Vanderbilt stumbled on to the dance floor, hauled himself upright and stared point blank into Whelan's black face. His eyes rolled and popped, as recognition dawned. Whelan shouted something at him he could not hear above the music and the noise generated by the crowd on the floor. Vanderbilt swung his right arm in a wide arc, aiming for the left side of Whelan's jaw.

Whelan would have seen the hook coming wearing sunglasses in the dark. He simply lifted his left arm and blocked the swing. Vanderbilt's wrist slammed into his upper arm, deadening Whelan's elbow and sending vibrations up into his shoulder. But he did not need his left arm any more. He balled his right fist, dipped his right shoulder and drove straight and hard into the space underneath Vanderbilt's ribcage.

There was bellow of pain from behind him. He swivelled the upper half of his body and looked back over his left shoulder. Toomes was falling to his knees, Grover hanging on to the right arm he had just dislocated from Toomes' shoulder. Grover released the arm and Toomes yelled again. Whelan nodded his thanks. Grover waved his right hand in acknowledgement. Whelan turned back to Vanderbilt, who was now kneeling on the dance floor. He placed the palm of his right hand on Vanderbilt's neck and pushed down hard. Vanderbilt's knees slid from under him and he met the floor with his forehead. He grunted, collapsed and then rolled over; unconscious, blood streaming from a wound under his hair line.

There were those in the crowd on the dance floor who could not fail to see what was going on. They simply ignored it. The spectacle in the centre of the floor was the entertainment. The dancers kept on dancing and the band played on.

Whelan hauled the unconscious Vanderbilt to his feet, put his right arm through the guy's legs and swung his torso up over his shoulders into a fireman's lift. Toomes, breathing hard and wheezing in pain and trying to support his right shoulder, simply did as Grover ordered. People still at their tables cleared a pathway, watched the quartet pass by and move to the wicket gate.

Around the dance floor, the scattered tables were collected and put back into position by the drinkers who had been sitting at them. They sat down again. And suddenly, it was like nothing had happened. The band played the refrain again, followed it with one more chorus and brought the dancing display to a breathless halt. The crowd ringing the dance floor, applauded and yelled and whistled. Those who needed their glasses re-filling, moved to the bar.

Whelan dumped the comatose Vanderbilt on the floor by the wicket gate, went out into the rain and called the Snowdrops. Grover offered to re-set Toomes' dislocated shoulder. The response was a roar of protest. He roared again, when one of the Snowdrops accidentally on purpose thumped his shoulder as he was escorted out to the jeep. Witnesses would have applauded. Toomes and Vanderbilt were universally considered lower than pond scum.

***

There were repercussions, of course. It took a day or two for Grover and Whelan to clear themselves of any responsibility for the commotion. Vanderbilt and Toomes got a month each in the Brig. Everybody on the base, from the CO down to the lowest grunt, had at least one grudge against Vanderbilt and Toomes. So nobody cared what happened to them. What did piss everybody off however, was that the future dance programme was put under revision. Punishment way above and beyond, was the common consensus. And endorsed by a whole swathe of Westcountry womanhood, who would not get the 'Luckies', the stockings and the booze they knew had been on offer.

Meanwhile, repatriation was delayed again. Nobody was going home to the USA.

CHAPTER FIVE

"Read this Sergeant Major…"

Lieutenant Berger pushed a piece of paper across the top of his desk. Grover picked up the typed sheet, stared at it with some suspicion, then looked up at the Adjutant. Berger nodded at him.

"Okay, you've taken a couple of days to think about this."

He paused. Grover scanned the page in front of him, put it back on the desk and looked up again. Berger continued.

"You've made it clear you want to stay in this neck of the woods. Well… the USAF is expected to provide a liaison officer for the Bristol Javelin engines project. No flyer on this base relishes the responsibility. So, our superiors have suggested that an Army officer who served with distinction during the late nonsense, and has a feel for the locality, should get the gig. Which makes you *The Man*. And if you want to take this on…"

He slid another three pages, stapled together, across the desk.

"Rules and regulations. Memorise them, and whatever the hell you do, don't break them."

Grover speed read the pages. Then leaned back in his chair. Berger's tone softened.

"I know you'll do well in the job, Ed."

"Sir."

"And finally…" Berger slid another page towards him. "This is about you and the 21st."

Grover spun the paper round on the desk.

"Just to remind you you're still in this man's army. Sign that one."

"Yes, Sir."

Grover signed his name in a box at the bottom of the sheet. Pushed it back across the desk and stood up. Berger checked the signature and held out his right hand. Grover shook it.

"Thank you, Sir."

"The best of luck, Sergeant Major."

Grover saluted and left the office. Still not out of uniform, but still on European soil. And officially in Bristol.

***

Blenheim Villas, Cumberland Road, sat facing a footbridge which crossed the river to Southville. Five small town houses, each of them with three floors, the top one an attic conversion, betrayed by the small dormer windows. There was a handwritten sign in the downstairs window of number 1.

No Blacks No Dogs No Irish.

Grover pulled *Salome* into the kerb outside number 5, opened the wooden gate, walked the half dozen paces to the front door and pressed the first-floor bell. The sound of footsteps racing down the stairs was followed by a moment's commotion in the hall. Then Rachel opened the door and beamed from ear to ear.

"Ed Grover," she said.

Grabbed him by the coat lapels and dragged him over the threshold. He picked her up, twirled her around a couple of times and put her back on the floor.

"Hey soldier. What you doing with my lady?"

Still holding on to Rachel, Grover turned to face Leroy Winston, the imposing black man from the top flat.

"Leroy," he said. "It's good to see you."

"And you Bro."

Grover let go of Rachel, stepped to Winston's outstretched hand, took it in his and allowed himself to be pulled into an embrace. Rachel watched the moment of reunion and smiled.

A smart, bright and funny brunette, Rachel's husky contralto fronted the six-piece house band at *Club El Paradis*. Winston was the club bouncer, and developing into a promising welterweight across town at the *Albion Gym* – owned and operated by Blenheim Villas' landlord Roland Bevan.

From whom apparently, Grover had to pick up the keys to the house and the ground floor flat.

"He would like to give them to you personally," Rachel said.

"Really? I figured you'd have them," Grover said.

"Personally, in person" Winston said. "Roly just can't wait to meet you again."

Grover could understand why, considering the problems which accrued during their last confrontation. He and Grover had fallen out a couple of months earlier. Not surprising, as Roland 'call me Roly' Bevan's back story was of interest to all sorts of people, including the frustrated local constabulary. He had a good war, beginning as a corporal in the Army Pays Corps, then transferring to the Quartermaster Section where he built up a lucrative black-market operation. Back in Bristol following the conflict, he segued into a pubs and property business. And was transformed into something of a local hero when he bought the row of derelict houses on Cumberland Road and re-built them, thus setting a challenge to the city council. Most of the re-building programmes had ground to a standstill. There were on-going rows about where the priorities lay – homes or city centre businesses. So, enter Roly Bevan. Posing on the front page of the *Western Daily Press* in his hard hat, as the man who got things done.

On Grover's previous visit to Bristol, he and Bevan had clashed over a bit of unpleasantness with a group of second-string hard men and 'entrepreneurs', when Bevan got the wrong idea of whose side the GI was on. Grover put that into perspective, and in the process met Rachel and Leroy, and Mrs Rawlins who had lived on the ground floor. Grover asked what happened to her. Rachel nodded at the pay phone on the wall.

"You remember she used to answer all the phone calls down here and shout up to us… The phone rang early one morning, a couple of weeks ago. It kept on ringing. It stopped as I got to the bottom of the stairs. Mrs Rawlins door was open and she was lying face down across the threshold. A massive stroke, the Coroner said." Rachel raised her right hand. Rubbed her eyes with her thumb and forefinger. "I liked her. She was a wonderful lady… She'd been a Tiller Girl; did you know that?"

She had to explain to Grover who the Tiller Girls were.

Winston helped him collect his bags from *Salome*. Grover nodded along the terrace.

"How do you get on with the folks in number 1?"

"Fine and dandy Massa," Winston said. "Cos Aa lives here." He grinned and dropped the 'Uncle Tom' accent. "As the lady said 'It's not me you understand, I have to think of my tenants. If it was up to me…' Only minor racist bullshit. I can handle it."

No one could dispute that. Winston had arrived in England in June 1948, twenty-five years old, one of the passengers on the *Empire Windrush*. He followed a friend down to the Westcountry, got himself a job in Palmers Timber Yard in the Floating Harbour and a room in a house in Southville. He was asked to leave after a visit from the police, following an altercation at work, which ended with him throwing the work gang yahoo off the dockside into the water. He was rescued by Roly Bevan, who knew what he had in the young bouncer.

The two men dumped the bags in the hall.

Grover got back into the jeep and drove across the city to St Philips – a quietly run-down suburb that had succeeded in being anonymous and neglected long before the outbreak of war. The sort of place from which an experienced operator like Bevan could work smoothly and un-noticed. Traffic lanes were still a major problem, despite half of the city being without motorised transport. Moving around was swifter by horse and cart. The three-mile journey took him twenty minutes.

Grover swung *Salome* into the car park behind *The Mighty Albion* pub and nosed into a space in front of the gym. A converted car workshop behind the pub, the place had been running since the late 1920's, a back street, unlicensed fights venue, where local hard men could earn themselves a week's drinking money, providing they won the bout. Bevan had bought out the previous owner, invested some money in the place, upgraded the boxing ring, secured permission from the city council to operate, and a licence from the British Boxing Board of Control to promote fights.

Allowing for a little irritation here and there, times were fine for Roly Bevan. He paid good money for his Neville Reed suits, Oxford shirts, Burlington Arcade ties and patent leather shoes. He dressed to make an impression. No fifty-bob tailor was coming anywhere near him with a tape measure.

His office was an eighteen feet square room on the floor above the bar of the pub. He had re-laid and sound proofed the floor, to ensure he would be undisturbed by the carousing from the bar and saloon below. And he had filled the space with bits of faux Hollywood – tapestry, chandelier, sofa and heavy oak desk. An oasis of pretend art deco class in a desert of bomb craters, dirty streets and grimy pubs. Not that Roly would be seen dead living around here. His home was a regency house in Clifton with a front row dress circle view of Brunel's suspension bridge. He kept his 1939 Mark V Bentley in a garage in the lane behind his house and drove to his place of business in a 1946 Austin 10.

Bevan had just finished reading the sports section of the *Daily Express*. He shuffled the broadsheet pages back together neatly, folded it and placed it on top of his desk as though it were still on the newsagents display stand. Even after reading, he hated his newspaper to be untidy. He looked down again at the front page headline

GRAFT AND FLOURISHING BLACK MARKET SCANDAL

The Assistant to the Permanent Secretary at the Ministry of Fuel and Power had taken a lady of his acquaintance to Brighton and Bognor Regis on successive weekends; courtesy of Danny Hedges, a black marketeer and small-time aspiring gang leader. In return for what, was not yet clear, but the *Express*, the *News Chronicle*, and the Assistant to the Permanent Secretary's wife, were up in arms. His Majesty's employee was in the process of being publicly humiliated at the enquiry set up by Leader of the House Herbert Morrison; while his wife had taken the two children to Capri for ten days, all expenses paid by *The News of the World*, to reveal all. It was a toss-up as to which – the cabinet minister or the Sunday newspaper – would get to a version of the truth first.

Bevan reached across his leather topped desk, flipped open the lid of a gilt cigar box and picked up a corona. The best that only black-market money could buy. He lit the cigar with a fat, gold desk lighter, sat back in his swivel chair and blew smoke rings at the ceiling.

The was a polite knock on the office door. Bevan sat up in the chair.

"Yes..."

The door opened a couple of feet and the blonde hair and the lived-in face of bar maid Lizzie Duke peered around it.

"Mr Grover's here Mr Bevan."

Bevan rose to his feet.

"Show him in Lizzie."

The blonde head disappeared and the door swung open. Grover stepped into the room. Bevan smiled at him with at least fifty teeth.

"Ed Grover. Welcome."

"You sent for me."

"Really? Did Rachel and Leroy make it sound so formal?"

Grover took a moment. Bevan went on.

"They're getting along fine, don't you think? They'll be good together. I like Leroy. He's got prospects."

He meant that. Whatever else he was, Roly was no racist. He looked at Grover, smiled gloriously again.

"It seems I have to report here for the flat keys," Grover said.

Bevan waved his left arm at the sofa.

"Sit down, Ed."

Grover did so. His host waved his right arm in the direction of the drinks sideboard.

"Is it too early?"

"Probably. Unless you have a bourbon."

Bevan looked hurt for a moment. Then he raised his arms and waved both of them.

"Really Ed. Do you honestly expect this office to be short of anything?"

Transfixed by the ongoing armography, it took Grover a while to reply. By which time, Bevan was at the sideboard raising a bottle of *Old Fitzgerald*, the key to Southern hospitality.

"Where the hell did you get that?"

Bevan looked hurt all over again. "Oh please…"

He poured a generous portion of the bourbon into a glass, and conveyed it across the room to his guest. Grover looked up at him.

"None for yourself?"

"In a little while." He sat down next to Grover. "So, you are my new tenant."

Grover nodded at him. "Thank you."

"Don't thank me, Ed. It was at Leroy's insistence. He likes you. And you know how much I value everything about him."

Grover sipped the whisky. Hell, it was good.

"You wanted me to collect the keys in person."

"Indeed," Bevan said. "I thought we might er… chew the fat for a while."

Grover sipped again. "About what?"

"Some ground rules, I thought."

"Do we need 'em?"

"It's best I think."

Grover breathed in and out. "So they are?..."

"I think we will get on terribly well, Ed. If you stick to your business and leave me to mine".

"Yes," Grover said. "That's probably best."

"Good." Bevan got to his feet again. "I think I'll have that drink now."

He moved to the sideboard.

"I was at the Filton bash three weeks ago," he said. "I get invited to these things nowadays. Good for business."

Grover was tempted to ask which business he was referring to. Instead, he swallowed the rest of his *Old Fitzgerald* and stood up too. Bevan poured something from a cocktail shaker he had already prepared, and moved to his desk. He opened a drawer, dug out a key fob, leaned forward and placed it on Grover's side of the desk.

"Flat 1, 5 Blenheim Villas. At your disposal. You will have to make do with Mrs Rawlins furniture I'm afraid. The flat has been cleaned since she died but the fixtures and fittings remain the same."

"Fine by me."

"Splendid." Bevan raised his glass. "Here's to the future."

He downed the cocktail and held out his right hand. Grover shook it and picked up the keys.

He was back at Blenheim Villas twenty minutes later.

"How did it go?" Leroy asked.

"He was excessively polite."

"Excessively?" Rachel said.

"In the self-effacing way we know he operates. So much so that we agreed on things."

"What things?"

"The ground rules," Grover said. "The status quo."

"Just be careful, Ed."

Grover dug the flat keys out of his pocket. "Okay. Let's see how Mrs Rawlins lived."

As Bevan had promised, the flat was spotless. The furniture was pre-war, in fact some of it pre the Great War. But it was clean, sturdy and the old armchairs surprisingly comfortable. Grover sat and contemplated his new surroundings. There was a knock on the door.

Grover opened it to reveal Rachel standing in the hall holding a tin tray of basic foodstuffs. A small jam jar of milk, half a dozen slices of bread, a chunk of margarine, a handful of biscuits and a desert spoonful of tea.

"This for now," she explained. "Until you can get to the shops tomorrow. Mind you, tea is still on ration, so we'll have to figure that out."

"No we won't, "Grover said.

He disappeared into the kitchen. Rachel put her tray down on the sideboard. Grover returned to the living room and handed over a large silver foil bag with the word *TEA* stencilled on the side.

"Liberated this from the Sergeant's Mess. I recall the tea problem from my last visit."

Rachel smiled her thanks.

"Meanwhile, you are cordially invited to supper on the floor above. 7 o'clock sharp. No need for white tie and tails."

CHAPTER SIX

At 8 o'clock the next morning, Grover was ironing. While unpacking his bags the previous evening, he had decided his rumpled dress uniform trousers were in no fit state to represent the US Army. At any function. After dinner, Rachel handed him the means to solve the problem.

Satisfied with the knife edge creases, he put the trousers on, shrugged into his dress jacket and examined the result in the hall mirror. He decided he scrubbed up rather well. Close to six feet tall, straight backed, square shouldered and a comfortable twelve stones plus a pound or two.

He studied the Bristol Street map he had picked up during his last visit to the city. And logged into the information he had stored away during his first recce a couple of months ago, when he had mapped out the city boundaries in his head, the bomb craters and blasted landmarks, the detours and the one-way systems. He remembered all the main directions out of the city – west to the coast, north to the A38 and Gloucestershire, east to the A420 and Wiltshire, south on the A38 again and the A37 into Somerset. He had done this sort of exercise more times than he could recall, as the allied advance pushed on through France, the Ardennes, the Rheinland and into eastern Germany. He had learned, wherever he was, to place himself in the centre of the map and set the map to the compass in his head.

Grover decided to avoid the city centre and drive out to Filton via Clifton and Southmead. Fifteen minutes later, with Durdham Down on his left, he turned onto Henleaze Road. Another ten minutes and he was through Southmead, approaching the A38 and the access road to the recently expanded aircraft factory.

The Bristol Aircraft Company had first gone to war in 1916. A string of successful fighters and bombers followed, and heading into World War 2, Filton had become the largest aircraft manufacturing unit in Europe. Teaming up with Hawker Aviation in Gloucester, the factory built thousands of Hurricanes. And now, the company's aero engine division had joined the jet development race, lengthening the runway by some distance and building Gloster Javelin engines for their neighbours up the A38.

Grover was met by Andrew Turnbull, Senior Aero Engineer and the Javelin Team Leader. He was in his mid-60s, short in stature, with close cropped dark hair, rows of thought lines across his forehead. He offered Grover a broad welcoming smile.

"How much do you know about aero engines Sergeant Major?"

"Nothing about jets," Grover admitted. "But something about Spitfires and Merlin engines."

"You were a flyer?"

"I wanted to be."

"This way…"

Turnbull opened the door of the design office, ushered Grover inside and called across the room.

"Gentlemen…" Half a dozen heads alongside and behind drawing boards looked towards him. "This is Sergeant Major Ed Grover." A series of 'welcomes' and 'hellos' followed. "I'll introduce you individually later."

He led Grover across the floor and into his personal office. Gestured to an armchair in front of the desk. Grover sat down. Turnbull moved round the desk and sat down facing him.

"You said you didn't fly…"

"I was nineteen," Grover said. "I'd just spent two years in the Tomah PD." He noticed the look of enquiry on Turnbull's face and explained. "The police department, Tomah Wisconsin. I came over here in 1940. Joined the Eagle Squadron in Suffolk. Like the rest of the guys, I wanted to get into the war. The MO said there was something wrong with my sinuses. I couldn't fly, so I joined the engineers, re-building the Spitfires that made it home."

Turnbull glanced down at the paperwork in front of him.

"You came to Bristol in '41. That's some distance from Suffolk."

"A friend was on a weekend pass. Visiting his uncle, who worked in this place, building Beaufighters."

"We had four Americans here before the blitz," Turnbull said. "One was killed. He was Italian… Primo. Can't remember his second name. He was always just Primo. The family lived in Bedminster. Near the *Rex* Cinema."

For moments, Turnbull was lost in remembrance. Grover too. He was never going to forget Good Friday

1941. From less than one hundred yards away, he had watched thirty kilos of high explosive blow the roof off the *Rex* and rows of seats into neighbouring gardens.

He heard Turnbull from some distance away.

"Sorry. What was that?"

Turnbull repeated the question. "Do you think that was him? Your friend's uncle?"

"I guess so."

Turnbull changed the subject.

"Tell you what… You ought to visit the chaps in 501 Squadron. They're based at the other end of the airfield. Began the war here in Spitfires. Moved to Kent during the Battle of Britain, then came back here in '46. The squadron is transferring to Gloster Meteors soon, but they have a handful of Spits in a hanger. One of them a trainer. Get Lieutenant Mills to take you up. I'll introduce you."

"Thanks. I'd like that."

"Alright, final thing. Impossible not to notice this… You are in fact a serving officer in the US Army. Not that I'm questioning your qualifications for the job you have undertaken, but erm…"

Grover helped him out.

"By the time the rest of the nation turned up, I was spending most of my days playing table tennis. There were fewer Spitfire sorties and more of them were coming back. So, I joined the Infantry." He scrolled back to June 1944. "And that was tougher than everyone expected. We'd all thought about it, but the reality hit us like a Mack truck."

Turnbull nodded again. Understanding what Grover was getting at.

"My son was killed at Arnhem," he said.

Silence took the room hostage. Then Turnbull spoke again.

"Too many sons were killed in Europe. Yet we keep returning to this."

Grover said nothing. Turnbull recovered and got down to business.

"What would you like to do this morning. Look at the books?"

"Hell no, that's not my thing. Show me around. Tell me what you're doing."

Spirits had lifted again.

"Right you are, Sergeant Major."

"And please, forget this rank stuff. I was told to turn up and make an impression. Actually, I think I'm over-dressed. I won't be back looking like this." He stood up and stretched his right arm across the desk. "My friends call me Ed."

Turnbull shook his hand.

"Andrew," he said.

Grover smiled. "Okay Andrew. Give me the five dollar tour."

"Meet my associates first," Turnbull said, and moved to the office door.

Grover met the engine designers, was given a guide to the factory floor and finally introduced to his office. Actually, a redundant tool store, built in 1916 to house the grinders, saws, stretchers, fabric cutters and piles of canvas used in the frenzied construction days of the *Bristol Fighter*. Located outside the finished engines exit door, it betrayed its recent history as a junk room. It had been given a coat of paint, and the drawing office had donated a desk, a swivel chair and a three-drawer filing cabinet. The GPO had topped the wish list with a connected line and a black bakelite phone.

Turnbull asked him how often he intended to show up.

"How often are the development meetings called?" Grover asked.

"Every month."

"Then that's when I'll show up, officially. Unless I'm summoned in between."

"We had the latest ten days ago. So, you're off the hook for a while. But do feel free to visit any time. You'll be welcome. And I'll answer any questions you have."

"Okay, one right now. Can we get an armchair in here, however old and battered? And replace this designer's swivel for something a little more comfortable?"

"Of course," Turnbull said. "Leave it to me."

***

The next stop was Gladstone Street Bedminster and the Morrison family.

Grover eased *Salome* into the kerb outside the shop, slid out of the jeep and scanned the front of the building. The place was looking good. With more food and household items coming off ration every couple of months, the two bay windows were full of brightly packaged stuff. Grover stepped into the shop porch and pushed the door open. The bell rang out cheerfully.

Arthur, round faced, grey haired and newly retired, stood behind the grocery counter. He looked Grover up and down.

"Good day, Sergeant Major."

He grabbed the hinged counter top, lifted it up and over and stepped into the middle of the shop floor. Grover moved into his embrace. Then Arthur dropped back a couple of paces and gave him a second inspection.

"Very smart. I assume then, you're going to dress up every time you visit."

"Not from day two. After today it will be smart casual."

Arthur turned and shouted in the direction of the kitchen.

"Ellie… He's here. And dressed like a dog's dinner."

Ellie emerged from the kitchen.

"My my," she breathed. "My oh my."

She moved onto the shop floor. Grover swept her into his arms and held on. He released her and stepped back.

"You look terrific," he said.

And she did. Fast approaching her sixty-fifth birthday, but the still dark-haired bob and the brilliant blue eyes made her look so much younger.

"Your timing Ed, is impeccable. I've been baking. Come on, both of you. The bell will go if somebody comes in."

Ellie ushered Grover and Arthur through the gap in the counter and on into the kitchen. She picked up the kettle and went into the wash house to fill it. Came back and put it on top of the iron grate in the fireplace.

The trio sat at the table, tea cups in front of them, the milk jug and tea pot between them. The tea was made, the madeira cake was sliced and they talked for a while, interrupted only by customers entering the shop. Arthur attended to that and Grover asked about Harry.

"He's well," Ellie said. "You must remember the wonderful Jerry Wharton?"

"Of course."

Who could forget Jerry Wharton? The existentialist, Marxist, homosexual Punch and Judy Man. A giant ball of entertainment, caring and committed to a cause he truly believed in – to make the world a better place. The man Grover had watched die of cancer in Weston Super Mare General Hospital. Jerry once explained his presentation thus…

Punch is the Bolshevik you see. The policeman is the Tsarist lackey. The Crocodile is the corrupt state. The kids don't get that of course. But one day I'll present the Punch and Judy version of the October Revolution. Then things will change.

"He left Harry and Mark some money," Ellie explained. "They share Mark's flat now. Along with all Jerry's books and his diaries."

"And that works?"

"Seems too. They're very happy. Both of them."

"Good."

"Take time to visit. They'd be pleased to see you."

Grover promised he would.

"Now," he said, "I need to buy some groceries."

He was persuaded to stay for lunch

***

He drove away from Gladstone Street shortly after 3 o'clock. Northeast, towards Redcliffe Hill and into gridlocked traffic. It cleared a little as he crossed the bridge over the river and turned west onto Commercial Road. Ahead on the right was the General Hospital and beyond that, the roundabout at the junction with Cumberland Road.

By then, the car in front of him was familiar. A Morris Minor Traveller, belonging to Melanie Davis, Zoe Easton's outdoor clerk at Fincher Reade and Holborne. Grover had spent some time in the law firm's chambers earlier in the year. An imposing three floor regency town house in All Saints Court, a small square off Clare Street, a couple of minutes' walk from the Assize Courts – the yard fortunately still ringed by historic buildings the Luftwaffe had failed to hit.

He remembered, on first acquaintance, standing on the cobble stones and marvelling at the solidness of the surroundings. People walked in and out of the buildings dressed in dark suits, carrying briefcases and envelope files and boxes of envelope files. There was a palpable aura of importance about All Saints Court. The processes of law were going on in these buildings. When he pressed the bell underneath Fincher Reade and Holborne's brass plate, the door was opened by a slim redhead with green eyes and a smile that would match any Rank starlet any time of day.

"I'm Melanie Davis," she told him. "Please come in."

Maybe he could catch Mel's attention…

The Traveller fishtailed in front of him and the back end swung through ninety degrees. The car slid to a halt as the front wheels bounced onto the pavement. There was an impact noise at the front of the car Grover could hear from the jeep. He stamped on the brake and pulled up just five yards short of the Traveller. He was at the front passenger door in seconds. He bent down and looked across the front seats. Melanie's head was turned towards him, her right cheek up against the steering wheel. He pulled open the passenger door, climbed into the car, slid his left hand between her head and the wheel, lifted it, eased her upright into the seat supporting the back of her head with his right arm. Blood was dripping from somewhere close to her right eye. He heard a voice behind him shouting into the car.

"We saw it all," a lady said. "My husband's just run across the road to the hospital for help. Is she all right?"

"She's unconscious."

"The legs of the soldier are underneath the car," she said.

"Soldier?"

"One of yours. He seemed to step, no fall I'd say, off the pavement in front of the car."

"An American soldier?"

"Yes, I'm sure." She looked up and over the roof of the car. "Ah... Help is arriving..."

The face of a woman wearing a white coat, ducked into Grover's line of site.

She peered into the Traveller, then opened the driver's door and introduced herself.

"Doctor Mason," she said. "And you are?"

"Ed Grover."

Mason glanced at his dress uniform sleeves. "Sergeant Major?"

That seemed irrelevant to the situation, but Grover said she was correct.

"Right Sergeant Major, let me take a look. Keep supporting the lady."

Grover sat back in the passenger seat, his right arm still behind Melanie's head.

"Unconscious," the doctor said. "No broken neck, but there will no doubt be serious concussion. And maybe some internal pressure. We'll get her across the road and take a look. Do you know who she is?"

"Melanie Davis. I don't know where she lives, but she works for Fincher Reade and Holborne, a law firm in All Saints Court."

The doctor looked to her left. "Ah, good… Give that information to these gentlemen."

She stood up as two porters arrived with a stretcher, stepped out of the way, and moved to the front of the car. Grover and one of the men, eased Melanie out of the car onto the stretcher. To the other, he repeated the information he had given Doctor Mason. Asked if he could follow them into the hospital.

"Yes of course."

The doctor called to him from the pavement in front of the car.

"Sergeant Major. A moment please."

"Just come straight to Casualty," the porter said. "It's a few yards from the hospital entrance."

Grover watched them cross the road. Fifty yards to his right, two black police patrol cars pulled up, blocking access from the bridge over the river. Then he moved to join Doctor Mason. Who pointed down to the soldier's torn right sleeve.

"Do you recognise the insignia?"

Grover nodded. "Same as mine. The 21st Infantry."

The soldier's torso and head were clear of the Traveller, the rest of his body was underneath it. The right side of his face was scraped and bleeding. There was more blood bubbling from the bridge of his broken nose. The shoulders of his uniform jacket were torn, the collar pulled away from his neck as if he had been caught by something and dragged a couple of feet.

"Do you know him?" the doctor asked.

"No. But I guess he'll be wearing dog tags."

"We'll take a look once we get him inside and onto a table."

She looked up and waved at the two porters, now on the way back.

Grover knelt down by the soldier. He had tripped over countless mauled bodies over the last seven years. He could not hear or see signs of breathing, but he knew the man was still alive. The dog tag chain was around his neck.

Grover stood up again. "He's not dead."

"Not yet," the doctor said.

CHAPTER SEVEN

An hour later, Grover was invited into a cubicle in Casualty. Melanie was sitting up, her face cleaned, wounds stitched. She smiled at Grover and winced in pain.

"Don't do that," he suggested.

Melanie opened her arms wide. Grover turned to the attending nurse.

"May I?"

"Of course. But gently."

He stepped to the bedside, placed his hands on the edge of the bed and leaned forward to be hugged.

"It's so good to see you Ed," Melanie whispered into his left ear.

"Hell of a way to get my attention," he said. "You going to be alright?"

Melanie pulled back and looked at the nurse. "The lady says so."

"The head x rays are fine. The scars on her face will heal. Unsurprisingly, she has a nasty headache and severe concussion. We'll keep her here for a while; make sure the headache is nothing but that. Then you can take her home."

"Er… yes of course," Grover said. "It will be a pleasure."

The nurse read between the lines. And hastily apologised.

"I'm sorry. I thought that you were…"

Melanie grinned. And winced again.

Grover pitched in. "We're good friends. And we work together sometimes. Of course I'll take her home, you just say the word." He turned back to Melanie. "I'm here for a while."

"You're not going back to the US?"

"Nope. Got a job?"

"A job? Dressed like that?"

The nurse interrupted the dialogue.

"I'll leave you to it." To Melanie she said, "You've got ten minutes, then I'll be back to take you to a ward." She shot Grover a stern look. "Don't get her excited, she needs rest."

The nurse swept out of the cubicle.

"Spill," Melanie said.

Grover did. In the ten minutes that was allowed they both caught up. He told her about his new job and about moving into Blenheim Villas. She gave him the latest on her extended family.

"My elder brother is getting married. He'll be leaving the city for the home counties. Lisa, his wife to be, works in the costume department at one of those film studios along the Thames. Merton Park. Which leaves…"

She breathed in. Grover interrupted.

"Don't tell me. See if I remember… You've got two parents, two grandparents, two brothers, one sister, two uncles, two aunts and four cousins. Right?"

"One uncle, one aunt and two cousins."

Grover began counting. "Two, four, six, seven, eight, ten, twelve members including you. That's great."

"You have a brother, don't you?"

"Kind of," Grover said. "But that's it. My father died when I was a kid. The rest of us... Hell, we had Christmas 1939 together. Eight months later I went to war, my brother married and moved to Detroit. My mother died when I was somewhere in Eastern Europe. And by the time I got to Berlin, I was uncle to a boy and a girl I've never seen."

"That's a story full of regret," Melanie said.

"No, it's not. I don't regret coming to England and fighting a war. Millions of us from all over the world signed up to that. And to all that happened. Now, home is light years and a whole ocean away. I don't have anything to go back for."

"I think that's sad."

"Not so Mel, it is what it is. Besides, I like it here. I like the folks I've met. This job gives me reason to stay. Without it I'd be back in the States."

"Doing what?"

"God knows." He smiled ruefully. "What do you get to do after you've helped save the world?"

"Perhaps that's enough," Melanie said. "There's certainly nothing greater."

"Yeah, but the pay is terrible. And it doesn't add anything significant to your resumé. A home for heroes is just so much bullshit, Mel. I don't want to go back to being a cop. Not now, not since Berlin. As for this man's army... Hell there are guys up in Fairford who can't wait to go to Korea."

His eyes darkened and he stopped talking. Melanie was concerned at the tone they were left with.

"You must have friends in the 21st," she said. "There's this thing isn't there? You've got his back, he's got yours."

"Sure. But it comes with a hail of bullets. And I'm done with that."

He lightened the mood.

"Look, I have to find out what I can about this GI. I'll do that and catch up with you on the ward later... Okay?"

"Yes."

He leaned down and kissed Mel on the forehead.

She said, "That's more than okay, Ed Grover."

***

He found the soldier and Doctor Mason in Intensive Care.

"Ah. Sergeant Major"

"I know the uniform is kind of formal," Grover said. "But I'd rather answer to Ed."

The doctor smiled. "In which case..." She hooked a thumb and forefinger under the name badge on her collar and titled it into Grover's eyeline. "Lauren. Senior surgeon in A and E."

She nodded in the direction of the soldier and handed Grover the man's dog tags.

"Meet Private Bradley Parsons."

Grover checked the tags and looked down at his countryman, hooked up to a cluster of machine parts working hard to save his life. The two men had gone through the same war, in the 21st. Slogged through the same mud and blood and bullets, in the same remorseless advance. But if he and this guy had met, it could not have been a moment of significance. He would have remembered that. The disconnection made him somewhat uneasy.

"He's not in good shape," the doctor said. "Head injuries, broken ribs, broken hip. We stopped the wounds bleeding, but x rays show he's bleeding inside his chest. We're trying to do something about that, but we're not having much success. In all probability he will just not wake up."

"In which case how long has he got?"

"You need a crystal ball for that. Minutes, hours… If this soldier has someone in the city who knows or cares for him, you need to find out quickly. Use the phone in my office."

Grover called Lieutenant Berger. He was not at his desk. It took Corporal Layne twenty-three minutes to find him. Grover counted every one of them before Berger rang back.

"Private Bradley Parsons, from Able Company, is AWOL. Has been for five days."

"Did you know he was here in Bristol?" Grover asked.

"No. He signed out on a 48 hour pass a week ago. Didn't tell anyone where he was going. The Snowdrops have been looking for him."

"Did you tell the cops?"

"Hell no. It's an army problem."

"No longer," Grover said. "The cops are on the case now. Parsons got himself run over in front of a bunch of passers-by."

There was a pause. Grover listened to the buzz on the line.

"Then we need to get him back," Berger said. "I'll send a Medical Unit to pick him up."

"If you move him, odds on he'll die. Then you won't find out why he's here and what he's been doing."

"So what? If he dies, we don't need to know."

"The Bristol Constabulary won't let that rest. And the lady who knocked him down works for the city's top law firm. They'll take the incident apart as well."

Another silence. This time the phone line crackled. Grover tried to move things along.

"If Parsons dies, there'll be an inquest. The army will have to turn up and explain why it didn't know he was roaming around Bristol. There'll be a police investigation. The lady might be indicted for manslaughter. The whole thing could spiral out of the army's control. At best it'll be a PR nightmare."

He paused and let the Adjutant absorb all that.

"Okay Ed, you're on the spot," Berger said. "What do you suggest?"

"Leave him here. Let the doctors get him through the night and maybe save his life. You have no deadlines. Let it play out. Let the cops at this end deal with the rights and wrongs of the accident. Don't let anyone mention AWOL. And if Parsons pulls through, then take him back without fuss and say lots of nice stuff about the Bristol doctors who saved his life. The 'special relationship' in action."

Berger did some more thinking.

"Alright… Meanwhile, anything you can do to find out what the hell Parsons was doing in Bristol… A bit outside of your remit I know, but we need eyes on the situation. I guess it's a kind of liaison."

Grover took some time over the proposition. Then asked a question.

"Have you got Parsons' military record there?"

"Yes."

"Then do this for me. Copy it and have someone drive it to the office in Filton. It'll be secure there. I'll pick it up first thing in the morning."

"I'll do that."

"Thank you, Sir."

"To make sure you're completely in the loop Sergeant Major, let me tell you this… Bradley Parsons was a long standing bunkie of Harvey Vanderbilt and Larry Toomes."

***

"It's so good to see you Ed."

Zoe Easton got up from the chair at the side of Melanie's bed and smiled at Grover. Dark, shoulder length hair, brown eyes and dimples in her cheeks.

"And looking so smart too," she said.

Smart is as smart is. But Zoe Easton smart was knock out. She fitted the tailored, grey pin-striped two piece with a cool and easy grace, irresistible to most of the men she knew, met and dealt with. A dozen years older than Grover with a drop-dead gorgeous maturity she wore without construction or artifice.

"And you," he said. Then managed to peel his gaze away from her towards Melanie. "Feeling better?"

"Much. How is the soldier?"

Grover stepped to the foot of the bed.

"He's not in good shape. May not last through the night. Sorry to have to tell you that."

The smiles and the good vibrations vanished. Zoe set to thinking. After a moment or two, Melanie gave voice to the problem.

"In which case, the question of manslaughter comes up."

"Not necessarily," Zoe said. She paused. Melanie and Grover waited. "Tell us how you saw the accident."

Melanie breathed in and out.

"That's the point. I didn't see anything until it was too late." She looked at Ed. "I was watching you and *Salome* in the rear-view mirror." She turned her head towards Zoe. "I dropped my eyes to look along the bonnet. The soldier… just appeared… in front of me. I braked, swung the car left. There was a thump, the car shook and then it hit the curb. The force of that shot me forwards and into the steering wheel."

"That's it?" Grover asked. "Nothing else?".

"No." She included both of her visitors in the rationalisation. "It's not good is it?"

"It's complicated," Zoe said. "And we have decisions to make." She looked at Grover. "Have you any idea who this soldier is?"

Grover nodded. "Private Bradley Parsons, 21st Infantry."

"The same outfit as you?"

"He's currently based at Fairford, waiting to be repatriated home."

"And having a last fling in the sinful city."

"Maybe…"

Doctor Mason created a gap in the curtains surrounding the bed and stepped inside. Her first regard was for Melanie.

"How are you feeling?"

Melanie managed a smile. "Much better."

"Still dizzy?"

"No."

"Good."

She dipped into a pocket of her white coat and produced a small brown leather wallet. Handed it to Grover.

"It was found in Private Parsons' jacket," she said.

Grover unfolded the wallet. It contained a couple of pounds, nine dollars, a photograph of a young woman, his latest weekend pass. And a piece of paper with hand written directions to a street in the city, but no house name or number.

"Peel Street," he said. "Any of you know where that is?"

Zoe and Mel shook their heads in unison. Doctor Mason helped out.

"I'd bet on Bedminster," she volunteered. "I have an outpatient who lives in Palmerston Street. There's a Russell Street. And Gladstone Street too."

Grover hooked up with this. The doctor took the response for confusion and went on to explain.

"English Prime Ministers back in Victorian times. Along with Robert Peel. Like most cities, Bristol has collections of related roads all over the place. Up near the cricket ground you can find half a dozen named after counties. Kent, Lancashire, Somerset of course. Then there's Dartmoor and Exmoor, a selection of trees in Redland…" She faded to a stop. "I've looked this up. Sorry, too much information."

"Not at all," Grover said. "I know Gladstone Street."

"Where the Emmersons live, of course," Mel said. "We all know it."

Grover stared at the photograph again.

"His wife perhaps," Doctor Mason suggested.

"No. He wasn't married. No girlfriend either, as far as we know."

"Do you think she might live in Peel Street?" Zoe asked

"Maybe."

He passed the photograph to Zoe.

"What do you think?"

"I don't know her."

"Didn't expect you would. That's not why I gave it to you. Take a good look."

Zoe did. Turned it over in her hand, then back again. And joined the dots.

"This is a recent picture," she said "It's sharp, not faded. There are no creases or folds or breaks in it. This must be someone he met recently."

"Right," Grover said. "That isn't a photograph of Parsons' childhood sweetheart. He didn't carry it down through the years and all the way across Europe. This must be a girl he came here to see on his weekend passes. A girl who may be the reason for him going AWOL."

"There is this too," the doctor said. She handed over a tiny piece of blue paper with one serrated edge. "It was in another pocket. A ticket of some sort. It might provide a clue to his whereabouts at some time in the last few days."

The paper seemed to be a raffle ticket. Just a number on it. Grover looked at the reverse side. The top right-hand corner hosted a tiny stencil mark. The word *EAVES*. He passed the ticket to Zoe.

"Any idea what this might be?"

Zoe scrutinised the paper. "It could be from a place called *Eaves Night*. A club behind the Hippodrome."

"Calls itself a club," Mel said. "But it's a glorified knocking shop."

"A what?"

Doctor Mason helped out "A whore house, in your parlance."

Grover looked at Zoe. "And you know this place?"

She grinned at him. "Contacts high and low Ed." She looked at the piece of paper again. "I imagine it's a cloakroom ticket."

Grover turned to the doctor.

"Would you mind leaving us to our deliberations Doc?"

"Of course. But I hate the abbreviation. Lauren is good. But if you must be formal, stick with the full Doctor Mason."

"Got that."

She took one more glance at Melanie. "In all probability you can go home tomorrow. So, make sure you rest." She looked at Grover again. "Have you time for a word in private?"

"Sure."

Lauren stepped through the gap in the bed curtains. Grover followed, pulling the curtains together behind him. The doctor led the way out of the ward and into the corridor. She dug into the pocket of her white coat and produced a small plastic bag of white pills.

"Benzedrine," she said.

Grover put two and two together. "Courtesy of Bradley Parsons," he suggested.

She nodded. "We found those in his jacket too."

"Okay…"

Grover began thinking. Unsure which of the rising questions he should address first.

Lauren Mason helped out.

"Given Private Parson's current situation… ie, that he can't help us in this matter; my first question ought to be, where did the pills come from?"

"Given we don't know the answer to that," Grover said, "we can only speculate. And maybe consider a couple of other questions. Was he using? Or was he dealing?"

"Either way, he may have needed a substantial regular supply," Lauren said. "We have had a handful of amphetamine cases in here. A couple were the result of over-dosing medicine prescribed by GPs."

"Mistakes?"

"We couldn't be sure. We gave both cases the benefit of the doubt. I talked with their GPs. They were satisfied. There is a flourishing black market in the city, like everywhere else. No doubt there will be somebody dealing somewhere. But as to the source… God knows."

"So you're suggesting?…"

For a moment she looked uncomfortable.

"I don't know of any source of criminal or black market Benzedrine in the city." She paused. Breathed in and out. "But, the odds-on choice of any insider who has cause to consider this would be…"

Grover completed the proposition for her.

"The US Army."

"Did you ever take Benzedrine during the push across Europe?"

Grover stared at her.

"There are reports…"

Grover nodded.

"At Remagen. The last bridge left standing across the Rhine. The Brass decided it would shorten the war if we took it. We'd get tanks and infantry across faster if we didn't have to build bailey bridges under mortar fire. The Germans had Remagen Bridge wired to blow. We didn't want to charge across it because we were waiting for tanks to arrive – at any moment we were told. So, we sat in shell holes and stayed awake, the medics doling out the bennies like Hershey Bars. Then the Germans realised they were on a hiding to nothing and decided to blow the bridge. Only a few kilos of explosives worked. And with us pinned down, they threw everything they had at it. Even V2 rockets, which missed by hundreds of yards and blew holes in the surrounding countryside. We eventually took the bridge, what was left of it, with forty percent casualties. I didn't sleep for three days. Historians reckon we shortened the war by a week. On Benzedrine. And we continued taking the pills. All the way to the River Elbe."

"No shortage then?"

"There were bucket loads flying in from Reykjavik." He looked into Doctor Mason's eyes. "Still are, I guess."

"Thus…" Doctor Mason rationalised, "The Air Force base would be the most likely source for Private Parsons. Unless he made regular visits to Bristol."

"Three weekend passes earlier in the year, and this one."

"Hardly enough to organise a major drugs racket," she suggested.

"Unless he had help at this end," Grover said.

"He'd need help at both ends, surely. Supply and demand. And he'd have to be an experienced master criminal to waltz into the city and set up an operation here, working over a handful of forty-eight hour periods. I'm no expert on the ins and outs of an American base, but I assume no one can freelance to such an extent in peacetime."

She paused the narrative. Grover waited. Lauren summed up.

"Let us suppose Parsons was just supplying. A bottle or two, here and there. Visiting Bristol once every five or six weeks. He might accomplish something like that smoothly, and make a few bob. Presumably he isn't searched leaving the base or getting back in."

"Under normal circumstances, no."

"In which case…" she left the prospect hanging in the air. And changed the subject. "I should call the police, Ed."

Grover nodded. Then asked her if he could buy some time. Lauren blew out her cheeks, slipped her hands into the pockets of her white coat and stared down at the floor. Grover asked her where Parsons' clothes were.

"In a locker, in a room behind the Intensive Care ward."

"Who searched his belongings?" Grover asked. "Anyone? What's the procedure?"

"Two nurses disrobed him. I was given the dog tags. A porter took the clothes away. He did nothing more than hang up the uniform, fold the rest of Parsons clothes, and leave his boots on the locker floor.

"And we assume he didn't find the bennies?"

"That's the most likely assumption. He didn't take them, which he might have done, had he realised what they were. And he didn't hand them to a nurse or to me. I found them because I looked in the locker. Beyond the dog tags, I knew nothing about him. So I went through his clothes, looking for some personal stuff."

Grover looked at the packet of tablets in his hand. Then back at the doctor.

"So… I'm asking, don't call the cops yet. Give me some time to talk with the army. Thirty-six hours. Parsons isn't going anywhere any time soon. Nobody can speak to him. Not even the cops. Let this ride a little bit. Please."

Lauren looked at Grover dead centre.

"Thirty-six hours. Unless, by some miracle, Parsons' wakes up and starts revealing all."

She turned through 180 degrees and set off along the corridor. Grover went back into the ward. Zoe had pulled a chair up close to the bed. Grover looked at both in turn.

"Tell me about *Eaves Night*," he said.

71

"Since the war, owned and operated by a second-rate chancer called Ronnie Eaves," Zoe explained. "Until a few months ago. He was shot down in the street outside the club by his girlfriend Ruby Willis. She emptied the contents of Ronnie's service revolver into his chest. He died on the spot. The place has lived on its notoriety since then."

Grover pondered. "Why would Bradley Parsons go there?"

"And how did he get in?" Mel asked. "Who would he know?"

"What do you mean?"

"These places operate under strict control," she said. "Licensed as late-night venues, members and guests only."

"Which means someone had to introduce Parsons?"

"That could have been done weeks ago," Zoe suggested. "How many R and R passes can a soldier get?"

"The 21st arrived in England on New Year's Eve. Around a third of them are still here. Forty-eight and seventy-two hour passes have been easier to get recently – a treat for the guys itching to get home. His record back in Fairford logs four weekends. Three times earlier in the year, and the latest seven days ago."

"If the current operator of *Eaves Night* has been behaving," Mel suggested, "the club visitor's book should tell us the sort of company your soldier has been keeping."

Grover looked at Zoe. "What are the odds on that?"

"Extremely long I would think."

"I'm an expert in long shots," Grover said. "I'm going home to change."

The two women looked at him. He posed, arms outstretched.

"Can't visit anywhere, dressed like this." He looked at Mel. "I'll check with Doctor Mason about picking you up tomorrow."

***

At Blenheim Villas, Winston reached the bottom of the stairs as Grover opened the front door. He was wearing jeans and a tee shirt under a loose jacket. He lifted the holdall he was carrying.

"Off to the gym," he said.

Grover asked him if Rachel was in.

"Up in her flat," Winston said, and stepped out of the house.

Grover changed out of his uniform, then climbed the stairs and knocked on Rachel's door. She opened it. Looked Grover up and down.

"That's less formidable. Come in."

He stepped into the hall. Rachel moved into the kitchen to fill the kettle.

Grover scoped the room, the same size and shape as the floor below, but with a hundred more personal touches. Posters of great musicians and singers on the walls. Peggy Lee, Nina Simone, Frank Sinatra, Billie Holiday, Benny Goodman, Duke Ellington, the Dorsey brothers. And a postcard size photograph of an old friend, Fidel Johnson – the much-missed sax player Rachel had worked with at the *Club El Paradis*. Until the early hours of one morning back in March when he was beaten to death for being West Indian.

73

Rachel's voice reached Grover from the kitchen doorway.

"I still miss him," she said.

A quartet of men the worse for drink, had unloaded on Fidel, kicked him to the ground, picked him up, swung him around and hauled him head first into a stone wall. He died in hospital two days later.

"Tea or coffee?" Rachel asked, from the kitchen doorway.

Grover turned to face her.

"Tea," he said.

"I have some Battenburg cake."

Grover had no idea what that was, but it sounded okay.

"Fidel had never heard of it either," Rachel said. "But he tasted it and got hooked."

"So, in his honour, I'd love some too," Grover said.

Rachel served the tea, and the Battenburg in thick slices. Grover declared that both hit the spot. He turned down a third slice of cake.

"Can I ask you a couple of questions?"

"Of course. Fire away."

"What do you know about *Eaves Night*?"

"The club? I sang there for a week. Oh… eighteen months ago. Hated it. Thankfully I was poached by the *El Paradis*." She was silent for a moment or two. "What's this about Ed?"

"It needs time to explain. How were the rules? Tight, or a bit… loose?"

"Bendy, I would say. It's a low rent establishment. Interesting thing though. Since the death of Ronnie Eaves, it's been run by a woman. His ex-wife, Sandy."

"Isn't that a bit weird? I mean with the Ruby Willis thing?"

"Ronnie fancied himself as a bit of an operator. Had women all over town. The consensus of opinion is that Sandy stayed with him, waiting for the right moment to take him to the cleaners."

"Which Ruby Willis served up."

"Yes…"

Curiosity seeped into her eyes.

"You're well informed for a stranger in these parts."

"Not as much as I'd like to be," he said. He stared down into his cup for a while. "And there's something else…"

He paused. Rachel gave him a couple of seconds then broke the silence.

"Go on…"

"Okay. You're in the music business."

"Yes."

"Club land."

"Yes."

She was waiting for Grover to get to the point. So he did.

"Can you get a fist full of bennies around here?"

She gave him an old-fashioned look.

"Can I?" she asked. "For you?"

"No, no no. What I mean is, are they easy to get hold of?"

"Bennies?"

Grover stared at Rachel for a moment. He opened his mouth to speak, but she beat him to it.

"Is this a hypothetical conversation? If so, it's likely to go on for a while. On the other hand, if you want to get something off your chest, please do and I'll try to empathise."

"As I said, it's a bit complicated. The why is best not revealed. I am not looking for bennies personally. In fact, I have a few milligrams downstairs. They are not mine, I promise. But I would like to know where they came from."

Rachel stared at him without blinking. He went on.

"They were found in the jacket pocket of a GI absent without leave."

"So ask him where he got them."

"I can't do that. Because he's along the road, in the General Hospital, in ICU."

"But I," Rachel said, "because I'm a stoned contralto, might know the answer to this."

"Are you?"

She grinned. "Touché."

Grover grinned too. "I just want to know if they're easy to get hold of."

"You're asking the wrong girl. Nobody takes anything, anywhere near the portals of *El Paradis*. The band, the staff, the punters. You should know this. Remember the boss, Daniel Zampa?"

He remembered. Recalled every moment etched. On the right side of the man – his side that is – every moment was sunshine. On the other, moments were at best unfortunate, at worst deadly. How could Grover possibly forget Daniel Zampa? A man with all the ambition of Al Capone, but much cleverer, more sophisticated, and maybe just a little less murderous.

"He hates drugs," Rachel said. "He is known for his personal interventions in business with users and dealers. You have to be well into the scene, and well away from Zampa, to know who to approach." She looked at Grover, tilted her head to one side. "Incidentally he knows you're in town."

Of course he did. Daniel Zampa ran things. All things. Grover switched topics.

"Nobody in the band needs bennies to stay awake?"

"The guys smoke some weed in the early hours, after the club closes. To come down. In a Dominoes Club in St Pauls."

"Dominoes?"

"Yes. It's a big thing among black people in south Bristol. A huge piece of Rastafarian popular culture. Would you like some more tea?"

CHAPTER EIGHT

In the Filton office, Grover stared at the reproduced, five inches by three photograph of Private Bradley Parsons. In focus once upon a time perhaps, but so muddy Grover couldn't even guess at the expression on his face. Not much use for waving in front of people with the question 'Have you ever seen this man?' 'Why is he standing in the fog?' would be a reasonable response from any putative identifyee. His military record was a litany of misery. Beating up a mess cook after a crap game dispute; suspicions of the unprovoked shooting of a German prisoner; a bout of fraternising with the locals which resulted in the suspected assault of a Belgian waitress; several nights in the brig for drinking and causing an affray. He began Operation Overlord as a sergeant, survived the slog across Europe but within eighteen months of the occupation of West Berlin, he had been busted to private and become a monster pain in the ass to everyone who had anything to do with him. Then suddenly, he transformed into a model serviceman – or so the Brass, the Snowdrops and his platoon buddies thought. And back in England, waiting to go home, his behaviour was all that the army expected.

Which resulted in the 48 hour passes, five days AWOL and his life hanging in the balance.

Grover had spent the previous evening at Blenheim Villas, restless. Rachel and Winston were working. He cooked and ate on his own. Pondering relentlessly on the difference twenty-four hours can make to a new chapter in a life which is supposed to be a breeze. Roly Bevan had set his stall out, Mel was in trouble, Bradley Parsons was up to something nefarious. All of this leaving him locked into an investigation of sorts, at the behest of his employer, the US Army. The sort of ingredients which made for a grade A unhappy ending.

Now out of uniform, he was in the clothes he had bought in the city a couple of months ago – a tweed sports jacket, shirt, dark blue flannels and comfortable, soft soled shoes.

Turnbull had been as good as his word. Grover rocked back in a much more comfortable, upholstered swivel chair and put his feet up on the desk.

And asked himself 'What now?

***

Eaves Night was a down market piece of real estate in *Stage Door Lane*, an alley around the corner from the Hippodrome. A narrow, two storey brick building adjacent to a partially cleared bombsite. Before the war it had been a flourishing ironmongers. Now it looked like what it was, a drab left-over place with a name tailored in light bulbs, some of which were missing.

A short, bald man in his late 50s, clad in a boiler suit, was waving a wash leather optimistically at the glass in the front door. The panes were coated with grime and almost opaque. He stepped back to consider his handiwork as Grover approached.

"Some job that." Grover said.

"Makes no difference, whatever I do," the man said.

Grover studied the wave of lightbulbs above the door and tried to imagine how *E ves ght* looked when the sign was lit up.

"We don't open until 8 o'clock," the man said.

Grover asked him if the boss was in.

"You want to talk to her then?"

"I'd rather not come back later."

"Somebody inside will show you to the office."

He stepped to his left, opened the door and waved Grover across the threshold. The lobby was no more or less than any expectations could harbour. It was fifteen feet square, decorated with purple flock wallpaper from the floor to a dado rail and above that, a lighter bluish purple to the ceiling; the exact colour of which, Grover could not establish in the half dark. The cloakroom was represented by a counter with a clothes rack behind it housing a row of metal coat hangers. Grover ventured onwards and pushed open the double doors ahead of him.

The place was bigger than he had expected, but in this case, big was no more beautiful than the lobby had been. The dance floor occupied two thirds of the space. There was a small band stage in the corner to his right – just enough room for a quartet, Grover figured – and a bar about the same size in an alcove to his left. A short, slightly built woman was cruising across the floor with a long handled, wide shouldered brush. She approached a wall, stopped, swung the brush, pushed the detritus she had collected to her right, turned through another ninety degrees, put the business end of the brush behind it and set off on a parallel course back along the floor. Concentrating on the job she was doing, she did not see Grover arrive, or hear him as he moved alongside her.

"Excuse me…"

He stepped ahead of the woman and into her line of sight. She dropped the brush.

"Bloody hell. Where did you spring from?"

Grover picked up the brush and handed it back to her. Apologised.

"I should think so too," she burbled. "Creeping up on a woman like that."

He apologised again.

"You're an American," She said. "Still over here."

"Can't deny that."

She softened a bit. He asked where the office was. She pointed in the direction of a door to the left of the bar alcove.

"Thank you," he said.

She bent once more to the task in hand. Grover watched as she glided away from him, then moved to the office door. He read the word *Private* and knocked politely.

There was a short delay before a husky female voice said 'Come in'.

Behind her desk, the boss filled the chair she was sitting in. Wide shouldered and curved in the all the right places, but big all over. She had the desk phone receiver to the ear facing the door and was mid conversation.

Grover closed the office door quietly and took a couple of steps forward. Ignoring his presence, the boss carried on talking.

"Of course I know that," she said. Then without looking up, "Put it down on the desk."

Grover stood still. Glanced around the office. A space twelve by twelve or thereabouts. Housing, along with the desk, a couple of filing cabinets, two armchairs and a carpet which had seen better days. And on the wall behind the desk, as if in pride of place, a collection of blown up and framed newspaper headlines, chronicling the shooting of the late Ronnie Eaves, and Ruby Willis' journey to her date with the hangman.

"He says that does he?..." She listened again. "Then tell him to piss off and try somebody else." With her spare arm, she waved in Grover's direction and pointed at the desk top. "No no no, bollocks to that... Just fix it."

She jammed the receiver back in place and looked up. Opened her mouth to say something, closed it again and changed the subject she had been about to address.

"Who the hell are you?"

"Ed Grover."

"A yank."

"No disguising that."

"I thought my tea was on the way," she said. "What do you want?"

"To ask you a couple of questions. If you're the boss that is."

She did her best to sit back in the over-flowing chair, but her body had no room to re-arrange itself. Grover's eyes shifted again to the headlines behind her. She noticed.

"Good aren't they. There to remind me of the best days of my life."

Grover was lost for words. His host waved at one of the armchairs. He sat down. He was given a moment to rehearse the opening gambit, by a knock on the door and the entry of the tea person. A woman who could have been the twin of the lady sweeping the floor. The boss thanked her and looked back at Grover.

"Would you like some tea?"

"No thanks. I'll pass."

The tea person left the office. The boss reached to her right, picked up the saucer in one hand, raised the cup with the other and sipped her tea. Grover noticed she was left-handed.

"I'm Sandra Eaves," she said and sipped again. "So… Do you live here? As opposed to over the water."

"I'm in the US Army."

"Dressed like that?"

"I have a liaison job."

Sandra drained her cup of tea and replaced it in the saucer. Put the saucer back down on the desk.

"So what are you liaising about? Here in my establishment that is."

"Bradley Parsons," Grover said.

"Never heard of him."

Not much of a beginning.

"Parsons has been here."

"So have several thousand people since the end of the war."

"He's a member of the 21st Infantry."

"Is he?" the lady asked.

Grover sensed more curiosity in the answer than the question merited.

"Your outfit?"

"Yes."

"And you've lost him?"

"Not exactly. We do know where he is."

No response from the boss. She appeared to be considering something. Grover ploughed on.

"He's in the General Hospital. A step away from dying."

That provoked a reaction. Sandra leaned forward across her desk, picked up a heavy glass paperweight, examined it for a moment or two, then put it down again.

"And what foolish thing did he do, to find himself in such a place and in such a state?"

"He was knocked down by a car."

Sandra let go of the wariness that had crept into her end of the dialogue. She sat back again.

"My friends and valued customers call me Sandy."

Grover produced the cloakroom ticket. Put it on the desk in front of his host.

"We found this in Parsons' pocket."

Sandy stared down at the number. "It's a raffle ticket."

"Look at the other side," Grover said.

She did so.

"Ah…"

"As I said, Parsons has been here. I'd like you tell me when that was. And respectfully to ask if you know why, and if he was with someone."

She shook her head. "I can't do that. I never met him."

Grover pushed a little harder. "Will the number tell you which night he was here? If he was a guest, presumably he signed in. Private club, private membership… Or do you ignore that?"

Sandy took a long look at him, and a while to decide if Grover qualified for help, or the traditional bum's rush. He waited. She made up her mind, reached for the phone, picked up the receiver and dialled two numbers. Grover counted the seconds. This was either the prelude to an act of cooperation, or a one-way ticket to the front door, courtesy of a couple of wide shouldered employees.

"Donald," she said into the receiver. "My apologies for bothering you. Can you please check the visitor entry book for last Saturday…? Yes. The name is," she looked up at Grover, "Bradley Parsons?" Grover nodded. "Yes, that's right Donald. Will you find out which member signed him in?... No that's all. Thank you."

She put the receiver back in its cradle.

"Donald. Keeps the books. An absolute treasure."

"Saturday," Grover said. "Why Saturday?"

"You were correct of course… Everything, every member, every guest, every drink, every day, is accounted for. In the book. In Donald's delightful copperplate. And each night has its own cloakroom ticket colour. Saturday is blue."

Which made for a perfectly sound system, all elements considered. It simply required two signatures in a book.

Which were not there however, according to Donald. He called back to say there were only five guests admitted last Saturday night. But there was no 'Bradley Parsons' recorded alongside an appropriate club member.

Sandy looked stricken for a moment or two, then smiled at Grover with all the ohms she could muster.

"So, there you have it Ed. No Mr Parsons in the book. And if he's not in the book…"

Grover had nothing he could say. Sandy took the silence for agreement. "Perhaps I could offer you a drink? Other than tea I mean."

Grover got to his feet. Sandy decided that agreement had morphed into disappointment.

"What can I do Ed, but apologise?"

Grover kept his own counsel. She rested her elbows on the desktop, raised her arms and opened them right and left.

"Truly sorry. I will of course, actively pursue the omission with all those on duty at the time. This is both embarrassing and a clear breach of club rules."

She prised herself out of the chair, ushered Grover out of her office and insisted on conducting him personally to the front door. She watched him travel all the way to the end of the alley before retreating into the club. She crossed the dance floor and stepped into Donald's small, cramped office behind the bar.

A solid man with an easy smile, he was expecting the boss. He offered her a slim ledger.

"Saturday night's record," he said.

"And let me have the records of all the other nights Private Bradley Parsons has treated us to the pleasure of his company."

The smiled drained from his face

"Private?"

"As in the United States Army."

"Oh fuck."

CHAPTER NINE

A similar measure of concern was making Sam Nicholson fret also. At high noon, in the old scarlet fever hospital, he and Rodney Pride were standing in ward 3, re-named *Brockley*. Washed, scrubbed clean and re-decorated.

"Impressive eh?" Pride said, glowing with self-congratulation. "And this is only the small ward. Across the corridor…"

He escorted Nicholson from the room and into ward 4, newly named *Failand*. Clean and spotless also. In spite of the attack of nerves which fired up his ulcer every moment he thought about this project, Sam had to admit he was impressed.

"Who did all this Rodney?"

"Three blokes who are now on a long holiday in Cyprus."

Nicholson looked out of a window. At a large wooden shed. The site HQ of a non-existent building company, its name stencilled in black paint along the wall he could see – *NEW WESTERN DEVELOPMENTS*.

"So that's our second piece of real estate is it?"

"Come on Sam, get on board for fuck's sake."

A tall, straight backed, grey-haired man, walked into the ward. His tailored suit was a navy-blue worsted, his shirt light blue, his tie a matching grey. He carried himself well.

He looked comfortable, and better than that, prosperous. Pride beamed in delight and introduced him.

"Sam, this is our main man. Richard Havers. He will be the first person our mothers-to-be meet."

Havers smiled, relaxed and comfortable. He held out his right hand. Nicholson shook it.

"Pleased to meet you, Mr Nicholson. I prefer surnames. We should keep all this as formal as possible. Hospitals have a rigid code of behaviour. I want us to adhere to those also."

Pride beamed again. "Adhere away."

Havers looked at Pride. Like an indulgent parent who has let a thing or two slide, but intends to pounce on the next irregularity. Pride got the message.

"Sorry doc. Mr Havers."

"Doctor Havers will do."

Pride nodded. "Okay, understood."

Nicholson looked on amazed. He had never seen Rodney Pride this relaxed and amenable.

"Good," Havers said. "I have a car outside, full of files and papers and paraphernalia. Will you help me unload?"

He turned and left the ward.

"Great, isn't he?" Pride said.

"As long as he's a real doctor," Nicholson muttered.

***

Grover knocked politely on the door of Turnbull's office. The incumbent bade him enter. He was handed the photograph of Parsons' girlfriend.

"Can you re-produce this for me?"

Turnbull studied the face in the picture.

"Who is she?"

"I don't know."

Turnbull looked at him sideways. So, Grover gave him a précis of the accident story.

"I'd like to find her. Another print would be useful."

"And you don't have the negative?"

"No."

Turnbull studied the picture again.

"Taken recently I'd say. It's sharp and clear. We can photograph it."

"How about this one?" He handed over the picture from Parsons' record. Turnbull stared at it.

"Really?"

"It's all we've got."

"Okay," Turnbull said. "I can re-produce it but I can't improve on it." He got to his feet. "Come with me."

He led Grover to the aero design records office. Stacked along one wall, from floor to ceiling, with wide cabinets and drawers.

"We keep copies of all plans, drawings and final designs in here." He moved to a door in the wall opposite. "And in here…" He opened the door and ushered Grover into a ten by twelve feet room.

It housed a 35mm camera rostrum, rigged above a modified drawing table. Turnbull clipped the photograph in place on the table. He opened a flight case in a corner of the room, and selected a lens and a camera. Scrutinised the frame counter.

"There are half a dozen shots left in this. Might as well use them up."

He put the camera into the rig, screwed the lens into place and looked down through the viewfinder.

"There's a light switch on the wall behind you, Ed. Flick it please."

Grover did. Light flooded the drawing table. Turnbull adjusted the lens focus.

"Okay… Tilt the table vertical a little. There's a wheel at the side."

Grover located the wheel and turned it.

"Stop. Too far…" Turnbull said. "We're dealing in tiny measurements here. Back a couple of degrees… And again… Good. Here we go…"

He took one shot, checked the focus, and took three more. He attempted to improve the shining hour with a couple of viewable shots of Parsons, bowed to the inevitable, unlocked the camera from the rig, re-wound the film roll and prised it out of the holder.

"Okay, we'll get this into the bath. You'll have the prints in half an hour."

Back in his own office, Grover decided the filing cabinet was in the wrong place. Moving it drove him into a complete reorganisation of the office. He was stripping the desk of its drawers, prior to heaving it though ninety degrees when the phone rang. He located it on the floor to his right, sat down next to it and picked up the receiver.

"You can collect Melanie this afternoon," Doctor Mason said.

"Thank you for that."

"And your soldier got through the night."

"That's good."

"It means, at least, that his prospects appear much better."

"Is he conscious?"

"Yes."

"Can I talk to him?"

"Absolutely not. Apart from being unable to put sentences together, he won't recall anything of the accident. At least not at this stage. I'll keep you up to date".

"I'd appreciate that."

"And may I remind you, the hours fly by. You are halfway through your grace and favour thirty-six."

Grover thanked her and ended the call. Considered that a trip to the hospital might at least offer a chance of seeing Parsons at first hand. He called Fairford and passed on the news to Lieutenant Berger.

"So far so good then," he said.

There was a knock on the office door.

"Got to go, Sir."

"Any other developments to me soonest, Ed"

"Sir."

Grover replaced the receiver and welcomed the visitor. Turnbull gave him an envelope containing the photographs. He took out the master, restored it to Parsons' wallet, and put the envelope in the left-hand drawer of his desk. He asked Turnbull if he would mind keeping this secret. Turnbull said he had no idea what Grover was talking about.

A second knock on the door announced the arrival of Howard Rockcliffe, the engine factory public relations person. A carefully manicured, short haired man, around five feet ten and dressed in the 'Full Monty'. Courtesy of the high street tailor Montague Burton, a gentleman could be suited entirely – a full three piece, plus a shirt and tie, for two pounds nineteen and six. A cut or two above the demob suit and the fifty-bob tailor.

"We have been invited to attend a function at the *Grand Hotel*," Rockcliffe said. "All three of us. Tomorrow at noon. To meet members of the local Chamber of Commerce, several luminaries and the City Council Leader."

"Okay," Grover said. "Do I need to bone up on anything?"

"No nothing technical. Nobody is going to quiz you about jet engines. You may get asked about how the Marshal Plan works, in principle of course. Just be the polite, helpful, straight talking GI we have all come to like."

"Right," Grover said with a certain wariness. He caught the smile on Turnbull's face.

"You'll enjoy meeting the council Leader," Rockcliffe went on. "He's a bit of a character."

***

The City Council Leader, was trying to stay manful and unworried. There was not much about this hospital enterprise – apart from the anticipated dividends – currently sitting easily.

The office chosen by Rodney Pride, was situated above an empty garage in a cul de sac opposite the Imperial Tobacco Factory in Southville. A place which swarmed with people at shift changes, but twenty-three hours out of twenty-four Baynton Close was just another street in a relatively anonymous neighbourhood. Two of Rodney Pride's associates were on the pavement, giving the garage and the office access door a coat of paint. Broken nosed bruisers in overalls with seams bursting at the shoulders.

Nicholson's Rover pulled up alongside the property. He had persuaded his partner in the scheme to leave his ostentatious hunk of Detroit metal at home.

"We'll never keep all this under wraps, if you coast around in that fucking thing," Nicholson had said.

The two men climbed out of the Rover. Pride nodded at his work force. Led Nicholson through the office door and up the stairs. He had fitted the place out simply, but elegantly enough.

"Our clients will have no reason to think this is a cheapskate racket," Pride said. "And as we have both floors, we won't be disturbed by tenants below." He pointed at the comfortably stuffed swivel chair behind the desk. "Try it for size."

Nicholson shook his head.

"Oh no. This is the first and last time I set foot in here. I'll fix stuff but I won't be seen dead in the place. The business is all yours."

Pride grinned at his discomfort. "Apart from the dividend every six months."

Nicholson managed to look him in the eyes. "In cash, personally delivered to my home," he murmured, as if the place was bugged. Which in that instant he decided was well within Rodney Pride's business parameters.

"This is where our secretary will sit," he said. "This is where we'll meet clients. All business will be done in cash. No bank accounts, no records, no paper trail. Safe as houses."

Nicholson could not help himself. "Christ, I hope so."

"Stop whingeing Sam for fuck's sake." He dropped into the swivel chair and grinned up at his partner. "Just get the hospital change of use through the council and leave the rest to me."

***

Melanie was sitting in the ground floor waiting room when Grover arrived to pick her up. She rose to her feet and presented him with a bunch of red, white and purple carnations.

"By way of thanks," she said.

"I should be bringing flowers to you."

"I tried for red white and blue," she said. "Purple was the best the florist could manage."

"Purple is my favourite colour." He smiled at her. She smiled back, not wincing this time. "Thank you."

"Let's hope Mrs Rawlins left you a vase at Blenheim Villas."

On the way to Melanie's house, they stopped to check. And found a tall, fluted glass vase under the kitchen sink.

"This place is more comfortable than I had imagined," Melanie said, the flower arranging done.

"Yes, I'll be okay here. Now let's get you home."

The whole family were in the living room. Two parents, two grandparents, two brothers and one sister, an uncle and two cousins, all yelled 'Surprise'.

Melanie turned to Grover.

"Not my idea," he said. "They did all this."

It was a good afternoon. Everyone was upbeat, thoughts of the uncertainty ahead temporarily banished. Zoe arrived in time for tea and cakes, accompanied by Clerk to the Chambers Neil Adkins. A middle aged, dark haired, brown eyed man; quick witted and swift on his feet, and indispensable in any 'what to do next' conversation.

For which, the KC, the Clerk and the Sergeant Major re-convened in Mel's tiny study. Grover was asked about the welfare of Bradley Parsons.

"He made it through the night."

"Good," Zoe said. "That's encouraging."

"Only in so far that he's not dead yet," Grover suggested.

Adkins shot him a baleful look. "Strong positive thinking, Ed."

"Apologies for that. But I need to talk something through with both of you. In absolute confidence."

Adkins looked at Zoe. She nodded. "Go ahead."

Grover took some moments to order what he was about to say. The legal team waited.

"Okay," he said. "This is information that you are not entitled to, as we speak, because you don't know the direction of travel yet. You will need to request it later, but knowing now, may help me to help Melanie. As long as the source of this information doesn't know you know."

Adkins respected the obfuscation, but cut to the chase.

"And this source is?"

Grover looked at them both in turn.

"I need you to treat me like a client in this. The information stays in this room. No disclosure… Your word, here and now."

"You have it," Zoe said.

"Neil?"

"She's the boss."

Grover took a deep breath.

"The source is the US Army. Private Bradley Parsons' military record. Parsons is no angel, although his recent behaviour had been beyond reproach. Clearly, my boss, wouldn't want you to know this. Especially at this moment in time, when there is only a remote possibility Parsons will pull through. In the unlikely event that he does, the Army, will apologise for any aggravation caused, buy Melanie eighteen yellow roses, ferry Parsons back to Fairford, and then on to the States. Where, well away from prying eyes, he will be court marshalled."

He paused. The other two remained silent. Grover picked up the story.

"If he dies, the coroner and the local constabulary will step in. Yes?"

Two heads nodded at him. He moved on.

"In which event I assume you will go into bat for Mel. In court if necessary. The US Army will hate that. You will question why all this is necessary, and driven by probable cause, ask to see the aforementioned military record. Whereupon the shit will hit the fan. The Marshall Plan aside, this is not a great time for the 'Special

Relationship'. We are still over here, albeit agitating to go home, fraternising with the locals, in some cases causing trouble and being a pain in the ass."

Still the legal team said nothing. Grover moved swiftly on.

"Parsons is AWOL. Seven days including today. That won't play well with the good burgers of the city."

For a moment Adkins looked pained. Grover wound up.

"And there is more. He is AWOL not just because he's the tricky bastard he is, but because he's into something he shouldn't be. Sandy Eaves, in her straight from the shoulder lying way, says she's never heard of Parsons. But adds that she will do her best to find out what the guy was doing as a guest at *Eaves Night*, and who signed him in. That's bullshit of course. She won't, because she already knows. But in the meantime..."

He left the rest of the sentence hanging. Zoe completed the supposition.

"She may be stirred into some action we will all be sorry for."

CHAPTER TEN

Grover in dress uniform, Turnbull wearing a sleeveless jumper under his tweed jacket, and Rockcliffe sporting another suit, shared a car from Filton to the Grand Hotel bash.

Sam Nicholson was the first to take the floor. He had no need to display any knowledge of the Marshall Plan project. Had simply to welcome it enthusiastically, wax a bit lyrical on how it had the potential to change the fortunes of the city, and hand the rest of the business over to the honoured guests.

Rockcliffe did not know much about the workings of the Marshall plan either. So he stuck to pouring large dollops of congratulation on the factory for gaining the confidence of Britain's North Atlantic partner and leader of the free world, and looked forward to Filton regaining its position as the major aero engineering outfit in Europe.

He introduced Andrew Turnbull, who did have something technological and of potential interest to say to everyone in the room. His short speech produced a lot of nodding heads, contented murmurs and hearty applause at the end. He handed over to the man in the dress uniform, who represented American interests in the project.

Grover simply said 'hello', informed the gathering that he was based at Filton in the room next to Mr

Turnbull, and that his job was liaise with anyone and everyone – British and American – who might at any time have questions to raise.

Whereupon, given the exigencies of rationing and the need for the gathering to be as simply catered as it was noble of purpose, all present tucked into sausage rolls, gala pie, egg and cress sandwiches and drinks.

Zoe sought out Grover. He was staring at the portion of pastry, processed pork and sliced egg sitting on his plate.

"Why do they call this gala pie?"

"It was part of the wartime drive for cheap celebration," she explained. "Try it. Simple and hearty."

"Not really," he attempted to protest with his mouth full. Then he managed to swallow. "I think I'll give the rest of it a miss."

He put his plate on the nearest table. Zoe changed the subject.

"You did well," she said, "You and your badge of office."

"Maybe," he said, looking around the room. "Who are all these people?"

"Local politicians, city councillors, fixers, financiers, members of the Chamber of Commerce. And the odd colourful character or two. You met a couple of them on your last visit. Roly Bevan's here somewhere. And I saw Daniel Zampa earlier. You remember him, surely?"

On cue, the most powerful man in the city slid into Grover's line of site, raised an arm and smiled. Zoe moved closer to Grover's side.

"Be careful young Lochinvar," she murmured.

He looked into her eyes.

"Sir Walter Scott," she explained. And began to recite
"*Young Lochinvar is come out of the west*
Through all the wide border his steed was the best
And save his old broadsword he weapons had none
He rode all unarmed and he rode all alone."

Grover stared at her. "How did he do?"

"He rescued a young bride from a man her father forced her to marry, swung her up onto his charger and rode off into the sunset. He was a knight of great purity and honour. A sole crusader, a romantic. The poem is all about love, the cold moments of battle, the good guy winning and the best of things saved."

Zampa began to make his way across the room.

No time for poetry this, Grover decided, however germane. And being no stranger to the ways and the workings of the person with all the available ammunition in his hands, he swiftly recalled how dangerous the man, now barely a few steps away, was.

Daniel Zampa, was in his mid-40s. Tall and wide shouldered, with jet black hair, black eyes and a pencil moustache like Zachary Scott. Born in Valetta, the only son of a Bristol nurse and a Maltese con artist who met in 1915. The family left Malta for Bristol when Daniel was five years old. Zampa *pere* did well between the wars. Converted a two roomed billiards hall into a basement drinking den and set up a protection business. Which flourished until the night his past caught up with him in an alleyway behind the *Gaumont* cinema on Baldwin Street.

Zampa was as clever as his father had been ambitious, and those who had ordered the killing were found swiftly and dealt with. He converted the billiards hall into a night club, and as soon as the war arrived, did the place up, re-painted the front door, renamed it *El Paradis* and jacked up the prices. He was cute enough to appreciate there was nothing like a war to boost entertainment revenue.

Despite being half Maltese, he was called up in 1942. Whereupon, he paid £250 to the examining doctor to stamp his certificate *Unfit for Service* because of a heart murmur; giving no thought to the heroics of his aunts and uncles and cousins in the middle of the Mediterranean, managing to put up a hell of struggle against Hitler's dive bombers.

Zampa was an equal opportunity exploiter. Membership of *El Paradis* was open to anyone with money to spend; regardless of class, creed, culture, skin colour or sexual orientation. The lights were low and the nature of the clientele never an issue. No questions were asked as long as their money was good. Discretion and patronage were assured at all times, in return for unalloyed acceptance of the ground rules. The implied threat was clear. And nobody, but nobody, welched on their tab.

"You have a new job I see," Zampa said. Then went on to elaborate. "And a new address. Roly Bevan phoned me."

"Courteous of him."

Zampa grinned, ignoring all that the last three words implied.

"That's good," he said. "Really. I'm pleased." He transferred his attention to Zoe. "Mrs Easton. Delighted to meet you again."

"Thank you," Zoe said.

Grover decided not to get irritated by this carefully constructed dose of 'hail fellow, well met'. He could take Bevan's laid-back charm for what it was; Roly wasn't all that dangerous. But Zampa was the polar opposite. So, he said nothing. Zampa moved the conversation along.

"You appear to have succeeded, Ed, in your ambition to stay in this country. If you need anything, give me a call. You never know…"

He let the rest of the proposal hang in the air.

Zoe intervened. "There's somebody I want you to meet Ed." She smiled at Zampa. "Please excuse us."

Zampa smiled in return. "Of course." Then looked into Grover's eyes. "Don't be a stranger Ed."

Zoe hauled Grover across the room.

"Just a minute ago I said be careful. Now I'm telling you to use those finely honed reactions of yours to ensure you stay in one piece. Zampa isn't inviting you to tea and cakes."

Sam Nicholson hove into view. Zoe nodded towards him.

"Spend some time with the Council Leader. He's not one of nature's noblemen. A small-time fixer, but relatively harmless."

Nicholson arrived and pumped Grover's right hand vigorously.

"Pleased to meet you Sergeant Major."

"Mr Nicholson."

"Call me Sam. And if there is anything I can do for you… Oil the wheels, that sort of thing, just let me know."

"Of course," Grover said. "Thank you."

He retrieved his right hand. Zoe apologised to Nicholson for having to pick up a conversation somewhere across the room, stepped away from the two men and disappeared into the throng. Nicholson wrapped an arm around Grover and steered him towards the drinks table.

It was close to 4 o'clock before the handshaking, eating, drinking and talking were over. Back in the car, Rockcliffe pronounced their labours most satisfactory. Grover asked to be driven to Blenheim Villas so he could change before making another visit to the General Hospital. A purpose which took on a whole different momentum when he picked up the note slid under his door by Rachel.

Doctor Mason phoned. She wants to see you soonest.

Grover didn't need more than a second to consider why.

***

"Bradley Parsons died two and a half hours ago," Lauren told him. "He bled out inside. We couldn't help him."

Grover stared down at the body of the dead soldier.

"There will have to be an inquest, I guess."

Lauren nodded. "I'm afraid so. What will the US Army think of the prospect?"

"The army will hate it," Grover said. "And the Coroner will be swamped with lawyers."

She looked at Grover. "Why? It's a straight forward accidental death. Isn't it?"

"That's what my boss would like it to be."

"But it isn't, of course."

Grover took a beat. Asked the doctor what happened next.

"We put him in cold storage here, until the post mortem. Which is then followed by the Coroner's Inquest."

"And that could be when?"

"In as little as a few days. It depends on what the pathologist discovers."

Grover breathed in and out.

"May I use your phone again?"

***

"Shit!" was all the Adjutant said.

He told Grover to keep abreast of the situation and ended the call. Looked out of the office window.

"Shit shit shit shit shit."

He hastily arranged a meeting with Colonel Whitmore, the 21st CO. Who asked if the army would be allowed to have Parsons back before the British pathologist got to work on him?"

"That's not likely, Sir."

Just about to celebrate his 50th birthday, Whitmore had been in the army since he had volunteered at the age of seventeen; gaining his first experience of the butchery of the Great War in August 1918, during the brutal allied counter offensive at the Second Battle of the Marne. More than a million American troops were thrown into the forty-seven day Meuse Argonne Forest offensive. 117,000 died. During the second US commitment to European war, Whitmore had masterminded the 21st recovery after Bastogne and the dedicated slog to the river Elbe. The men liked him, and had gone to hell and back for him. Now, along with the majority of veterans, he was looking east again, poised for yet another conflict in a country far away. While he was simply longing to go home to Idaho, at least for a while, to meet his first granddaughter.

"Should we get our own doctors and a lawyer to Bristol," he asked.

"I think that would be a mistake at this point, Sir," Berger said.

"Because…?" For a moment irritation got the better of him.

"Might be considered something of a knee jerk reaction by the Brits, Sir. And that might give rise to a question or two."

"Yeah…" The Colonel pondered. "How much do they know about Parsons? The authorities."

"According to Ed Grover, the doctors know a little but the cops don't know anything. Parsons did spend time in a club called *Eaves Night*. Ed found the place and talked with the owner. She denied he was ever in the building. He doesn't believe her."

"Then neither should we," the Colonel said. He stood up and started to prowl around the office. "What the hell was Parsons up to?"

"We have reason to believe he visited the club on at least two, maybe three occasions earlier in the year. But we don't know why? Hell, maybe he just wanted a drink and some company?"

Whitmore stopped prowling. "You don't really believe that."

Berger looked uncomfortable. "Okay," he said. "But Parsons could have just been enjoying himself."

Whitmore snorted. The two men were running out of 'maybes'. The Colonel looked straight into the Adjutant's eyes.

"We need to do the next right thing."

Berger didn't flinch.

"Even if that means handing Parsons over to the Brits?" he asked.

"Look at it this way?" Whitmore said. "Do we really want the bastard in this man's army?"

Berger summed up.

"Then I suggest we leave Sergeant Major Grover to poke around for a day or two. He's our guy on the spot. He's not stupid. He did well in Berlin, and he was a cop back in Wisconsin."

Whitmore returned to his desk and sat down. Did a couple of circles in his swivel chair. Berger waited.

"Alright. Your show, Steve," the Colonel said. "For now. Get back to Grover. Tell him to do everything on tiptoe. And keep both of us posted."

CHAPTER ELEVEN

Which for Ed Grover, was either a very good thing, or a very bad thing. This liaison job was supposed to be an easy gig, not a relationship hot potato. He decided to sleep on it.

The mid-day sausage rolls and egg sandwiches, and the memory of the gala pie had lain heavily most of the afternoon. Under the circumstances, baked beans on toast were enough of an evening repast. He sat down to eat, listening to the radio – the Ray Noble Orchestra and the late great Al Bowly recording of *The Touch of Your Lips*. Followed by *Goodnight Sweetheart* and *I'll String Along With You*. Grover had first become acquainted with that great soaring tenor voice in Berlin, when he heard *The Very Thought of You* on BBC radio's *Forces Favourites*.

He switched to the BBC Home Service and *The Brains Trust* – the line-up Julian Huxley, CEM Joad and Archibald Bruce Campbell. The latter, considered by the BBC to be 'the man who could talk about anything', was regarded as essentially low brow by hardcore brains like Joad and Huxley. During one broadcast, the team was asked to define what an allergy was. Campbell leapt into the fray before the other two and said, "I suffer from an allergy. If I eat marmalade, my head steams." Huxley and Joad were incensed by the injurious crassness and only just made it to the end of the programme. The following week Campbell seized the initiative again, by announcing at the head of the show, "I've had over 200 letters from people with the same problem."

Grover had not heard of any of the three brains on offer, and was amazed by the idea that some BBC department head truly believed that listening to the received wisdom of sociologists, scientists, philosophers and retired admirals would be remotely entertaining.

Returning to the Light Programme he caught the end of a comedy show featuring Al Read who said "Right monkey" and "You'll be lucky, I say you'll be lucky" a lot. He was followed by *Educating Archie*; the programme leaving Grover baffled by the concept of giving a ventriloquist a radio show. Surely the essential skills of a vent act were not displayed over the air waves.

In the end, he gave up because the dialogue handed out to the human performers was not remotely funny either.

He retired to bed and immediately began thinking. About having to tell Mel and Zoe of Bradley Parsons' death, the complications it had stirred up, the varying degrees of 'I'll help all I can' from Sandy Eaves, Sam Nicholson and Daniel Zampa. All the while having to beat out of the park the ever-present question of what the hell Parsons was up to and why.

He was still punching the pillow at midnight. Ten minutes later, he got out of bed, dressed and took himself for a walk.

Which brought another cast of characters out of the darkness.

He walked west along Cumberland Road for a couple of hundred yards, then turned right onto Albion Dockside. Behind him, the street lamps were out, but there were pools of light leaking from the Marina to his left and the dry dock to his right. The night was warm, the temperature above average for mid-May. In front of him, moonlight coated the surface of the Floating Harbour, the water rippling and distorting slightly.

Grover stopped to drink in the sight in front of him. The noise of his shoe heels seemed to echo behind him. It took him a moment to dismiss that idea before he turned to look back. Someone, or maybe a shadow of someone, disappeared behind the Boat Chandler's to his left. There was movement also, from behind a Vauxhall parked to the right. Behind the car a line of thick, spikey bushes bordered a path which swung away through some more shrubbery; beyond which, the path straightened out again, heading into the darkness of a pub car park.

Grover backed slowly towards the dockside behind him. A few paces short of the water, he stopped. Looked towards the Cumberland Basin and then in the direction of the city centre. He decided that anyone who might be standing in the distance was no immediate threat.

A couple of steps away a cast iron bench was bolted into the concrete and facing the water. He needed surprise on his side. If he sat down, whoever was behind the chandler's, the parked car, or in the shadows, would be emboldened into action. Maybe encouraged to break cover.

But nothing and no one stirred.

Grover made a decision. He stood up, turned around, called out.

"Come on. Let's do this. And whoever is left standing can go home to bed."

To his right, at 2 o'clock, a man stood up behind the Vauxhall, holding a pickaxe handle. He threw it up into the air, let it twirl and caught it again. The action was supposed to impress. To Grover's left at 10 o'clock, the man in the alley behind the chandler's stepped out into view. Fists bunched, he held up both hands and rotated his wrists. Silver and gold knuckle dusters caught the moonlight. Straight ahead, slightly behind the other two and blocking direct exit back to Cumberland Road, was the biggest character of the three. He raised his right hand. Flicked open the blade of the knife he was holding.

Grover, the decorated soldier, experienced combatant and trained killer, took stock.

The knuckle duster man was clearly a poser. He probably had a selection of gold-plated teeth also. But knuckle dusters hurt like hell and broke bones. It would only need one swing to connect and the game would be over. The man with the flick knife looked like he weighed more than the other two put together. But he was short, muscle bound, and probably slow. Face to face, one to one, he would go down easily. He was the farthest distance away and likely to be the last into action. The juggler with the pickaxe handle was tall, lean and looked agile. He would be tougher. But Grover decided he out-weighed and out-massed him, and if he got inside the man's reach, there was a chance he would go down too

They had chosen the right amount of space between each other. He could see all of them in wide shot. But any closer and his view would be narrowed to two. And to take on one at a time he would have to be close enough to make out the colour of their eyes. Grover calculated the odds. He decided that even at three to one, his assailants were being optimistic.

As he had expected, Knuckles weighed in first, coming in slightly to his left. He swung high and hard, mis-judging just enough. Grover swayed back out of the way. The knuckle duster came close, but the force of Knuckles' right arm swing had pushed his shoulder through ninety degrees. His weight was in the wrong place and he could not recover quickly enough. Grover bent his knees slightly, stepped to his right, balled his right fist and punched it into the space underneath Knuckles' rib cage. The man yelled and buckled. Grover slammed the edge of his left hand down onto the back of Knuckles' neck. He slumped to the ground. Just as Pickaxe Man swung from Grover's left, towards the side of his face. Grover ducked under the swing and charged. Wrapped his arms around the man's torso and kept on going. Straight into the half-glazed door of the Boat Chandler's. The force of the collision whiplashed the man's head backwards through the glass in the door, slicing a cut into the side of his neck. The pickaxe handle hit the ground. He was out of the game. But Knuckles was back again, closing on him from behind. Grover bent down and grabbed the pickaxe handle. Waited until he could smell the man's sweat, then spun round one hundred and eighty degrees, transferring all his upper body weight and power into the swing. The handle hit Knuckles between the fourth and fifth ribs. Grover heard them break. He swung the handle upwards in an arc, like the follow through in a golf tee shot. The action broke the man's jaw, drove his bottom set of teeth into the roof of his mouth and whipped his neck up and backwards. He was unconscious before he could feel any more pain. Out of the game also.

So far, Flick Knife Man had made no contribution to the contest. Now he decided there was no way he was going to. Grover slid the pickaxe handle forwards in his right hand until he got the balance he needed and stepped towards him. The man backed away, gaining speed, then turned and ran into the darkness behind the pub, heading for Cumberland Road.

Knuckles had dropped to his knees, trying to stem the blood from his neck.

Grover turned around, walked back to the dockside, and sent the pickaxe handle soaring through the air into the floating harbour. He sat down on the bench. Took time to let the adrenalin charge subside. The moon hung in the sky like a painting on a stage backcloth. Across the water, a car drove slowly along Hotwells Road behind the pollarded trees, headlights dipped, the noise of the engine filtered by the distance across the harbour. It slipped behind Palmers Timber Yard and disappeared out of sight.

Suddenly, everything was just so goddam peaceful.

Nonetheless, Young Lochinvar decided not to wait around. He stood up, eased his shoulders back and forth, rotated his neck a couple of times, and left his two assailants where they lay.

He met Rachel and Winston outside Blenheim Villas, as they returned from the *El Paradis*. The trio reconvened in Rachel's flat for coffee. Winston asked him if he'd had a good evening.

"Three guys jumped me in Albion Dock?"

"Who did what?" Rachel asked, stepping from the kitchen with a tray of mugs and a milk jug.

"Three men attempted to inflict damage on our neighbour," Winston said.

Rachel put the tray on the dining table.

"Are you hurt?"

"No. They were big and wide and thought they were tough, but they were second rate. I got two of them and the third one ran away."

Rachel handed out the coffee.

"Why did this happen? It wasn't random surely?"

"No."

"They must have been watching the house," Winston suggested. "Saw you leave and followed"

"Why?" Rachel asked.

"Because I've annoyed somebody," Grover said.

"Who?... I mean, Roly doesn't seem to mind your presence. And you haven't crossed swords with Daniel Zampa. No one else in the frame, is there?"

"People are lying to me about Bradley Parsons."

"Which people?" Rachel asked.

"You need to report this to the cops," Winston said.

Grover was silent.

"You are going to," Rachel said.

Grover remained silent.

"You're not, are you?"

Grover explained why.

"There's no point. I've no idea who those guys were, or where they came from. I'm poking around in what's likely to become a manslaughter case. And I don't want to add to my profile. A GI throwing his weight around in an English suburb, however defensible, will please neither the local cops nor the US Army. One wrong step and I'll get dragged back to Fairford and sent home on the next plane." He watched his friends absorb that, then ploughed on. "I'm in trouble whichever way it goes. I seem to have rattled somebody's cage. Impelling this person to send three employees to me with a message. In effect, get out of whatever it is I've gotten into."

"And that is?..." Rachel asked.

"I've no idea. A racket of some sort, I guess. Important to someone I probably don't even know. The meeting on the dockside was never intended to be a polite invitation to leave town."

There was some supping of coffee and some frowning. Then Winston shifted the mood.

"You need an ally," he suggested. "And there is one man in the city who knows everything that's going on."

Rachel looked mildly terrified.

"No no," she said. "He might be our boss, but confessing all to him could be the wrong thing to do. Totally. Besides, he might be the one who…" She could not give voice to the rest of the proposition.

Grover nodded. "Yeah, there is that."

"This is serious Bro," Winston said. "How is your current relationship with Daniel Zampa?"

"Only one way to find out," Grover said.

CHAPTER TWELVE

The *Club El Paradis*, sat at the end of a row of dwellings running from the Colston Hall stage door towards the top of Christmas Steps. Grover walked uphill along the cobbled back street to the door. There was a red and gold striped canopy over the pavement stretching from the club door to the edge of the road. Six feet wide and all of four feet long. Not exactly *The Talk of the Town*, but the place deserved credit for trying. At noon, the doors were already open. The cleaners were in and the band was rehearsing. Grover walked into the lobby.

Fifteen feet square, wood panelled and painted dark red. There were two doors to the right. One featured a central panel with a lady flamenco dancer in a swirling red skirt above the word *Bailaoras*. The other, her dancing partner in a tight black suit and Cuban heels, bore the legend *Caballeros*. Behind the hostess counter, there was a mural of a hillside dotted with long spiky cacti, Mediterranean palms and white walled villas. A lush Technicolor fantasy probably bearing no resemblance to reality. But hell, who in the entertainment business was concerned about that.

Grover moved on into the lounge. The designer glory of the room was another mural; this one encompassing the entire three hundred and sixty degrees of all four walls, doors, entrances and exits. The terraces of a bullfight arena. The dancing happened on what was supposed to be the floor of the arena. On the stage, the Xavier Carrera Rumba Band were rehearsing, swinging their way through *Begin the Beguine*. Five of the musicians were black – the drummer, the base player, the saxophonist, the guitarist, and the pianist. The sole white guy played clarinet. Xavier, real name Elijah Eugene Carson, was a huge Trinidadian who on the night conducted in a white tuxedo, swivelling his hips centre stage.

He saw Grover cross the floor. Still conducting with his right hand, he waved with his left. Grover waved back, moved to the door of Zampa's office and knocked on it.

He was invited to enter.

Daniel Zampa was at his desk, signing some paperwork. He paused, looked up and beamed across the office.

"Ed. Just a moment."

He appended his signature to the letter in front of him, put it to one side, speed read the next one and signed that. Screwed the top onto the expensive fountain pen he was using and placed it on the desk. Then he sat back in his chair.

"So soon Ed. Nonetheless welcome of course." He pointed at the sofa. "Sit down, please."

Daniel Zampa's office was expensive 1950s catalogue stuff. The shelves and the cabinets were made out of the latest laminates faced with wood. The desk was a beautifully crafted, circular affair, supported on a central tubular steel column with splayed feet. The chair Zampa was sitting in had black leather covered cushions inside a steel mesh shape, like a scooped-out egg. The narrow back curved as it stretched upwards, to support the occupant's spine; the arms, curved to match, spread out gracefully. The sofa against the wall Zampa was facing, had six-inch steel legs, which flattened into small plates where they rested on the carpet. The sofa arms and cushions were black leather covered too.

Grover recalled being impressed with the décor the last time he was in here.

He sank down into the sofa – so luxuriously upholstered it took every occupant, however able bodied, several seconds to get up out of it. No swift exits from this office. Zampa had all the time in the world to run any encounter as he pleased.

"Would you like a drink?"

"No thank you. Too early for me."

"It's never too early for a good malt whisky," Zampa said. "So please forgive me if I order one for myself."

He picked up the phone receiver on the desk. Dialled a couple of numbers and waited.

"Ah Sidney. Bring me a whisky and water please." He looked back at Grover. "Are you sure...?" Grover nodded. Zampa spoke to Sidney again. "No that's it, thank you."

His ordering done, he looked back at Grover.

"Out of uniform I see. Does that mean this visit is…" He chose the rest of the sentence carefully. "… as you Americans say, off the books?"

"Yes."

"Then I'm glad you're here."

Zampa chatted away amiably for the next minute or so, before a polite knock on the door presaged the entry of the barman, carrying a small tray with whisky and a jug of water.

"Sidney, this is Sergeant Major Ed Grover."

Sidney might have been aged anywhere between 60 and 90. Graceful though slightly stooped, thinning silver hair, but eyes that shone brightly. He looked in Grover's direction and dipped his head graciously.

"Sir."

"Pleased to meet you Sidney."

"Thank you, Sir."

He checked that everything was as Zampa had requested, put the tray on the boss's desk, nodded farewell to Grover and left the office.

"Good man Sidney," Zampa said. "He worked for my father, back in the good old days. When a bargain meant something." He added a little water to the whisky in the glass. "You know the sort of thing. A favour here a drink there, handshakes and secret deals. I'll take the south of the river you take the north. You settle with the man I'm after I'll nail this loser to the warehouse floor." He swallowed some whisky. Sighed with satisfaction. "Ah… Best the Scottish Isles can produce." Then he wound up the summary. "Not the way to operate now, of course. These days it's low profiles, no turf wars, no unilateral action. And no stirring up the police."

"Day to day business in south Chicago, the Bronx and Miami."

"But not here, Ed. Not in my neck of the woods. Everything that happens in this city, passes across my desk. Nobody rampages round these streets improvising."

118

Zampa looked at Grover dead centre and offered the nuclear-powered smile that no recipient ever forgot. Several megatons brighter than the welcome rendered by Roly Bevan a couple of days earlier, but not accompanied by the eyes.

"I'm like a friendly society. I hold all the markers and the mortgages. In difficult moments I tidy up, lend support, close the gaps, cover the financial holes."

"All of which sounds like an excellent service."

Zampa considered the implications for a moment. Then brushed that from his eyes and replaced it with a look that would chill the coldest steel.

"Ed. We both know I am not your ordinary common or garden freelance. However, as you have experienced, *El Paradis* clients do number among their ranks, breakers and enterers, fraudsters, forgers, bent accountants, tax dodgers, people whose deeds and personal preferences are frowned on by the majority of citizens, and many others with assorted histories. And all their secrets are safe with me. Unless, or until, they step out of line. I have no interest in drugs and prostitution, pushers and pimps. In fact, in the past I have been known to take a prominent stand against such pond scum."

"And you get a percentage of everything that grows in the garden."

Zampa smiled, approving of the analogy.

"And I ensure that all the weeding is done properly and no one plants anything in the wrong spot. Nothing grows in this city unless the head gardener approves."

No proud boast that, but Grover wondered how comprehensive his information was. Zampa spoke again and supplied the answer.

119

"Which is why I can appreciate how unfortunate this unpleasantness with your GI is... Don't look surprised. Did you think I wouldn't have heard?"

This was the big moment. Grover had to lead. He wondered how much of a fishing trip Zampa was on. Decided to test the waters.

"Bradley Parsons was AWOL. Had been for close on a week. It began with his fourth weekend pass this year."

"So, he was no stranger to the city."

"That's correct."

"Do you know what he got up to?"

"Not yet."

"Or who he came to see?"

"No."

Zampa was irritated by this. Uncharacteristically out of the loop and genuinely curious. No going back now. Grover decided to share.

"We know who he came to see last weekend."

Zampa kept his eyes glued to Grover's. Waited.

"He was a guest at *Eaves Night*."

Zampa did not move for several moments. Then he drained the contents of his glass and put it back on the tray.

"Are you sure about that?"

Grover nodded.

"I suppose you have been to the club?" Zampa said.

"I have."

"And?..."

"The owner operator did a passable imitation of surprise. Checked with some guy called Donald. And then -"

Zampa interrupted. "Expressed shock and concern that there was no record of your GI being there."

"Apologising throughout."

Zampa straightened up in his chair.

"Leave it with me."

Grover shook his head. "It's not that simple."

"Actually, it is," Zampa said. "I assure you."

"Not right now."

The laid back Zampa slipped a little. He leaned forward, elbows on the desk.

"You know how this works Ed… I sort out this kind of thing. Swiftly, cleanly. The ripples don't spread."

"They already have," Grover said. "Parsons died yesterday afternoon. A post mortem is happening as we speak. The cops are about to get involved. A case of manslaughter is just over the hill. Fincher Reade and Holborne are prepared to act for the car driver. The KC wants all of it out in the open. The US Army lawyers want the whole thing shut down. Now, I have no idea what a conversation with Sandy Eaves will dig up. It could open a whole can of worms. Which even you may not be able to bury."

The look in Zampa's eyes radiated 'Don't fuck with me'. He had said all he wished to say, for the moment, so he waited. Grover took a long look at him. Tailored navy blue pin stripe suit, with a maroon jacket lining, and matching waistcoat. His body language added 'I've got all the time in the world'.

Grover had been on the receiving end of the club owner's iron clad determination before and he took a deep breath. Most people on the sofa, even if not under threat, would have been nodding in agreement by this time. Grover managed to allow the sofa to absorb some of the strain.

"Nobody in this can afford a scandal," he said. "It's a PR nightmare for the Army. We're all still overpaid, oversexed and over here. A renegade GI involved in some local criminal activity is dead. And someone in your organisation may be freelancing. The whole thing could burst wide open."

"Sandy Eaves is small fry," Zampa said.

"Yes," Grover agreed. "And it's small mistakes which bust up rackets."

Zampa suddenly looked dangerous. Nobody called him a racketeer. Grover ploughed on.

"Fincher Reade and Holborne would love to take all of you to the cleaners. Personally, I don't give a shit if it goes wrong. I'll get sent home out of the way, but you'll go to jail for twenty years."

Zampa raised his right arm and pointed straight at Grover. The extended finger like a spear that couldn't miss its mark; a look in his eyes that would chill the coldest steel.

"Don't you try and threaten me Ed Grover," he whispered. "I once told you that no one talks to me the way you have just done, without at the very least, getting a marker next to his name. Well this makes two."

Grover scrolled back down the years to Bastogne, temperatures way below freezing, the Ardennes snow pocked with blood and guts. It was a marker he'd locked away, to be recalled when things got tough. Along with the emaciated bodies of women and their dying babies in a crushed and war-torn western Europe. Zampa was never going to get the better of a resolve born of those images.

"This is a two-way street," Grover said, "Neither of us needs to act tough." He pushed a little harder. "And it won't work for me. A close friend of mine may be stuck in the middle of all this. I need to know stuff. Not simply have it buried."

He waited for a reaction from Zampa. Nothing.

"Okay… I have encountered blackmailers and black marketeers, two-bit chancers, extortionists, thieves and murderers on my way to here. I'm not surprised by any of the rackets going on. The world is in turmoil. I spent twelve months in Europe trying to prevent what was left of the Third Reich from killing me. And then another five years struggling with the starvation, misery and fear left behind. Your operation would not register on that scale of atrocity at all."

He paused again. Still no reaction.

"Here's the thing. The US Army trained me to kill. For what I believed was a just cause. But in the mud and the crap and the blood, I lost track of what that was all about. We all did. But once we realised the rule was simply kill or be killed, we got on with it. I cannot quantify my personal contribution to the war effort. I've locked it up in the 'done and dusted' box and thrown away the key."

Zampa watched, waiting for Grover to finish. He did.

"I don't want to be your best buddy." He paused and gathered his last few words together. "But I need your influence and your help."

Zampa took an age to respond. Not blinking. Even, it

seemed, not so much as breathing. Grover sat still, waiting for him to telephone the nearest hit man. Instead, Zampa offered his assessment of the situation.

"Sandy Eaves is not a member of this organisation. She's the ex-wife of a Z list freelancer. Her club is a shithole. She's no threat to anyone. And she knows what will happen if she crosses me."

"So, do what you do and get me some information." This time Grover's eyes connected with Zampa's. "Please."

Zampa suddenly beamed at him again.

"You are going to be around for a while, right? Let me organise a temporary membership. For you and any guest you care to bring along. The best table every time."

The swift changes of mood were unnerving. And now the politeness routine was too much to bear. Zampa was happy to wait for a response. Grover had nothing to say. So Zampa sailed on.

"You don't know what to say. Think about it." He picked up the phone receiver again. "Let me get someone to escort you outside."

Grover levered himself out of the sofa cushions.

"Don't do that," he said. "I'll find my own way."

Back in the street, he paused to take a deep breath. And another and another. His heart rate began to slow down.

CHAPTER THIRTEEN

"The kid's a natural southpaw," Patsy Halloran said. "Look at that."

Leroy Winston was sparring with Bill Hefty, a welterweight from Knowle.

He had taken thirteen wins from eighteen fights, most of them on points. He was never going to be in the same league as the Jamaican.

"Billy's your traditional right hander see," Halloran explained to Grover. "Wants to circle right all the time. Which means he keeps stepping into the way of Leroy's power punch, the straight left."

Winston swayed back out of Hefty's reach, then stepped inside and swung his other major asset the right hook.

"And that one," Halloran said.

Hefty staggered to his right. Patsy moved to the ringside.

"Okay boys that's it." He heaved on the ropes and pulled himself into the ring. Moved to Hefty, helped him out of his head guard and handed him a towel.

"You all right?"

"Yes Patsy, sure. Just didn't see it coming."

"You never do Billy."

Winston stepped to Hefty. "Alright Bill?"

"Sure. I'll see you in the locker room."

He crossed the ring. Halloran looked at Winston and pointed in Grover's direction.

"Your neighbour."

Winston pulled off his head guard.

"Give me a couple of minutes to shower, Ed and I'll be with you."

He climbed out of the ring and followed Hefty to the locker room. Grover looked around. Roly Bevan had worked his magic on the old place.

The ring was in the centre of the floor. One corner of the gym worked as the weight management centre, with a string of lifts and pulls, press benches, rowing machines and simple old-fashioned skipping ropes. In the space running left towards the next corner, there were three heavy bags and a couple of speed balls, hanging from an iron ceiling bar. A series of wooden cupboards containing head guards, hand wraps, gloves, medicine balls, chest exercisers and first aid kits, stood ranged along the opposite wall. And there was a glass fronted cabinet, which housed the trophies won by members of the gym, past and present.

Halloran joined Grover on the gym floor. Now in his late 50s, bald except for a fringe of close-cropped grey hair ringing his head like a collar, Patsy carried too many extra pounds for his five feet eight frame. Once a promising flyweight, too many parties while on the rise and too many drinks on the way down had left their mark.

"Leroy's the real deal," he said. "You see, as a leftie he moves in a mirror image of the normal right hander. It's a big tactical advantage. Unless you're up against

Sugar Ray Robinson." He pondered for a moment or two. "There's a Cardiff welterweight looking for a fight. I think Leroy's ready." He looked Grover up and down. "Have you ever boxed?"

"A bit, in the months before D Day. And when I was in the police force back home. I watched a lot when I was a kid," Grover said. "You remember Ralph Giordano?"

"Oh yes. Nicknamed 'Young Corbett the Third'. Welterweight World Champion in '33 and '34. Moved up to Middleweight and got that belt too."

"I saw him do it. He beat Fred Apostoli for the World title in '38."

"Boxed with a hand he broke a week earlier in training. Won on points." Halloran drifted back down the years. "Giordano was one of the greats."

Roly Bevan called from his office door.

"Reminiscing doesn't get the work done Patsy."

Halloran looked beyond Grover across the gym floor. "Sorry Boss."

"Don't worry Patsy. I agree with you, about Leroy. He's ready." He moved towards the two men. "Are you here to see me Ed? I do hope so."

"I wanted to catch a word with Leroy before he goes to the *El Paradis*."

"Oh dear. I am devastated. How is the flat?"

"Fine. The neighbours are great and I don't mind Mrs Rawlins' furniture."

Bevan dismissed Grover with a wave.

"Patsy, let's talk about this fight you're suggesting"

He shepherded the trainer into his office.

Left to his own devices, Grover mooched about a bit. He found a cupboard with boxing gloves in it. Selected a ten-ounce pair and put them on. They felt comfortable and easy on his hands. He bent his arms at the elbows and rotated his shoulders half a dozen times. He squared up to a punching bag and jabbed it a couple of times with his right fist. That worked. He felt the power in his upper arm as he jabbed and the rebound force from the bag as he made contact. He jabbed again, twice, then swung a left hook. His glove hit the bag with some force. It reverbed up the length of his arm into his chest. It was powerful and stimulating. He stepped close to the bag, dropped his head and worked a series of left and right punches into the leather. He stepped back, let his arms drop and breathed in and out.

Leroy called across the gym.

"You should take this up again."

Grover turned to face him.

"Sorry. I just couldn't resist."

"Don't apologise Bra, you got style."

Grover clamped his right hand into his left armpit and pulled off the glove. Then used his right hand to pull off the left. He stepped to the cupboard and returned the gloves to their place. Winston moved closer.

"You want to see me?"

"Yeah. I have a question." He took a moment to phrase it. "Have you seen anyone passing bennies at *El Paradis*?"

"Christ no." He stared at Grover, gobsmacked by the suggestion. "Nobody, but nobody, makes that kind of mistake. Not even the simplest of chancers. Zampa would have his balls on a skewer... Come on Bra, you know this. *El Paradis* has its share of colourful characters, but not one of them could be tortured into breaking the house rules."

"Yes, I know. Maybe I just needed to hear you say it."

"Well now you need to believe it. Without reservation. Come on. You can buy me a salad."

***

In Berger's office, Colonel Whitmore was laying down the law.

"That's how simple it is Steve The Army can't risk an investigation, let alone a court case. A guy called Maddox is flying here from Reykjavik as we speak. An army lawyer. Meanwhile, our orders are to make sure your man in Bristol keeps a lid on all of this."

"Sir."

"The United States Army, Judge Advocates General Corps, is the oldest law firm in America," he said with some flourish. "Founded by George Washington in July 1775. Since then JAG Officers have had jurisdiction over all army legal affairs and courts martial."

"That's perhaps a little difficult to enforce in the country of an international ally," Berger suggested.

"Bullshit Steve. You've heard of the Uniform Code of Military Justice?".

"Yes, Sir. Comes into force at the end of this year."

Whitmore was warming to his subject. "Yeah… The most comprehensive change in the history of US military law. Individual soldiers will now receive every legal safeguard available, exactly like the civilian legal system. In other words, Private Parsons, obnoxious, violent, sonovabitch that he was, was our boy. And we want him back, no questions asked."

"I'm not sure you can do that, Sir."

"Then what the hell is the fucking 'special relationship' about?"

"It's kind of a two-way street Colonel."

"Okay," Whitmore bellowed. "We help them build their jet engines. So, we get what we want in return. Hell, we saved their fucking asses in 1944."

"Sir, I think what Mr Churchill was really trying to say about us, as allies, was that -"

The phone on the desk began to ring. Berger silently praised the fates for their interruption and grabbed the receiver.

"Lieutenant Berger… That's okay corporal… Who?… Who's he?… Oh yeah?… Has he now…. Alright, put him through."

Whitmore got to his feet. The Adjutant held up his left arm. Whitmore looked at him, paused, then sat down again. Berger listened for some time with the receiver glued to his ear, before speaking again.

"And I'm supposed to know who you are, am I? Because forgive me, I don't recognise the voice at all… Oh you do? And why is that?"

The voice at the other end of the line apparently sharpened up. Berger looked across the desk at a swiftly boiling Whitmore. Berger listened again, this time for close to a couple of minutes.

"No no," he said finally. "Not at all. I'll pass this on to the people who need to know… And goodbye to you."

He put the bakelite receiver back in its cradle and stared at it. Whitmore glared at Berger, waiting. Outside, a Gloster Meteor buzzed the airfield, creating a blast of hot air and the smell of used rocket fuel.

Finally, Berger sat upright in his chair, Whitmore barely holding on to what was left of his patience.

"How the hell do civilians get our telephone numbers?" the Adjutant grumbled.

"AT&T have directories all over the world Lieutenant."

Berger put his elbows on the desk, lifted his hands and rubbed his eyes.

"There's been a development Colonel."

"Who was on the phone?"

"Some gangster."

Whitmore stared at Berger.

"Offering us a deal."

***

Grover walked across the cobbles of All Saints Court to the chambers of Fincher Reade and Holborne and pressed the first-floor bell. He took a step back and looked around him. Two elderly men in wigs and gowns walked across the square, seriously engaged in conversation. About legal matters Grover assumed. Although maybe they were discussing the soccer results from the previous night. Maybe they were…

He heard the door open behind him, and spun round to face a slim, clean shaven, delicate looking young man in a tailored grey suit.

"I'm Ed Grover," he said.

"Ah yes. You are expected," the young man warbled. "Please do come in."

Grover smile graciously and stepped over the threshold. He was asked if he had been here before.

Grover replied politely. "Yes indeed."

"Then you probably know the way. But as I have been invested with the job of escorting you to the boardroom, please do follow me."

Grover followed the young man up the stairs. Somewhat side-tracked by the memory of the last time he did this, following Melanie's backside in a calf length tight skirt and her sensational legs in nylons with seams.

His guide opened the boardroom door and ushered him into the room.

"I will let Mrs Easton and Mr Adkins know you have arrived," he said, stepped back, and closed the door behind him.

The board room was dominated by a heavy mahogany table, surrounded by matching armchairs. The senior partners of Fincher Reade and Holborne, going back over a century, looked down from the walls in gilded frames. There was history here. Clients and adversaries alike could not fail to appreciate it. Grover remembered the lunch he was offered some months back, spread on the table. Coffee, brie and smoked salmon sandwiches neatly presented in triangular sliced sizes, fresh vegetables with dips. Clearly, there was no iron fist of austerity clamped around Fincher Reade and Holborne.

He wandered round behind the chairs, estimating the room to be twenty-five feet, or thereabouts, by fifteen.

He surveyed the table. The most important people at any gathering in this room, sat in the two large armchairs at the head and the foot. So, he chose one of the smaller armchairs midway along the table's length.

To find himself staring across it at the be-whiskered Gabriel Fincher, who sat down in this imposing room for the first time in 1825 and made plans. Messrs Reade and Holborne had hitched their wagon to his star somewhere along the way and gone on to leave a substantial legacy. The firm was one hundred and twenty-five years old. Rich, prestigious and comfortable, in a building which cocooned and kept warm the clever people who worked in it, like an old sweater. Only one of the incumbents bore the founder's name – the Head of Chambers, Alexander Reade, the great great great grandson of the man on the wall behind him. Grover picked out Herbert Reade, who looked down at him with unblinking Victorian confidence. The confidence which built huge machines, mills, potteries and mighty bridges. And steamships, which sailed to conquer and colonise a fifth of the world. The British were good at this stuff, he reflected. They savoured tradition. Like warm clothes in the night air, best when they're old and shaped by the years to fit.

There was a knock on the door. Grover looked across the room. The door opened and the young man poked his head around it.

"Would you like tea or coffee?" he asked.

Mindful of where he was, Grover did not hesitate.

"Tea," he said.

"Rington's of course," the young man said. "But would you like their Earl Grey blend?"

Not to be outwitted, Grover dived in to the discussion.

"That's the scented stuff with bergamot," he said.

"Indeed it is, Sir. Especially blended one hundred years ago, by a Chinese Mandarin speaking gentleman, for Lord Grey at the family seat in Northumberland."

"So I've been told," Grover said. "I understand that the bergamot was added to offset the preponderance of lime in the estate water."

The young man looked a little fazed for a second or two.

"I'm sure you are correct, Sir." Almost on the edge of a dither, he went on. "So that would be your choice?"

"Yes please."

"Very good."

The young man disappeared, leaving the door slightly ajar behind him. The reason for this was demonstrated two minutes later, when Neil Adkins slid into the room carrying a tray, expertly pushing the door open with his left elbow.

"Good day, Ed."

"Hi. Where is er…"

"Young Anthony?" Adkins said. "Still in the kitchen. A little traumatised I think, by your encyclopaedic knowledge of English tea."

"I got a lesson a couple of months ago, from Ellie Morrison."

Adkin walked around the table.

"How is Ellie? In the best of health, I hope."

"She is."

"And young Harry and his friend, Mark is it?"

"Both well."

"That's good to hear."

Adkins placed the tray of tea cups, milk jug, sugar bowl and tea pot – under a tea cosy of course – in front of the guest.

"You can't forget the word bergamot," Grover said. "Or is it pronounced bergamoh?"

"No, it's bergamot. But sensitive of you to consider that nonetheless. Milk?"

"Yes."

"And how many sugars?"

"Two."

Zoe swept into the room. "What have you done to young Anthony? He's in the kitchen, weeping."

"I think that was my fault," Grover said.

"What did you do?"

"I got a rise out of him. His accent his demeanour. His Englishness, I guess. I'll apologise to him."

"We are all going to need a special dose of that Englishness before we're through. I have just had a phone call from your Commanding Officer."

CHAPTER FOURTEEN

At 9.30 the following morning, Captain Francis C Maddox, stepped into the Filton office. Grover stood up.

"Sergeant Major Ed Grover, Sir" he said.

Maddox grinned. "I'm a lawyer, Ed. A JAG officer, not a regular soldier. And from what I hear, I gather you're endeavouring not to be. So, let's drop the rank shit." He held out his right hand. "Frank Maddox."

Grover shook his hand. Maddox pulled up the chair behind him and sat down.

"Enjoying this job? he asked."

"I was hoping too."

"But there's a substantial spanner in the works, right?"

"A dead GI, with bennies in his pocket."

"Ah…" The bennies were news to Maddox. "And is this known?"

"Only to me and a surgeon at the General Hospital. But she will have to tell the cops. Within hours probably."

Maddox pondered.

"Well, we won't get away with denying it. Was Parsons a user?"

"We might get that answer from the post mortem."

"How long have we got to wait?"

Grover shrugged. "Hours… Minutes maybe."

Maddox sat back in his chair.

"Okay, tell me all about it."

Grover gave him the story of his 72 hours in the city, omitting the late-night encounter on the dockside. As he finished, he opened a drawer in his desk, fished out Parsons' wallet and passed it to Maddox. The lawyer looked inside. Pulled out the photograph, now creased and scratched.

"Who's this?"

Grover took a moment to answer. He had decided on discretion over this issue. The less the Army knew about the girl the better. There was no point in poking a stick into what might turn out to be the proverbial hornet's nest. At least not at this time. He had done his best to make the photograph look older than it was. The copies Turnbull had made were lying in a desk drawer, alongside the two pictures re-produced from Parsons mug shot.

"No idea," he said.

"Is this a girl from home?"

Stick to the simple truth, Grover thought.

"Might be. You'll need to check that."

Maddox looked straight at Grover. Neither man blinked.

"That's all you can offer, Ed?" Maddox asked.

"You know as much as I do, Frank."

Maddox changed the subject.

"Okay. This guy Zampa…"

Grover stared deep into Maddox's eyes. The lawyer explained.

"He called us. Offering a deal. He'll keep the peace if we extricate Parsons and send him home soonest."

137

"That sounds like his kind of endeavour," Grover said.

"Would he do it?" Maddox asked. "Keep the peace I mean."

"I'm sure he would. He's got a kind of grace and favour thing going with the local cops. He's running a dipped in bronze racket. Keeps his people in line, doesn't make mistakes. Because if anything falls apart, the cops will drop on him like a megaton bomb. And I imagine we wouldn't want to be involved with anything like that."

Maddox ignored the hint of sarcasm.

"You're suggesting we stay away from Zampa."

"Can you afford to get caught up in the affairs of the city's crime boss?"

"Of course not. Officially."

Grover shook his head. "This isn't the south Bronx. You can't play those kind of games here."

Maddox crossed his left leg over his right and thought for a moment.

"You have friends in these parts, clearly."

"Good friends," Grover said. "From early in the war. And some new ones."

"Enemies?"

Grover chose to dissemble, hoping the brief hesitation would not give him away.

"I've spent a lot of time here since February," he said. "Which is why I was offered this job."

"You were happy to take it?"

"Yes."

"And you have an inside track to the city's top law firm."

Grover smiled at the advocate.

"But no influence." He rationalised. "I'll take your pitch to them, if I think it's the way to go, but I won't be able to affect any decisions they choose to make."

"Meanwhile, one of your friends is the lady who killed Private Parsons."

"She works for the law firm. And they'll put everything into defending her against the manslaughter charge if it comes her way."

"Are you siding with the wrong people here, Ed?"

"No. But I'd really like to find out where the bennies came from and what Parsons was doing with them."

The phone on the desk rang. Grover picked up the receiver.

"I have the results of the post mortem," Doctor Mason said. "Your soldier was 20/20 fit. Nothing wrong at all. No alcohol or Benzedrine in his system. No signs of habitual drug use. All interior organs were fine, except for the ruptured spleen. That's what killed him."

Grover assimilated all that. Lauren interpreted the silence for a line fault.

"Ed. You still there?"

"Hang on a minute please," Grover said. He took the receiver away from his ear, placed the palm of his left hand over the mouthpiece and looked at Maddox. "The surgeon. Post mortem results are in. Nothing suspicious."

Maddox held out his right hand.

"Give me the phone."

Grover thought about that for a moment, but could not come up with a reason for doing otherwise. He handed the receiver across the desk.

"What's his name?" Maddox asked.

"Her name," Grover said. "Doctor Mason."

Maddox leaned back in his chair, transformed instantly into everybody's cheery uncle.

"Doctor Mason," he said. "I'm Frank Maddox. A US Army lawyer. I'd like to talk with you." He listened. "Now if possible, or as soon as."

He looked across the desk at Grover, grimaced, and waved his left wrist in a limp sort of gesture. Then listened again.

"Ah. When?" Listened once more. "Two hours…" He looked at his wrist watch. "Let's say high noon." A final moment. "Ed Grover will point the way." A beat, then he closed the conversation. "Thank you."

He handed the receiver back to Grover. The avuncular stuff disappeared and Maddox switched into JAG mode.

"Okay, starting right now you're off the case. Drop any investigations you're involved in. From this moment, total concentration on the Filton project."

Grover breathed in. Maddox leaned forwards in his chair.

"Any of that you don't understand?"

Grover understood all of it. The message was clear. And orders were orders. Or at least they were supposed to be. This was not the moment to rip up the rules and regulations. The Judge Advocate Generals Office was no playground.

He cut back to the summer of 1945. An alley off Potsdamer Platz in Berlin. A girl, fifteen or sixteen maybe. Skinny kid, in a tattered green dress. Raped and strangled. She had no identification papers. They were stolen by the killer to delay any investigation.

"I recognise her," one of the MPs said. "There's a floating black market along Unter Den Linden. She's part of it. Don't know her name. Just another street kid."

In that moment, he decided nobody was 'just' anything. 'Just' was not good enough. Sure, it was difficult to care seriously about anybody in a charnel house. But no sixteen-year old girl should perish in a shithole back street, unknown, un-mourned, forgotten. He asked Lieutenant Berger, for permission to investigate. Two days later, newly promoted Sergeant Major Grover, he was re-located to Tempelhof Airport. He appreciated the pay hike, but he was angry at being moved. He wanted to do something about the dead girl. The army wanted him out of the way.

Later, he found out why.

The Snowdrops discovered something else in the alley. A button from a US battledress tunic. Either somebody had appropriated a tunic from somewhere, or somebody in Baker Company was missing a button. Twenty-four hours later, Baker Company dress paraded. All buttons were present and correct on all tunics. Action into the matter was suspended. But at the time, there were two men in sick bay. One of them was Private First Class Leo Vanderbilt – who was pulling a stroke, and out of sick bay a day later. And nobody gave a shit. Not a moment of thought, or a second or two of sympathy, for a stringy girl starving in a cellar and dying on a bomb site.

Right now, Grover decided, he was in to stay. There were friends of his involved in this. Mel was in trouble.

And Beelzebub himself was negotiating a deal with the US Army.

"Understood Sir," he said. "Clear as creek water, Sir."

Turnbull offered to drive Maddox into the city. Grover was left in the office to contemplate.

The whole thing was such a fucking charade – Zampa getting into bed with the US Army, to solve their problem for them. Why would he think of doing that? Answer… he wouldn't. Unless there was something at stake. Something so impossible to lose, he was prepared to risk all the stuff he had patiently put together over the years. The control he had taken over the city's crime world, the money he had hard earned, the money he had spent, the people he had roped and stung, the influence he now gloried in. Why was he betting the farm on helping to sort out a problem with a dead GI? Why was Private Bradley Parsons so important? What was there about him that held a bunch of people with real clout scared shitless?

He called Doctor Mason. Told her Maddox was on the way. She asked for Grover's assessment of him.

"He's one of the Army's top lawyers, Lauren. A man who can smile with his whole face and slit your guts at the same time. My advice is, don't elaborate on any answer you give to any question. And don't volunteer anything you think he should know if he doesn't ask about it."

"There's not exactly a lot to tell, Ed. Does he know about the Benzedrine tablets?"

"Yes. And the picture in the wallet."

"Then there is nothing to explain other than the medical intervention."

"Trouble is, there's a lot more to this thing than just a hit and run," Grover said. "There's a battalion of people with their bowels in an uproar over the fate of Private Parsons. I tell you, it borders on the supernatural."

"What about you?"

"I'm out of it. The Lone Ranger."

"Who is he?"

"He rides around on a horse wearing a mask."

"I don't understand."

"Don't bother. If I give you my home telephone number, will you ring me this evening? Even if it's only to tell me you're not allowed to do so."

"Of course."

"Thanks Lauren."

Grover gave her the number. She recited it back to him. And promised to call. He sat back in his chair

Then he remembered the name of the other soldier in the West Berlin sick bay with Vanderbilt. Private Bradley Parsons.

CHAPTER FIFTEEN

Just after 1 o'clock, two dark green Morris Oxford saloons – *Pride Rides* taxis with all logos and licence details removed – turned off Brockley Combe Road into the old scarlet fever hospital grounds. The new wrought iron gates, the left bearing the legend *SITE ACQUIRED*, the right the words *FOR DEVELOPMENT*, were open. The holed and rutted track with grass growing up the middle, had been scalped and flattened; the bumps levelled and the surface spread with hardcore. With each driver under strict orders to look after his precious cargo, the cars moved slowly and slid gently to a stop in the courtyard outside the entrance to *Brockley* and *Failand* wards.

Doctor Havers stepped to the first car, Matron Harper to the second and helped the six mothers-to-be out of the vehicles. The two car drivers, collected the six suitcases and portered them into the building.

Inside *Failand*, they were introduced to duty nurses Alice and Cassie, who in turn presented them to the six clients already ensconced in the twelve-bed wards. Names and greetings were exchanged, beds were allocated. Doctor Havers completed his meet and greet.

"I am sure you are all aware how confidential this must be," he began, his bedside manner impeccable. "I am afraid you won't be able to receive visitors while you are here. However, making your stay as friendly and as comfortable as possible is our premier concern. The staff will make sure you have everything you need and, hopefully, all that you may request. I will be in charge of your health throughout the time you are here and I will be present at every birth. Now, I will leave you to get to know Matron Harper, Alice and Cassie, and each other."

In his office opposite the new birthing room along the corridor, Havers was greeted by a smiling Rodney Pride, who took his right hand and pumped it up and down.

"Marvellous. Operation Intro completed."

Havers grimaced at the ludicrous codename, but kept his own council. He did after all recognise the commercial rewards that beckoned.

"Yes, he said.

"Proper planning doc. Sorry, Doctor Havers."

"I was not expecting to say this Mr Pride, but -"

Pride interrupted, "Rodney please…"

"Mr Pride," Havers insisted. "But I must acknowledge the work you have done here. I take my hat off to you in that respect. The organisation is quite remarkable."

"The result of three miserable years in the army."

Havers could not help himself responding to that.

"You learned all these skills in the army?"

"From the first battle of El Alamein in '42, through Libya, Tunisia, Sicily and into Italy. Three years of killing, and avoiding being killed – mostly by dodging the column. I learned how to survive and how to organise. Did a bit of gun running to the Italian communist resistance. Mercifully, got shot in the chest at Monte Casino…"

"Mercifully?" Havers was captured now.

"Well yeah. I was invalided back to Alexandria. At death's door apparently. They were worried about me. Why the hell I don't know. They didn't think much about my welfare all the time the Afrika Corps and the Italians were shooting at me. So, lying on my back in hospital, I had plenty of time to work out what I was going to do back home. I've lost count of the number of schemes I came up with, but this, along with the taxis, was favourite." He looked around the office. "I knew about this place you see. Decided that once I was back and established, I'd put the old thinking cap on again. And… bingo."

"We do seem to have everything in place," Havers said.

Pride grinned. "In which case…"

He moved to the door, then turned to face Havers again. The doctor held up his right hand.

"I take it, however, you won't be visiting on a regular basis."

"Absolutely, Doctor Havers. Of course not. You're the boss here."

Havers allowed the last sentence to pass without remark. Pride was not finished however.

"But remember, Pride's Regs begin as of now," he said. "All who come here to work, do so from the other side of the combe, via the track through the woods between here and Wrington Warren."

Havers was annoyed that Rodney Pride felt he needed reminding.

"We have accomplished that every day for the last week," he said with some irritation.

"Good to hear," Pride said. "I'm off then. To lock everything up tight."

He left the room and closed the door.

Havers breathed a sigh of relief and sat down in the chair behind his desk.

The taxis which ferried the women to Brockley Combe were leaving. Pride got into the cab he had used to drive himself to the hospital and followed in their wake. He drove through the gates facing Brockley Combe Road and stopped. Got out of the car. Pulled the gates closed, so that that the signs bolted on them offered the complete message *SITE ACQUIRED FOR DEVELOPMENT*. He collected a length of chain from the boot of the Morris, wrapped it round the uprights where both gates met and snapped on a substantial deadlock.

***

"Right Sam. Now we are in business."

Pride and the city council chief were sitting in the Baynton Close office. With the outreach part of the business temporarily suspended, Brenda the secretary was on gardening leave in Cornwall. It was time for a catch up.

Pride slid two pages of accounts across the desk. Nicholson stared at them as if they carried the plague. Pride grinned.

"Go on, take a look…"

Nicholson stretched his right arm and picked up the papers. Pride rolled on.

"Alright, let me draw your attention to the second page. Initial client payments, twelve by 500 pounds.

That's 6,000 pounds in total. Costs so far, including the building transformation, equipment, wages and er, what I believe you call 'disbursements' 3,850 pounds. Balance good so far right?"

Nicholson, concentrating on the pages, muttered something he didn't catch.

"Final payments by 1000 pounds," he went on. "Another 12,000. Cash on delivery…" He grinned again. "Delivery eh? Get that?"

Nicholson had to admit it all looked as it should, given that the whole set up was illegal. It was three days since the business had extorted the last five hundred pounds down payment from the last clients. A couple whose son's platoon had managed to walk ashore at Sword Beach, only to be met head on by the 24th Panzer Division thundering up the road from Caen. It was a fierce and extremely bloody encounter. A lot of young men died on the road to Caen.

There were no sons in the Nicholson family, but he did have three daughters. All of them married and off his hands, at last. He could not recall much pleasure in the process of bringing them up. Not that his contribution had been extensive. It was woman's work after all.

He looked up from the pages.

"What happens in here now?"

"I'll take away the accounts and the…" he waggled his right wrist "… delicate info, in a day or two, and lock the office up tight. There's no trail in this direction that anyone can follow. According to Havers, a couple of our clients will drop in five or six weeks. At which point, we'll open for business again. Got to keep the beds full Sam."

Nicholson handed the pages back and stood up.

"I have a meeting at the council house in twenty minutes," he said.

Pride was annoyed by his associate's lack of excitement.

"For God's sake Sam, this is a cash cow. At least it's going to be. Each time we roll out the once expectant mothers and make room for the next batch, the overheads go down and the profits go up."

"I know what the figures say. Well done. I have to go."

He left the office as briskly as he could.

At the Council House, his mood improved considerably. Thanks to the arrival of official papers, duly signed – concerning the 'Town and City Authorities Contingencies' clauses in the Marshall Plan 'Local Administration' section – the revised upwards city budget for 1950 to 51 was satisfactorily enhanced. Not that he could look forward to getting anything from it beyond some 'expenses', but he was certain there were other ploys to be investigated. Like re-building work tendering, doling out contracts, arranging priorities, and a selection of other opportunities therein.

His day was improving. By now, his wife would be out of the way, visiting her sister in Didcot. He had no afternoon duties which needed his attention. And he was hungry. He decided, given that the paperwork was complete, it was time he and Ed Grover touched base, socially speaking. *The Green Man* pub in Clifton was relatively up-market with a good chef and decent service. Nicholson called Filton, issued an invitation to lunch, and stepped out into the sunshine.

The two men sat down at a corner banquette with a view across the substantial garden. To begin with, Grover was alarmed by the onslaught of agreeability. But slowly Nicholson reigned in the bullshit. And by the time the steak and fries had been consumed and the apples with cream were delivered to their table, neutral observers would have taken them for a couple of friendly work colleagues on a business lunch. Grover turned down a third glass of merlot. Nicholson finished the bottle himself, ordered coffee, leaned back against the banquette cushions and reminded his new best friend of what he had promised at the Grand Hotel bash three days earlier.

"Remember, I said if there was anything I could do, I'd be only too pleased to help make introductions, oil wheels, that sort of thing."

Grover looked at him, trying to assess just how on the level the council leader was. He decided to test the new alliance.

"You keep up with most of the things that happen in this city."

"Of course. Absolutely."

Grover dug into the inside pocket of his jacket and produced the photograph of Parsons' girl.

"I'm looking for this young woman," he said.

Nicholson looked at the picture. For a moment Grover thought his host had got the wrong idea. There was a split second when Nicholson appeared more interested in the prospect than he should have been. But a moment later he simply asked 'why?'

"There was a road accident last week, a few yards from the General Hospital."

"I didn't hear about it," Nicholson said.

Just as well, Grover thought, considering everyone involved was trying to keep it quiet.

"A man died. Her boyfriend."

Nicholson asked him why he was concerned in this. Grover kept it simple.

"He was a friend of a friend," he said. "And she has disappeared. I've got time on my hands. I'm just helping out." He pointed at the picture. "That photograph was found, in the man's jacket pocket, along with his wallet. This is a long shot I know, but maybe you've seen her around."

Nicholson looked at the picture again.

"Pretty young thing," he said. "But no, I've never seen her. I'm sure I'd remember if I had. Tell me who the man is, was. Perhaps I'll recall his name."

"Bradley Parsons."

Nicholson pondered. "I know erm… Walter Parsons. But he's fifty something, with a wife and six kids. Clearly not him." He pondered again. "Er… Len Parsons. He's my milkman. He's in his 20s. Just finished his National Service… That's it. Sorry."

Grover hadn't intended the dialogue to get this chummy. Nicholson was not going to be any help. Unless…

"Sam," he ventured. "Are you acquainted with any Americans in Bristol?"

"No, just you."

"Do you know anyone who is?"

"Er… No. Why do you ask?"

Grover busked an answer.

"Oh… Just looking for a comrade. Somebody to hook up with perhaps."

Suddenly, Nicholson was all conviviality once more. He called over a waiter and asked for the bill. Grover dug into a pocket. Nicholson held out his right arm.

"Absolutely not. You are my guest. I'll take responsibility for this."

The two men walked out of the pub. Nicholson asked Grover where he was parked. He pointed at *Salome*.

"A Jeep. That's your official vehicle?"

"I like her," Grover said. "I built her, with help from a friend on the air base."

"The friend you mentioned a few minutes ago?"

"What?" Then he caught up. "Yeah, that's right." He changed the subject. "Once again, thank you for lunch. Let me return the favour soon."

"What is it you say across the pond? I'll take a rain check."

Grover smiled. Nicholson lifted his right hand and thumbed over his shoulder.

"I'm over there."

Grover watched him move to the handsome maroon Rover. Nicholson fiddled around for a while in the front seat. Grover decided it was no concern of his, climbed into *Salome* and fired up the engine. Took one last look at the city council leader and swung the jeep towards the car park exit.

He stepped into the entrance hall of 5 Blenheim Villas fifteen minutes later, to find Rachel about to slide a note under his door.

"Your timing is perfect," she said. "I just took a call from Mel. She and Zoe would like to see you at Fincher Reade and Holborne."

"Thanks."

Grover looked at his watch. Almost 3 o' clock. He had time to make it.

"See you later," Rachel said. "Afternoon call. We're rehearsing a couple of new numbers."

Inside the flat, Grover mused for a while. On Sam Nicholson, and why he had asked a relative stranger to lunch. Decided in the end he had no reason other than to believe it was no more than a friendly gesture from a man he was going to have to deal with as liaison duties progressed.

***

Mel conducted Grover into Fincher Reade and Holborne's boardroom.

"Good to see you back at work," he said.

"Thank you, Ed."

She looked at the American Drop Dial Wall Clock stationed between Gabriel Fincher and Archibald Reade. 3.25. the hands said.

"Time for tea, I suggest."

Grover had this English tea thing down tight now.

"Never say no to English tea," he said.

Mel stepped to the phone on the table and picked up the receiver and dialled two numbers.

"Anthony… Yes, it is. Earl Grey tea for the boardroom please… For two… Yes, he is… Fear not, that would be splendid."

She replaced the phone receiver.

"Young Anthony has offered us chocolate bourbons, if that is all right for you. I told him it was and he need have no fear."

"Did that do the trick?"

"We will have to wait and see."

Less than a minute later, Anthony entered the room, rock steady.

"Good afternoon Mr Grover," he said.

No hand trembling as he set down the tray. He looked at Mel.

"Just ring if you would like something else."

He left the room without tripping over the threshold. Mel waited until the door closed behind him.

"Things are hunky dory, Ed. With Anthony I mean. However, not much progress with the photo identification yet. So far, all the people behind the doors we have knocked on have said the same thing. 'Don't recognise the girl, and the bloke could be anybody'."

"Who have you got working on this?"

"Myself and a couple of other outdoor clerks. Hal and Rita. I pulled a few strings in the chambers over the courtyard. Both have pictures of Parsons and the young woman. We have…" she searched for the right word, "…extended… a part of the job description. In this case, stretching the concept of 'office support duties' into a little detective work."

"That's my gig," Grover suggested.

"No. If you go prospecting around Bedminster sticking your foot into doorways, however politely, we will all get into bother."

Grover opened his mouth to protest. Mel pasted a stern look on her face and held up her right hand.

"But me no buts, Ed. Let's begin doing this by the book. Or at least as close as we can get to it."

Grover nodded with as much grace as he could muster. Mel accepted this.

"I have no doubt, there will come a moment when some er… re-thinking, is called for, but until then… Oh hell, drink your tea."

Grover reached for a biscuit.

"Give Hal and Rita another twenty-four hours," she said.

Two chocolate bourbons and two cups of tea into discussions, the phone burbled. Even the phones in Fincher Reade and Holborne had taste.

"We found the sister-in-law's cousin Margaret in Peel Street," Hal said. "Number 14. Showed her the photograph."

"Are you sure about the identification?" Mel asked.

"Margaret is. 'The picture's a bit fuzzy,' she said, 'and I haven't seen the SOB since I left the States, but it's him alright.' She said she did not know he was in the army, or where the hell he was."

"Not exactly a gushing response," Mel said.

"Rita suggests I come around and give you the complete SP, while she trawls a couple more streets with the picture of the young woman."

"Where are you now?"

"In a phone box near Victoria Park."

"Get a cab. I'll raid the petty cash."

She put the receiver back in place and relayed Hal's message to Grover. He slumped in his chair.

"Everywhere we look is a dead end."

Mel got to her feet. Collected the cups and saucers together on the tray.

"I'll order some more tea."

Grover got to his feet, crossed the office and opened the door for her.

"You put your thinking cap on," she said.

He left the door an inch or so ajar. He moved around the room, seeking inspiration from the pictures on the walls. He ended up facing Gabriel Fincher.

"Well Gabe, old sport," he said. "What do you think? What would you have done, back in the day?" Gabriel stared at Grover unblinking. His face chock full of Victorian majesty. Grover sighed. "We have to do this without you, I guess."

Zoe walked into the office. Grover looked sheepish. Zoe smiled at him.

"We all do that from time to time," she said. "Come in here and ask him for advice."

"Does he ever help?"

"Sometimes. If you get him at the right moment."

Mel came back into the office. Hal arrived four minutes later, having been conveyed to All Saints Court by a *Pride's Rides* taxi. 'Very efficient' he pronounced it and handed over a receipt the driver had signed.

"Not cheap however," Mel said as she scanned it.

"Rodney Pride would steal the dollars from a dead man's eyes," Grover said.

Hal looked at him, a little alarmed at Grover's reaction. Mel made the introductions. Hal regaled all three with what he and Rita had discovered so far.

Concluding with sister-in-law's cousin Margaret's last words on Bradley Parsons.

"Rita said they were unexpected. Her mood changed. As if she regretted the words she had used before. She mumbled something about 'the ties that bind'. Well he was family I suppose."

"That was it?" Grover asked.

Hal shrugged. Zoe asked him what Rita was doing now.

"I left her knocking on doors in Palmerston Street. She was going to come back here once she had finished. Or straight here, if she made some progress."

***

Rita had made no progress at all.

Dispirited, she was walking across a cleared and levelled bomb site; once the workplace of a small engineering firm making gromets for the motor industry, now in temporary use as a car park. Re-building was slow in this neck of the woods. And for the first time in motoring history, Bristol had more parking spaces than it could fill. There were half a dozen vehicles dotted around the area.

Rita unlocked the door of a neat, dark grey, four year old Hillman Minx and slid into the driving seat. She gathered her skirt and coat together, tucked them into the car alongside her and closed the driver's door. She chose a key from a key ring, inserted it into the ignition and turned it to the right. The engine fired. Rita depressed the clutch, engaged first gear, dipped the accelerator, let out the clutch out and the car moved forwards. She swung the wheel through thirty degrees, pointed the Hillman towards the car park exit and upped the engine revs.

The car exploded, burst into flames, and rose up into the air. A thousand pieces of it blew across the car park. The broken chassis and the engine block dropped back onto the tarmac.

CHAPTER SIXTEEN

"Who the hell do we know capable of doing this?"

Detective Sergeant Tom Goole stared, unbelieving, at the wreckage in front of him. His boss DCI Bob Bridge had no illusions.

"You may recall, Sergeant, three million men fought in the recent conflict. Two thirds of them got through it. And came home experts in all kind of violent skills. Blowing up things being one of them."

Bridge was wider in the shoulders than Goole, with dark hair and dark eyes. He had a scar across the bridge of his nose and over his right eyebrow; the legacy of an encounter with a razor gang when he was young beat bobby, back in the 30s. He headed the constabulary's Serious Crimes Team. An elite squad, based in the Bridewell at the western end of Broadmead. The only historic building still standing in that part of Bristol. Somehow the Luftwaffe had missed it.

Approaching his mid-50s, Bridge was an experienced copper with a direct approach to the job of catching criminals. And he did this with some of the best officers culled from the Bristol, Bath, Somerset and Gloucester Constabularies. All of them hand-picked and as tough as they could be moulded. He led them, with an understanding of human nature that had been absorbed through years on Bristol streets. And the SCT was developing a reputation for not having to call in detectives from Scotland Yard to deal with crimes like murder.

This, however was somewhat different.

"Do you think the bomb was made by the bloke who did this?" Goole asked. "Or did he go to somebody who makes them?" He paused to reflect. "Bombers and bomb dealers on the manor. Christ."

Goole was light on his feet and a couple of inches shorter than Bridge. Slim, fair haired, with blue eyes, solid cheek bones and a square jaw. Fifteen years old at the outbreak of war he wangled his way into the Home Guard for the final two years of it. Whereupon, he went straight into National Service. In Malaya, where he learned a lesson or two about human nature. Back home, he joined the police, much to his mother's despair and his father's amusement. He had been with the SCT since his promotion from DC a year earlier. He did recall bombs dropping from the sky, but this was his first experience of a bomb attack, on the ground and close up. And it had shaken him.

"The explosion was violent, right?" he said. "So how come there's so much of the car still here. In pieces yes, but big pieces. I thought bombs blew everything to smithereens."

"I imagine that's the theory," Bridge said. "And to answer your first question, we don't know anybody capable of doing this. We have a select client list of fences, thugs, thieves, muggers, buggerers and murderers, but no one who's shown any capacity for this kind of thing. We're going to need an expert to help us find who did this." He was staring at the car chassis. "However…"

Bridge cast his eyes over and around the wreckage.

"What?" Goole asked.

"Look at where the car is, Tom."

Goole was puzzled by the premise.

"It's on the ground."

"I mean the way it lies. It's not in a parking bay. Look at the white lines around us. At the other cars. There aren't many of them, but they are all parked where they are supposed to be, in the right spaces, between lines."

"But not this one," Goole said.

"Right," Bridge said. "Given our limited experience of bombs and bombers, we could hazard this at least. Look around. Does it appear that this car blew up, flew through the air and landed here?"

Goole took time to survey the car park.

"No. The big pieces of wreckage are confined to this spot. The concrete around it is scorched."

"Which means, Sergeant?"

"It blew up in this position. Right here. At an angle, across two parking spaces. We're not exactly pushed for space here, but I imagine the lady wouldn't have parked like this."

"So?..."

"She had moved," Goole suggested.

"Or was on the move," Bridge said. "The car blew up while it was moving."

"You mean with some sort of timed device?"

"Maybe something that was triggered as the car started to gather speed. I tell you, we need an expert."

Bridge looked around him. At half a dozen uniformed PCs, three sleek black Wolseley 6/80 patrol cars, two vans disgorging people in overalls and white coats. And an ambulance standing by, in the hope of being presented with a body to take away. Another man in overalls moved toward the detectives with two pieces of a number plate. He wiped a layer of black smoke from them and held them up for the detectives to see. The piece in his right hand read 'WT', the bent piece of metal in his right read 'K 298'.

"I picked it up," he turned and pointed across the car park. "About fifteen yards away."

"Find out who that reg number belongs to," Bridge said. "Meanwhile Tom, have a scout around. It's going to be ages before the boffins find out what happened." He pointed across the site. "Set two of the uniforms on a door to door. Get another couple to check the reg numbers of all the other cars, trace the owners and find out how much they know, or don't know. Bring the rest over here, get them to circle this car and move away from it checking the ground as they go. I'll find out from the ACC what our official view is on all this."

He sat in the front passenger seat of the nearest Wolseley and called the Bridewell. He was swiftly summoned to a meeting. And told to prepare for a late night.

***

No senior member of Fincher Reade and Holborne was going home either. Or the Head of Chambers at Frazer and Charlton across the courtyard.

Hal was in the board room being grilled by his boss, Jeremy Charlton KC and Alexander Fincher. Zoe was in another room with Mel and Grover. He was looking out of the window, at nothing in particular. Mel was sitting at a table, in some distress.

"We must not blame ourselves, or each other," Zoe said. "This was a decision we all took together. In concert with all senior partners."

Grover nodded at the window. "What about those guys over there?"

"Those guys too," Zoe said.

The phone on the table by Mel burbled. She jumped in her chair. Zoe moved to the table, picked up the receiver, listened for a moment said 'Yes', and replaced it.

"Our turn now," she said.

Hal had been dismissed from the boardroom. Jeremy Charlton detailed the decisions arrived at. Alexander Fincher nodded in agreement as Charlton spoke.

"The death is tragic. And given the modus operandi we agreed to, perhaps not altogether avoidable. However, both Rita and Hal were authorised by us to work, on loan to Fincher Reade and Holborne, in their capacities as outdoor clerks. Doing legitimate research for a firm with which Frazer and Charlton collaborates a number of times during the course of a year. This was an enquiry sanctioned, quite correctly, by a King's Council. This was not an active police case, and thus no interference by us in any official investigation…" He paused. Breathed in and exhaled. "In other words, apart from the murder of Rita Caton, no wrong has been done."

All in the room absorbed this rationalisation in silence. Charlton allowed it to fill, before he spoke again.

"Clearly, when asked, we must explain to the police what Rita was doing on our behalf. In essence only. We need not reveal the identity of our client…" He looked at Grover… "Or anything we have discovered. Unless of course, the police, in a search of their own, tread the same path we did and encounter the same people. We must, however, cease all we were doing on behalf of our client…" He looked at Grover once more… "With immediate effect."

Silence still cloaked the room like a pea souper. Fincher nodded. Charlton rose to his feet.

"Thank you for listening to me. And 'good evening' to you all."

He walked out of the boardroom. Fincher surveyed his employees and wound up the proceedings.

"As you can imagine, young Hal is extremely distressed. We must all appreciate that." He turned to Grover. "I'm sorry, Ed. Genuinely so. But we must part company now, I'm afraid. To put it directly, you are on your own. Until such time as we require you to assist us in the car accident business."

"Of course," Grover said. "At any time."

Fincher took in the whole room.

"Then I will say 'good evening' also.

He nodded at each in turn and left the room. Zoe recovered first.

"How about a drink?"

Mel stood up, shaking her head."

"No thank you. I'm going home. No doubt I shall see you in the near future Ed."

"No doubt."

Zoe and Grover watched Mel go.

"How about you, Ed."

"I guess we need to talk," he said.

"But not here," Zoe said.

Grover remembered his other evening commitment.

"I don't suppose you'd like to re-acquaint yourself with Blenheim Villas. I have drink there. And Lauren Mason promised to call me. Not much of an invitation maybe…"

"But nonetheless irresistible," Zoe said. "Lead on."

***

Grover's accommodation received Zoe's seal of approval. The bourbon was greatly enjoyed. An hour was spent reviewing the situation and agreeing to co-operate unofficially, in some way. The coal fire and the drink made the room glow.

"So?..." Zoe directed a whole world of 'what's next?' at Grover.

"Until I can come up with something to do or, conversely, do something which gets me court marshalled and sent home, I have no idea."

He heaved himself off the sofa to the coal scuttle. Transferred some coal onto the fire.

"We need to find the girl in the photograph," Zoe said, while re-filling the bourbon glasses. "She might be the key to all this."

On his knees by the fire, Grover stared into the flames.

"This what?" He swung round and sat by the hearth. "Maybe the girl was just Bradley Parsons' part time squeeze. Maybe Sandy Eaves is just a low rent club owner trying to make a couple of bucks, and not a player in whatever is going on. Maybe Daniel Zampa will get his evil deal done with the US Army and the whole… whatever it is, will just get buried."

"You don't want that," Zoe said. "Neither do I."

She held out his re-filled glass. He got up, took it from her and sat back on the sofa.

"So, I guess I'm supposed to go back to Filton, and wait for someone to 'liaise' with."

"Do you get paid for that?"

He looked up at the ceiling, raised his arms up and outwards.

"Somebody along the chain pays for this. Apart from that I'm just Sergeant Major Ed Grover, on a few dollars a week."

"A few dollars is cheap for an ambassador.

Grover raised his glass. "Here's looking at you kid."

They drank in silence for a while.

Lauren Mason did not ring.

"I will be around for Mel," Grover said. "If I can help. You can count on that."

Zoe said 'good night' at half past 8.

Grover turned on the radio.

The BBC Light Programme offered *Variety Bandbox*. Jack Hylton and his Orchestra played the programme in and out. Dorothy Squires sang *I'm Walking Behind You* and Lita Rosa bounced through *How Much Is That Doggie In The Window?* Frankie Howerd topped the bill.

Grover had come across him before. An outrageous eight minutes, based on catch phrases and innuendo and the word 'titter'. Tidied up of course for the BBC. At Wiltons Music Hall or the end of the pier, Grover imagined he could let rip during the second house - *a titter ran round the building, until the janitor caught him and threw him out.*

Still, Lauren Mason did not ring. Not even by the time Grover got into bed at a quarter to 12.

CHAPTER SEVENTEEN

"I'm sorry, Mr Grover, but Doctor Mason has not come into work this morning."

He was facing the Duty Receptionist at the Casualty desk. He explained that Doctor Mason had arranged to ring him the previous night and he became concerned when she did not.

"The Registrar has taken over her shift," the receptionist she said. "Let me see if I can find him."

She did. Doctor Regan pitched up a couple of minutes later.

"Ah you're the American," he said.

"Guilty," Grover said.

Regan got straight to the point.

"Lauren called me at 6.30 this morning. Hideously early. Said she would not be able to get into work. That she would explain later. And asked me to stand in. That's it. Although I have to admit we are all a little concerned."

"Can someone give me her home phone number."

"Talk to reception about that. Anything else? We're a bit busy back there."

"I'm afraid we can't hand out phone numbers," the receptionist said. "I would normally ring her and seek permission, or ask her to call you. But of course, there's no point in doing that, as… er, you're here and she's…not."

She looked confused and a little uncomfortable. Grover tried to help out.

"Can you call again while I'm here?" he asked.

The receptionist pondered for a moment.

"Yes, yes, of course."

She consulted a list sitting under the raised counter, and dialled Doctor Mason's number. Listened for a while, then took the receiver from her ear and held it out to Grover. He listened to the ringing tone and bowed to the inevitable.

"There is nothing else I can do, Mr Grover. But I will tell Doctor Mason that you came in, as er, as soon as she does." She apologised again. "Sorry… We will have to possess our souls in patience."

***

Jeremy Charlton KC was sitting in DCI Bridge's office, facing the detective. Goole was standing out of his direct line of sight, leaning against a four-drawer filing cabinet.

"The car belongs to Rita Caton. A lady who works, or rather worked, for us," Charlton was saying. "She was doing research for a case we were considering taking on."

There had been little information tossed around the room on the way to this point, and Bridge was not impressed with Charlton's dismissal of the bombing incident.

"What was that case about?" he asked.

"I am not obliged to tell you." Charlton said.

"Unless I deem it germane to an enquiry we're conducting."

"It is not."

"I'm allowed to be the judge of that," Bridge said.

Charlton smiled without opening his mouth or letting it show in his eyes.

"Not in this matter. We have decided not to pursue it. And we have informed our client to that effect."

"And why is that?"

"Chief Inspector, may I remind you that I agreed to this meeting, here, in your office."

"Because away from the practice was expedient," Bridge said. "Not obvious to clients and employees, and less arousing than having the plod roaming your corridors."

Charlton gave way on that, but felt impelled to hold the high ground.

"Away from a very busy practice," he emphasised. "To ask me half a dozen questions. Which I have answered."

He rose to his feet. Bridge did so too. In the corner, Goole straightened up.

"We may have to talk with you again," Bridge said.

"Oh I think not, Chief Inspector." He turned to Goole. "Sergeant…"

Goole moved to the office door and opened it.

"Thank you," Charlton said, and stepped across the threshold.

Goole closed the door behind him. Turned to face his boss.

"Supercilious bastard. Just because he gets paid thirty-five quid an hour…"

"And the rest," Bridge said.

"Do you think he actually knows what his outdoor clerk was doing?"

"Of course he does. But he's never going to tell us."

Bridge sat back down in his chair. Goole crossed the room and occupied the other.

"Private law chambers business," Bridge said. "No criminal intent or investigation. We have no reasonable cause to pursue the matter."

"But we're investigating a bomb explosion. Deliberate murder. Of one of his employees. There has to be a reason for that." He ran his fingers through his hair, breathed in and out. "Charlton can't really be so detached. I mean, one of his staff goes out to ask a few questions and gets blown to bits. Why? What the hell was she doing that was so dangerous? What was it that got somebody so worked up?"

The desk phone rang. Goole picked up the receiver.

"Detective Sergeant Goole… Who?... Ah…" He took the receiver away from his cheek and pressed it into the collar of his jacket. Looked at Bridge. "A friend of ours is downstairs. Sergeant Major Ed Grover."

"Well, we can't leave him there, can we?"

Goole spoke into the receiver again.

"Send him up."

Bridge looked round the room. "Get him a chair from next door."

Goole despatched himself to do that. Returned with a government issue, moulded plastic seat. Bridge asked him if that was the best he could do.

"The only one DC Campbell and DS Shaw weren't using."

"Make sure our guest gets the comfortable one."

There was a polite knock on the door. A uniformed PC opened it and ushered Grover into the room. Bridge stood up and moved around his desk.

"Ed Grover."

He held out his right hand. Grover shook it.

"DCI Bridge." He looked at Goole. "Sergeant."

"How are you Ed?"

Grover said he was fine. Goole pointed at the cushioned wooden chair and told him to sit down. Bridge asked him the reason for his visit. Grover spent five minutes explaining why he was once again in the city for reasons other than a short visit. The two detectives congratulated him on his new job. Then waited to be told the real reason for this rendezvous. Grover decided to begin at the ending of the story. Said he believed a friend of his was missing and wanted some help to find her. Goole suggested that he had come to the wrong department. Grover agreed that perhaps he had, but he'd be obliged if the gentlemen in this room could exercise some influence in the matter.

Bridge looked at Goole. He sat down in the plastic chair. There was a moment or two while everybody waited for everybody else. Bridge took the lead.

"Last time we talked, was what, two months ago? Just after you laid out a serial child molester with a police truncheon. We agreed that the action was in both of our interests and parted on friendly terms. If I remember rightly, I asked if you had any plans. And you said you liked it here, and hoped you could stay."

"I figured, that as I had played a significant role in the defeat of the Nazi hordes, the British authorities might cut me some slack."

"But they didn't, clearly."

"We're still working on that."

"Meanwhile, you're out of uniform."

Grover explained that, except for formal occasions, his present position vis a vis the US Army and his liaison role at the Filton Aero Engines factory, did not require dressing up. Impressed though the Chief Inspector was, he said he needed to know more.

"There's a back story to all this," Grover volunteered. "Your Traffic Department is dealing with a road accident outside the General Hospital three days ago. A soldier was run down by a car. He died twenty-four hours later. I witnessed the accident and I expect to be called by the Coroner to testify. This is probably way below your remit and unless one of you makes a habit of reading all internal bulletins, you won't know about it."

He paused. Bridge picked up his cue.

"Ring Traffic, Tom," he said. "And get the story. Not here, across the hall."

Goole left the office to do so. Bridge said that the death of Bradley Parsons sounded like a job for the US Army and the Coroner, rather than the Special Crimes Team. Grover agreed, but said there was a collateral damage problem. By which time Bridge was a little less interested in the tale than he had been at the beginning.

"Why don't you get to the point Sergeant Major?" he asked.

"Someone I met at the hospital has gone missing,"

Grover said. "At least I believe she has."

"She?"

"Doctor Lauren Mason."

"Missing since when?"

"Since around this time yesterday."

"Twenty-four hours.?"

"Yes."

"Well that's a case for Missing Persons. Or rather it will be. No one is missing, officially, until 72 hours from the time he or she was last seen."

"This has to be different," Grover said. "Lauren Mason is the leading consultant surgeon in the General Hospital Casualty Department. She was rostered on at 10 o'clock this morning. She didn't show up. She hasn't answered her home phone. I believe she's in trouble."

"And you want us to look for her?"

"No. I want you to ask the hospital to give you her name, address and phone number."

"Ah," Bridge said. "So that I can give the information to you."

"That's correct."

"And then you will, by yourself, pursue whatever this is."

"She's a friend."

Grover knew that would not pass muster. He was short of a good negotiating ploy. Bridge was looking at him with the patience of Job. He sat back in his chair radiating 'all the time in the world'. Grover had to give up something. But not before he was sure he could trust the two straight arrow coppers he was dealing with.

"I need your word on something," he said.

Bridge sat upright again.

"Ah. We're negotiating now, are we?"

"The bomb business," Grover said.

Bridge stared at him. Then found some words.

"Are you part of this conspiracy of silence?"

"I can tell you why Rita Caton was asking questions," Grover said. "But I want a deal. Your help to find Doctor Mason."

The response arrived in slow motion. Bridge processed Grover's proposal. Weighed it a little. Then nodded in approval.

"Alright. Go on…"

Grover had information the Serious Crimes Team needed to know, but giving them the what and the why was likely to ruin all his credit with Fincher Reade and Holborne. On the other hand, if Lauren Mason was in trouble, the SCT could start there, armed with the rest of the information available. He repeated that he wanted Bridge's agreement to treat the rest of the tale confidentially. The DCI said he was in no position to promise that, but bearing in mind their collaboration earlier in the year he would lean towards it. The two men sat in silence for a while. Grover chose his words carefully.

"Rita was asking questions about someone else who is missing." he said. "A young woman."

"Her name?"

"I don't know it. None of us do."

"Us?"

"We believe she may be the girlfriend of the GI who was run over."

"Who are us?"

"Just some people of the same opinion. Can we leave that until later?"

"Okay, let's be clear about this. Rita Caton was blown up because she was asking questions about a missing girl?... That's it?"

"Wherever that girl is," Grover summarised, "Whatever she knows, whatever she is up to, is so important, that someone's prepared to kill to avoid questions being asked."

"And bombs are pretty bloody final," Bridge said.

"These guys are deadly serious," Grover said. "Do you know how it was done."

"Not yet. Rita got into the car, turned the engine over, drove a matter of yards and the car exploded."

DS Goole came back into the room.

"The situation is as described. Doctor Mason was the attending physician after the accident. And depending on the Coroner, there could be a manslaughter charge on the way. None of our business, according to Traffic."

"Except that Doctor Mason is missing," Bridge said. He looked at Grover. "And so is a chunk of what you know."

"I need to know where Doctor Mason is," Grover said. "And if she is well. If she is, anything else I have to say will be of little or no significance. If she is not…" He paused and looked at Bridge dead centre. The detective did not blink. Grover ploughed on. "If not, and you open an official investigation, in the course of which you ask me to tell you all I know, I will have to do so."

"Thus, your relationship with the army, and with your conscience, will be clear?" Bridge suggested.

"Something like that, yes."

Goole looked at his boss. "What have I missed?"

"Later Tom."

Bridge put his elbows on his desk, raised his arms, made a steeple with his fingers and tapped the end of his nose. He considered for a bit longer, then dropped his hands.

"Okay Tom. Call the General Hospital and get Doctor Mason's address and phone number. You and I will take an informal look into the situation." He nodded at Grover. "Our friend here will assist us, if needs be, in our enquiries."

***

Lauren Mason lived in a three storey, semi-detached Georgian property near the Zoo. A slightly more understated residence than the mansions facing the road snaking across Clifton Down; but nonetheless, as with the dwellings around it, clearly the home of a professional person. At the very least, a substantial income was a basic requirement.

The Wolseley 6/80, with Goole sitting alongside the driver, and Bridge and Grover in the rear seat, pulled into the curb outside 16 Morland Road. The two detectives got out of the car and surveyed the property. It was a handsome house, with access up a flight of stone steps to an imposingly wide, dark green, front door. Grover was ordered to stay in the car. Bridge lifted his head and craned upwards in slow motion, as if assessing how many rooms the building hosted.

"Four bedrooms minimum, I guess," he said.

The detectives climbed the steps, Goole pausing to look down into the courtyard in front of the basement window.

"A kitchen down there," he said.

Bridge rang the doorbell.

He and Goole waited for someone to arrive at the door. In vain. Bridge rang the bell once more. A voice floated from the left.

"Are you policemen?"

An amply proportioned, middle aged lady, with long dark hair was standing on the doorstep of number 17.

"Do you want to speak with Lauren – Mrs Mason?"

Goole led the way back down the steps, and up those to the lady's doorway. He introduced himself and Bridge. The lady pointed towards the parked Wolseley.

"I saw the police car from my window," she explained. Then with excitement rising in her voice she asked, "Would you like to come in?"

"Actually, we'd like to get in next door," Goole said. "To talk with Doctor Mason."

"Is it important? I ask that, because I have a key, you see."

"Yes," Bridge said. "We believe it is. Mrs…"

"Maitland," the lady said. "Emily Maitland. I'll get it."

She disappeared into number 17, rattled some keys on a hook in the hall and re-appeared with a handful on a ring.

"It's one of these," she announced.

She stepped between the two detectives and led the way back to the door of number 16. Explaining as she travelled.

"Something odd happened last night. Lauren arrived home at 8.45. Parked on the other side of the road." She pointed at a blue Riley Roadster. "That's it there." She set off up the steps. "Shortly afterwards, another car pulled up. Big. Brown I think."

At the door Mrs Maitland began trying keys on the ring.

"Two men got out of the car, walked up the steps here and rang the bell."

Goole offered to assist. She clutched the key ring tightly and held it close to her chest.

"No. No thank you. These are my responsibility. I'll do this."

She concentrated on the business again. Keys three and four worked their magic on the deadlocks. She opened the door and led the way inside the house.

Goole called out, "Doctor Mason."

Mrs Maitland interrupted.

"No no no. She's not in. She left the house with the two men who got out of the car. Just a few minutes after they arrived."

"Without any fuss," Bridge asked.

"No fuss. One of the men opened the rear door of the car and she got in."

The detectives stared at her.

"Oh dear," she said. "Do you think I should have…? Oh dear oh dear."

Bridge held out his right hand. "Would you take those two keys off the ring and give them to us, please?"

Mrs Maitland nodded and began fiddling with them.

"Allow me," Goole said.

Now in some distress, Mrs Maitland handed over the key ring. Goole liberated the two keys, passed them to Bridge, handed back the key ring, and offered an arm.

"May I conduct you home Mrs Maitland?"

He escorted the neighbour back to number 17. Bridge waved at the Wolseley, beckoning Grover and the driver to join him. The four men congregated in the hall.

"Tom. You and PC Grafton… Begin downstairs in the basement and work upwards. Ed and I will start at the top and work down." He offered Grover his best 'now listen' look.

"I know," Grover said. "Don't touch anything. Don't move anything."

He and Bridge climbed two flights of stairs. On the top floor they trawled the four bedrooms, and a rather over designed bathroom with huge Italian tiles and pretend gold fixtures and fittings.

They met Goole and Grafton in the living room on the floor below. Elegant and carefully furnished, running the depth of the house. Centred at the front by a floor to ceiling window, with French doors at the rear, opening onto a stone floored, wrought iron balcony. A sofa and two large winged armchairs, embraced a marble Adam style fireplace. Another sofa took advantage of the view looking down into the garden. To the right, was the study, taking its width from the rest of the room and the space created by the landing above. It stretched back twelve feet or so, to the point at which the stairs above began to drop. A mahogany desk sat at right angles to the view from the sash window looking into the garden.

There was a reading area under the slope of the stairway, hosting an armchair flanked by a couple of small tables with mahogany stemmed candle lamps sitting on them. The bookshelves housed copies of *The Lancet*, articles and textbooks. As well as a selection of Victorian romances and the complete works of Arthur Conan Doyle – scientific papers and magazine articles along with his Sherlock Holmes novels.

The papers on the desk sat tidily, pens and pencils in an Edwardian ink stand. A Remington Rand portable typewriter, with a sheet of paper in the carriage seemed poised for action.

The consensus in the living room was, that whilst the place looked like the fabled *Marie Celeste*, there were no conclusions to be drawn. Lauren Mason was simply not there. Where she might be, was a source for debate.

Goole was despatched to talk with Mrs Maitland, PC Grafton back to the Wolseley. Bridge and Grover sat down, side by side, on the sofa facing the fireplace.

"Come on then Ed," Bridge said. "Give."

He turned his head and looked at the concern in Grover's eyes.

"Oh that's good. That's the best 'what can I possibly tell you officer?' expression I've seen in ages."

Grover tried to look at ease. Bridge continued.

"I don't know what we have here. I accept that you don't either. But you do know how we got to this point."

"No, I don't. Not this bit. Doctor Mason is in trouble and I have no idea why."

Bridge gave up a little ground.

"Ed. You are, as you say back home, between the rock and the hard place. And being the well-meaning bloke, you're known to be, you're hating it. I don't want to fight you over this. As a matter of fact, I don't need to. I can just arrest you."

"On what charge," Grover asked. "I haven't done anything."

"Well let's see. Not answering questions, withholding evidence, wasting police time. All stuff which can get you into the Bridewell overnight at least. And I can find a Magistrate who will give me another 48 hours to hold you if I tell him you are a suspect in a murder case. And then when I dress it up a bit, add a little colour – a bomb and a blown-up car – we could find ourselves enjoying some days together."

He paused. Watched Grover thinking.

"Now putting myself in your Adjutant's boots, I can imagine all sorts of bother coming down the pipe. One dead American soldier. Another a step away from a court appearance. Problems there, for all concerned I would have thought. You had nothing to do with the bombing, in the sense that you didn't actually do it. But back down the road a little, you set something in motion. Which in turn, led to us, sitting here on this sofa, passing the time of day."

Grover could not deny any of that. Bridge took all the time in the world over the next word.

"So..."

Grover gave him a carefully considered response.

"I'm going to wait for the Coroner to pronounce. What I have to say to you, will depend on what he decrees, and or, what he leaves out."

CHAPTER EIGHTEEN

The Bristol Coroner's Court was an example of over the odds Victorian Gothic excess, with a touch of French Empire. Built in 1858 by the local Methodist Circuit as a school for poor children, and probably designed to frighten them into learning. Two storeys high, tile hipped, with out of line ridges, cross parapeted window sections, elongated gables, and huge angle buttresses at each end to hold the preposterous edifice together.

It had been the home of all enquiries into unexplained deaths since the end of the war. Some people – mostly living elsewhere in the city – hailed it as an historic building. Others hated it. The locals living in Stokes Croft bestowed no merit on the building at all. Called it *Dead End Hall*, this probably influenced by the proximity of the cemetery over the road.

The Coroner, in the corseted grip of a dark grey suit and a high collar, was as cold and efficient as everyone in the court expected. Upright and formal, his voice as firm as the figure he presented, he dealt with proceedings thoroughly but swiftly.

"The Coroner's Court has been drawn into this case," he summed up, "because of a series of circumstances apparent at the moment the road accident occurred. One witness, Mrs Clara Tennant from Southville described the moment thus. 'The soldier appeared to

183

step off the pavement without taking any notice of the traffic conditions, or perhaps, stumble off the pavement and fall into the path of the car.' This, a Morris Traveller driven by Miss Melanie Davis on her way to work, well inside the speed limit, which is 30 miles per hour on that section of road. Miss Davis said she did not see the soldier 'until the last moment', as he appeared to fall into her line of sight ahead. Another witness, Sergeant Major Grover has testified he saw the Morris in front of him brake suddenly and swerve to the left. He managed to stop the vehicle he was driving – an American Army Jeep – without hitting the car in front of him, and went to the aid of Miss Davis who was unconscious in the driving seat. He was made aware of his fellow soldier's plight after Miss Davis had been released from her car and his attention was drawn to the seriously injured man, by Doctor Mason who proceeded to attend to him. The soldier was taken to the General Hospital Accident and Emergency Department, barely one hundred yards from the scene, operated on by Doctor Mason then taken to Intensive Care where, according to a statement by the hospital authorities, he died twenty-four hours later."

He paused to take a drink of water.

"And now to the unusual element in this case. Doctor Mason ordered a post mortem, to check whether the dead soldier was under the influence of drugs or alcohol at the time of the accident. We have not heard from doctor Mason personally, as she has not returned to work since leaving the General Hospital on the evening following the soldier's death. The police have been unable to trace her."

He paused once again to give his conclusion some weight.

"This case is open to scrutiny as death by accident, or death by misadventure. However, I am not convinced by either assumption. And adding to this, the disappearance of Doctor Mason gives further cause for concern. I have decided to record an Open Verdict. Notwithstanding, I am releasing the body of Private Bradley Parsons to the United States Army."

At the back of the room, Frank Maddox smiled.

***

"Necessity, is the mother of intervention," DCI Bridge said.

Grover was on the carpet, thread bare though it was. Finally, out of credit with the Senor Crimes Team.

"So we have to call a halt to this, Ed. You have no place in this investigation. Whatever it is and wherever it's going. You can't freelance any longer."

Grover had no choice but to accept he had reached the end of the tether. He nodded in surrender. Bridge picked up the phone receiver and dialled 0. He ordered tea and biscuits for three, put the receiver back in place.

"And we want more than just a few words. We want the whole nine yards."

Grover smiled. "I remember the day I explained to you what that meant."

Bridge smiled back. "I don't have to be told twice. Ed, we need all of it. Up front, in words of one syllable. Remember, if push comes to shove somewhere along the road, you are likely to be the only one in this room on the wrong side of this."

Grover told the two detectives everything he knew. The whole story as he had experienced it, from beginning to end. Both Bridge and Goole were by turns amazed, gobsmacked, angry and outraged, reflecting on how much of a dazzling scenario the GI had managed to pack into less than a week. Bridge arranged in order the mental notes he had made during the narration.

"Question one. How much of this have you told your superiors?"

"They know about the bennies, and the photographs. But I didn't tell them I had copies made. Nor what Hal and Rita were doing. The army has no reason to link any of the Parsons thing to the bombing. They have him back, and as far as they're concerned, it's over. However…"

Bridge raised his right hand.

"No speculation right now. Let me get through these questions. Number two. "Have you any idea who ordered the business in Albion Dock?"

"I figured it was Sandy Eaves."

Bridge pondered, then grunted.

"Question three. Your people at Filton. How much do they know?"

"They all know about the accident. The head of the Design Team knows about the photographs. He re-produced them."

"Where are they?"

"The army has the masters. There are two sets, well one now, at Fincher Reade and Holborne. The rest are at my place."

"Okay, Doctor Mason… How much does she know?"

"As much as we do. All of it."

"And that's why you think she has disappeared?" Goole asked.

"Yes," Grover said. "She was an easy target."

"So were Hal and Rita," Bridge said.

"And all they were doing was routine stuff with the pictures. If stopped, that was bound to go away. And it has. They didn't know the back story."

Bridge considered for a moment or two.

"And you think Mason wasn't killed because she did? And whoever picked her up needed to know what that was?"

Grover looked at each cop in turn. Goole was the first to speak.

"She may have talked by now," he suggested. "And the bad guys may know all we know. Add to that, what they already knew before the bombing…"

He paused, lost for a moment in the 'what we know' chronology. His boss and Grover waited. Then Goole found his ending.

"What I mean is, they know more than we do. And as soon as they find that out, they will have no need for Doctor Mason. Maybe that's happened already. Maybe she's dead. In which case, we have another murder on our hands. With no leads at all."

There was another moment or two of pondering. Grover tried to help.

"There is another angle," he said. "Parsons' girl. The girl in the photograph. She could be alive. It might be safe to assume the person who put the bomb in Rita's car knows she is. And the bombing was simply a device to put an end to the investigation."

He got no response from the detectives.

"Look guys, the bennies and the bomb are linked. The conduit was Parsons, and now, it must be his girl. And we, you, might be able to find her."

"To ask her what?" Goole said.

"Why somebody was killed for asking questions about her?"

There was knock on the door. Goole stood up, moved to open it and revealed a canteen lady with a tray. He said 'thanks', took it from her and turned back into the office. The canteen lady closed the door. Bridge made space on his desk for the tray. Goole passed the tea around. Bridge picked up a rich tea biscuit.

Then he scrolled back down the conversation.

"Ed. A couple of minutes ago I stopped you after my first question. After you said 'However…' You were about to say something else."

Grover looked at Bridge and put down the biscuit he had just selected from the plate.

"Yeah. Haven't you wondered how the US Army got the Parsons business tied up so swiftly, with no problems?"

"The lawyer," Bridge said. "Maddox?"

Grover picked up the biscuit again. "That's the guy, yes."

"Well, I guess he's got connections."

Grover crunched the last of the biscuit in his mouth, sipped his tea, and nodded as he swallowed.

"Yes, but not at his end," he said. "Back in Fairford,

Maddox and the CO were in a bind. And short of ideas. An AWOL grunt, with a pocket full of Benzedrine, gets knocked down by a lawyer's outdoor clerk. And not any old lawyer, just the best KC in town. An accident which might morph into a manslaughter case if and when he dies. With all the possible attendant shit which might collect. Meanwhile there's a humongous deal with aircraft engines going down, financed by the good old US of A. And a whole bunch of questions no one except Parsons can answer. Where do Maddox and the CO go for help?"

He waited for a reaction from the two detectives. Goole shrugged. Bridge did a John Wayne 'go ahead' gesture.

"Maddox needed a Bunkie," Grover said.

"A what?" Goole asked.

"You'd call him a partner in crime. But he's more than that. The guy you want for a Bunkie, is the one man, who, however miraculously, can live in the lap of luxury while every other SOB is roughing it."

Goole and Bridge were no wiser. They waited for the reveal. Grover supplied it.

"Maddox was offered help," he said. "By Daniel Zampa."

Goole was thunderstruck. Bridge looked deep into Grover's eyes.

"Zampa?"

"The one and only," Grover said. "Called him on the phone. And Maddox agreed to sup with the Devil."

"You omitted this from your confession a few minutes back," Bridge said.

"No, I didn't. I was about to tell you, but you went on to question two. Zampa knew all about Bradley Parsons before I went to see him. Put me firmly in my place and a few hours later, rang the airbase."

"And they agreed something between them?"

"Yeah."

Goole found his voice.

"Do you think that was the disappearance of Doctor Mason?"

"I don't think Zampa did it. Too many people would have to be involved. I think he provided the security."

He watched with some satisfaction as the two detectives looked puzzled, then at each other. Grover recalled his encounter three months earlier with James and Jonathan – Zampa's closest associates, and the two coolest hard men he had ever met.

"He has two guys in bespoke suits, with impeccable manners, who could relieve an elephant of his tusks and leave the beast smiling."

This was way beyond Goole's comprehension and only just clear to his boss.

"And?..." Bridge asked.

"So, if I'm right about this," Grover said. "There's only one other direction to look in."

Bridge looked at him dead centre.

"The US Army have Doctor Mason," he said.

"Bingo."

"Jesus Christ," Goole breathed. "I mean no. Really?"

"We all agree nothing was touched in her house, right?" Grover said. "And Doctor Mason walked out of her door in the early evening sunlight, got into a car without any apparent distress and was ferried away. Nobody else lurking about."

"You can't be sure of that."

"Do you think Mrs Maitland would have missed him?"

Goole pondered the proposition for a couple of seconds.

"No, probably not," he concluded.

"The one happy prospect we can cling to in this theory, is that the army will have no intention of disappearing her completely. I think Doctor Mason will be delivered back to work eventually, with a more than plausible reason for her absence."

"Meanwhile," Bridge said. "Bradley Parsons' corpse is back at Fairford."

"Draped in the US flag, and ready for his plane trip home."

Bridge reached for another rich tea biscuit. Goole stood up and began to wander round the room.

"Can they get away with this?" Goole asked. "Are we going to let them?"

"You have to admire the smoothness of the operation," Bridge said, biscuit poised. "Job done. No investigation, no recriminations."

Grover got to his feet.

"I don't. I think it stinks. You still have a blown-up corpse. And I have a person to find."

He left the room before either detective could say anything.

CHAPTER NINETEEN

He leaned into the door of the Emmerson's shop on the corner of Gladstone Street. The bell rang as it opened. Ellie Morrison beamed at him across the counter.

"Ed. What a wonderful surprise." She called towards the back of the shop. "Arthur, put the kettle on."

Grover protested that he did not have time for tea. Ellie would have none of it. She lifted the counter flap, reached out and grabbed an arm.

"Yes you do. Besides, there's someone I'm sure you'd like to see."

He bowed to the inevitable and allowed himself to be shepherded into the kitchen. At the table, Harry smiled and stood up to greet him.

"Ed…"

Grover stepped into Harry's outstretched arms. Both men remained enfolded in the embrace for a long time. Finally, Grover stepped back

"You look good," he said.

"I am. Thanks to you."

"Hell no." He looked at Harry's mother. "It was all down to the lady who runs this establishment. She never gave up on you."

Harry looked at Ellie. "Not even when I did."

Ellie smiled. Grover asked Harry how Mark was.

"He's good," Harry said. "We're both good."

Arthur stepped into the room from the scullery, holding up the kettle.

"Filled as ordered," he said. And placed it on the hot plate of the leaded grate.

Ellie motioned Grover to sit down.

"Okay," he said. "But I really don't have much time. I'm on a mission."

He dug into the inside pocket of his jacket, took out his wallet, opened it and laid the photographs of Parsons and the young woman on the table. Ellie peered down at them.

"Your friend from the lawyer's called on us. Showed me the picture of the man," she said. "I didn't recognise him. None of us did."

"What about the girl?"

There was a shaking of heads around the table. Grover had one question left to ask.

"Do you know a lady living in Peel Street called Margaret? Maybe she's a customer."

Thinking caps went on again.

"Maggie," Arthur said. He gestured with his thumb. "Maggie. Lives halfway along on the right."

Ellie smiled. "Of course. Maggie. A nice lady." Then concern crept into her eyes. She looked at Grover. "Is she in trouble?"

"No. But I'm not sure she's levelling with us. I need to talk with her Ellie. Can you build a bridge?"

"I can try. Do you want me to come with you?"

"Please."

"She doesn't have a phone. We'll just have to show up on the doorstep."

Five minutes later, Maggie Templeton was ushering Ellie and Grover into the parlour at 14 Peel Street. She invited them to sit down. Asked if they would like a cup of tea. Grover was about to say 'no'. Ellie beat him to it and said 'yes'. Maggie said she would be moments only and left for the kitchen.

"Tea helps to break the ice," Ellie said. "I thought you'd caught up with this ritual."

Grover acknowledged his mistake. He looked around the room. It seemed a little dark. The small street facing sash window was not able to collect and spread enough daylight. A thickly cushioned sofa and two armchairs made a semi-circle in front of the open fireplace. Antimacassars along the back to protect the upholstery from Brylcreem. All the men without a short back and sides used it. As the cinema advert used to sing out,

Brylcreem – A little dab'll do ya,

Brylcreem – The girls'll all pursue ya,

They'll love to run their fingers through your hair…

A hefty mahogany sideboard stood against the wall facing the window. There was a caged canary in the corner of the room next to it. Grover moved to the cage.

"That's Charlie," Ellie said.

As if in response to hearing his name, Charlie hopped up onto his swing and trilled at Grover. A beautiful, melancholic sound.

"I don't know how old he is," Ellie said. "He seems to have been here for years."

Grover turned to face her. He asked if Maggie was married.

"Her husband died at Tobruk," Ellie said. "They were married just before the 8th Army was shipped to North Africa in '41."

Grover scoped the room again. There were photographs on the sideboard. All of adults. Lots of a slim dark-haired man. By a car in the street, on the beach at Weston Super Mare, sitting on a bench in the back garden. And in the park, in uniform. There were no pictures of children. Ellie saw Grover wondering.

"No children," she said. "Maggie hasn't married again. George was the love of her life. They were childhood sweethearts. That's the way it is was with many women, Ed. My two aunts lost their fiancées during the First War. They lived next door to each other in Southville, spinsters to the end. Emily died first. Thelma less than two months later, from a broken heart."

Charlie trilled again. Ellie looked in his direction.

"He seems company enough for Maggie."

The lady returned to the parlour a couple of minutes later. Tea was dispensed, cups and saucers passed around. And Maggie asked how she could help Grover.

"Did you hear what happened to Rita Caton?"

Maggie nodded. "The lady who came visiting, yes. It was all over the papers."

"I hope you don't mind me asking… But did you tell the truth about Bradley Parsons. Did you really not like him? I ask this, not just because it's important. But the way Rita relayed it to her friend Hal, I sensed that you, er… weren't comfortable with the questions, or the explanation you gave."

Maggie sat in silence. Ellie tried to help.

"Please Maggie." She gestured at Ed. "This man is one of the best. We met in 1941, during the Easter blitz. He fought from D Day until the end of the war. He spent five years in West Berlin, helping total strangers stitch their devastated lives back together. Just two months ago, he did the same here, for Harry. He saved us, our family. Trust him. And if you can help him, in any way, please do that."

It was one hell of a speech. Grover sat stock still throughout it. Eventually Maggie's response was delivered.

"I thought I was protecting Brad," she said. There was the trace of an American east coast accent in her voice. "I wish I had tried harder. He was a good man, deep down. I can guess what you think of him. Wayward, undisciplined, a chancer, a cheat, a criminal…"

"That's what his military record says," Grover offered.

"It doesn't come close to the real Brad," Maggie insisted. "At least not the Brad he turned into during the last couple of years. The Brad who looked after Hanna – the girl in the photograph."

She paused. Ellie and Grover waited.

"Can I see the picture again?"

Grover fished a copy out of his wallet. Margaret stared at it for a long time.

"Hanna Gunther… She was born in Buffalo, upstate New York, in 1924. Her parents were German immigrants. Her father worked in construction, her mother took in sewing. When Hanna was twelve, her father was killed in an accident on a building site. Her mother Alys moved them both to a rooming house in

Queens. She got a job cleaning the place. Alys' parents lived in Berlin – middle class, well off, supporters of the Nazi regime. In 1936, things were good in Germany for such people. Her mother persuaded Alys to go back home, sent her the money for the trip. Alys got a job as housekeeper to a neighbour, Hanna went back to school, speaking her second language. Two months later, Hitler marched into the Rheinland, and if you know your history Mr Grover, you will recall that everything began to change. Hitler ramped up the lebensraum nonsense and the anti-Jew project. Her parent's nearest neighbour, her father's closest friend, was a Jew."

She paused to pick up the saucer in front of her and sip her tea.

"While Alys was collecting Hanna from school one day, her parents were arrested. Accused of knowingly associating with a Jew. They had lent their neighbour some money. Alys and Hanna didn't go home. They moved in with the old lady whose house Alys was keeping in order. All three spent the war together. Until the Russians attacked the city in '45. The terrified old lady died of a heart attack as the house was shelled, on the eve of Hanna's twenty-first birthday. Alys had gone out to scrounge some flour to make her daughter a cake. She didn't come home. Three days later, Russian soldiers arrived in the street. Hanna was raped by one of them, rescued by another. She was living in the cellar when the Americans took over her section of the city. The army gave her a job, as an interpreter."

She put down her cup and saucer.

"Which was when she met Bradley. He looked after her, helped her out, during his time in West Berlin. When he got word he was going home, he asked her to go with him. The army helped with a new passport – she is an American citizen – and she was flown out on a mercy flight by the USAF. Bradley managed to get her here just before Christmas last year. Then there was some hold up with his US repatriation, so Hanna stayed here for a while. She got a cleaning job at Doctor Broughton's surgery." She looked at Ellie. "You know the place. Brad used to bring food parcels and money on his weekend passes. Then two weeks ago, Hanna moved out. Said she and Brad would be leaving the country within days." Margaret stopped speaking, suddenly locked into some thought inside her head. "It seems that wasn't true. And now, she must be out there somewhere, by herself."

She stared towards the window, as if in some symbolic gesture.

"Still, she's a survivor. She's tough."

"Or she's back in the United States," Ellie suggested.

Grover shook his head. "Without Bradley? I don't think so. The rest of the 21st don't go home for some weeks."

Ellie brightened a little. "Did Hanna spend time with anyone else while she was here?"

"Not that I knew."

"No one at all. Not even a passing acquaintance?" Grover asked.

Margaret spent some time considering this.

"Well, perhaps someone at the surgery. But if so… I mean, she never mentioned anyone. She did like working there. Got on very well with all the staff. Especially the other GP, the new bloke… er Doctor Hassell."

"But you haven't the slightest idea where she might be?"

"I can't imagine," Margaret said. "I'm so sorry. I liked the girl. She was bright and funny. I liked having her in the house."

Grover stood up. Apologised to Margaret for bothering her. She waved the apology away and ushered her visitors to the front door.

Outside, in the street Ellie asked, "What's the next move?"

"The next move, Ellie, is to have some lunch and figure out what the next move is."

"Alright, home. There's some fish in the fridge. Good for the mind, fish. Gets you thinking."

The cod with mashed potato was terrific. Brains whirred around the table. Arthur came up with a suggestion.

"Why don't you pay a visit to the doctor? Well the surgery at least. You might get some sort of lead."

***

Grover located the medical practice of Doctors Broughton and Hassell at the end of Palmerston Street. The ground floor at the front housed a waiting room and a surgery; one of the rooms at the rear was a second surgery, the other an office, and behind that, looking out into the back yard, there was a kitchen.

"I'm afraid I can't tell you anything about Miss Gunther," the receptionist told him. "You will have to ask Doctor Hassell about her. He is the home visit person this afternoon, but I expect him back…" she looked up at the clock on the wall, "within the hour. The surgery will be closing then, but I'm sure he will make time to speak with you."

The receptionist and her desk sat with the rear wall of the room behind them, looking towards the window facing the street. A row of plastic chairs ran along both walls left and right. A low table in the centre of the room was laden with magazines and cheap kid's toys. There were half a dozen patients in the waiting room. An elderly man who seemed to be having trouble with his right leg, two middle aged women, one dabbing constantly at her eyes with a handkerchief the other staring fixedly across the room, a young man with a bandaged wrist, and a young woman with a very unhappy three year old wriggling in her arms.

This was Grover's first experience of the new National Health Service, pioneered by the Labour government. As yet primitive, unwieldy, not up to full speed, but free to all.

He selected an ancient copy of *Reader's Digest* from the magazines on the table and took a seat. Mercifully, the baby was the next patient to be seen. He began to cry as his mother carried him into Doctor Broughton's consulting room. He came out fifteen minutes later, much quieter.

The clients slowly dwindled down to the man with the painful right leg. The receptionist, looked at the clock on the wall, left her desk and moved into the hall to lock the front door. Doctor Hassell returned to the surgery as the man hobbled in to see Doctor Broughton.

Doctor Hassell recognised Grover, before he had time to introduce himself.

"You're the Army Liaison Officer at Filton," he said. "I was at the Grand Hotel introduction last week. Pleased to meet you once again." He pointed at the chair to the right of his desk. "Do sit down."

Grover did. Breathed in and out. The doctor opened the conversation. He asked how Grover knew Hanna Gunther was a patient at the surgery. Grover said he had no idea she was. He knew she used to clean the place and that she lived with Margaret Templeton. Who had pointed him in this direction.

Doctor Hassell took all that in.

"Miss Gunther gave up the cleaning job two weeks ago, or thereabouts. Although she's still registered as a temporary patient. And I'm sure you realise I cannot discuss anything concerning her medical record with you."

"Let me ask you this. Was she in good health when you saw her last?"

"Oh yes, absolutely."

"She hadn't consulted you, complaining of anything at all?"

"No. What's this all about?"

"Did you spend any time talking with her, outside of the patient relationship?"

"No."

"As an employer?"

"That's Doctor Broughton's area, not mine." He was losing patience with the conversation. "Again. What is this all about?"

"One more question please."

Doctor Hassell shook his head, deciding to put an end to the encounter. He rose to his feet. Grover did the same and snatched one more sentence.

"Did she ever mention a man called Bradley Parsons? Brad."

"No." The doctor was all out of empathy. "That's enough. I have patient's notes to write. I must ask you to leave."

"Hanna Gunther has disappeared," Grover said. "I believe she is in danger."

Whatever the doctor was about to say next, stalled on his lips. He looked long and hard at Grover. Grover did not blink.

"She has left her address in Peel Street," he elaborated. "A top KC is looking for her. Along with the city's Senior Crimes Team. The man she was going to marry is dead. He was supporting her. If she is still alive, she has to be somewhere. Maybe on her own."

An over-dramatised version of the situation. But it had the desired effect. Doctor Hassell sat down again. Pulled his thoughts together.

"I apologise Sergeant Major."

"No need to do that," Grover said. He sat down also. "Let me ask you once more… Was she in the best of health?"

"Yes," the doctor said. "For a woman who was almost four months pregnant."

***

Grover needed to know where Hanna Gunther was. How she was when last seen. The visit to the doctor although informing, was not the best next move in terms of results.

With permission from the receptionist, Grover phoned Fincher Reade and Holborne. Mel was in the office. Grover relayed his conversation with Doctor Hassell. Not that he expected Mel to leap into action, but advice from an insider if you're about to break the law was always helpful.

"It's progress, at least I think it is," he said. "And I guess you ought to know as much as I do. Besides, I need your advice."

"Fire away. Don't be bashful."

"Okay… This new information. Is it something I can keep to myself and investigate?" He imagined Mel shaking her head in disbelief, but ploughed on. "I know that sounds a dangerous idea. But if I call the police and reveal all, where will it place me? Will they order me to butt out? Or will they read me my rights and sling me into the hoosegow?"

"They'll probably do both of those things," Mel said. "And you haven't actually kept this to yourself so far, you've had the generosity to share it with me."

"Knowledge after the fact that's called isn't?"

"Not in this case, but it should be. Sleep on this. I'll meet you for breakfast at Carwardines tomorrow morning. 9 o'clock."

CHAPTER TWENTY

He slept the sleep of the restless and the unjust. Awake every couple of hours, despairing eyes dragged to the luminous face of his alarm clock. He was up and out with the dawn. Five minutes later he was sitting on the bench on his favourite piece of dockside. Highly unlikely, he calculated, that a trio of hard cases would pick on him at 6 o'clock in the morning. And if they did, hell he was spoiling for a fight anyway.

This major bout of unreason had no basis to it. He was simply pissed off with the world and what it had crapped onto his desk. The overwhelming attack of responsibility he had assumed for the welfare of Hanna Gunther, was not his to shoulder. Besides, what had he accomplished so far – beyond getting someone blown to pieces – was not much more than zero. But there was the bottom line. Rita was dead because he gave her a photograph to help with the poke-around for information.

The SCT had not come up against bombings before. The combined experience of detectives on the team in this line was minimal. They were going to have to call in experts.

Then his mind kicked into another gear. With a question he had not asked himself so far. Which was the 'go to' place to find an explosives expert? The answer was so simple. His employer had hundreds of them.

The first Carwardine's Coffee House opened in Bristol in 1842. Currently in Corn Street, it had managed to flourish unscathed throughout the war. And on desperate, blacked out nights during the blitz, had been open all hours to forces personnel, the Home Guard, Air Raid Wardens, and emergency workers. A great morale booster, eternally famous for the pungent fumes of roasting coffee beans which the populace could smell several streets away.

Sitting in the window alcove with a view down to Baldwin Street, Mel could see Grover was restless.

"Alright, Ed. You look as if you'd rather be anywhere but here. Come on, tell me the rest."

"I need an explosives expert," he said.

"No no," Mel said. "The police do. And they'll get him from somewhere. The army probably." Then she looked into Grover's eyes, added two and two together and made four. "No. Not from your army. Our army."

"I figured I could do some research of my own."

"Research? Is that what they now call meddling in business which is none of your concern?"

A waitress in a crisply laundered uniform delivered coffee and toast to the table. The conversation was suspended.

"There's something else," Grover said as the waitress retreated.

"There always is," Mel said.

Then her body language changed. She looked uncomfortable. She slumped back into her chair. Grover couldn't fail to notice the switch.

"You think this is the worst idea in the world," he said.

Yes, Mel did. But that was only part of the problem. She began choosing her words carefully.

"You…" she said. Then paused to get the next bit right

Grover stared at her. "Me what?"

"This is difficult enough. Don't interrupt."

"Okay," he said. Surprised at the purpose in her voice.

Mel looked down at her mug of coffee and the plate of toast. She reached for the mug, changed her mind and looked at Grover.

"We have a connection," Mel said. "Don't we?"

"Of course."

"And, I feel, that we are close.

"We are."

Mel took a deep breath. And got to the point.

"So, two things… One. This idea is barmy. It's a dead cert, nailed on, dipped in bronze way to get into trouble, and worse. I don't want you putting yourself in harm's way. I mean why would you do that? All over again. Didn't you get enough of that in Europe? Or do you need this kind of danger. Is it some sort of drug? Whatever… please don't put this absurd scheme into operation."

She paused.

"And two?..."

Mel looked straight into his eyes. "Can we spend this evening and possibly the whole night together?"

Grover stared at her. A blaze of adrenalin kicked in. He began to nod and grin, at the same time. And somehow, Mel could not stop. Anxiety had taken over. She babbled out one long sentence.

"Unless of course the first proposition is better in which case ignore the fact that I feel the way I do about you and get on with it because it's something a man's gotta do only don't get hurt."

She picked up a slice of toast and took huge bite, chewing fit to bust. Lifted the coffee mug, drank, swallowed, put the mug down and stared out of the window.

Grover said, "You're fabulous."

"Really? I mean… really?"

"One hundred percent, totally fabulous."

"And?..."

"I would love to spend the whole night with you."

"And the other bit? The Don Quixote bit. Where you ride into danger and take your life in your hands."

"Oh, that bit."

"Yes."

"I'm prepared to talk that over."

Mel relaxed and smiled at him.

"God this is ridiculous. We're doing this in Carwardine's."

"The place had survived much more damage than we can inflict," he said.

She asked him what his plans were for the day. He cleared his throat and said he was going to Fairford. Mel opened her mouth to object. He held up his right hand, palm towards her, as if he was about to swear an oath.

"I need to talk with my best buddy Henry," he insisted. "He won't repeat anything I say to a soul. And he might tell me something I need to know."

"And that is?"

"I don't know."

"You don't know what you need to know?"

"I'll know what I need to know when I know what it is."

Mel rode along with the linguistic hocus pocus.

"What if you never get to know what you need to know?"

"Then I will have to plough on into the not-knowing."

"Gotcha," Mel said. "You see, in spite of my pleas, you are resolved. You're going to mount your white charger and - "

Grover held up both hands.

"I'm not," he said. "But I need to find out if the US army had a hand in the bombing of Rita's car. She was doing something for us. For me. With no idea of the danger."

"None of us had any idea of the danger," Mel said.

"This experienced soldier thing works the other way too. I should have known, or at least sensed enough, to figure out the odds on it happening. This city is full of men who drifted back from the war with Lugers taken from dead Germans. Men who thought they were coming back to a home for heroes. That wasn't so, was it?"

"Alright," Mel said. "Answer me this. Are you going to do something foolish?"

Grover hesitated. "I swear I will try not to."

"Slit your throat and hope to die?"

"Yes."

"Say it," she ordered.

Grover raised his right hand.

"Slit my throat and hope to die."

Mel grimaced. "That's the best I'll do isn't it?"

Grover reached across the table. Took both of her hands in his.

"May I go to Fairford today?"

"How in the world can I stop you?"

***

Shortly after 10 o'clock, Salome and Grover were on the A420 and clear of the city.

Fifteen minutes later, he swung the jeep onto the A46 and headed northeast into Gloucestershire. Inside the Fairford base, he went in search of Master Sergeant Henry Whelan.

He found him in Vehicle Maintenance Bay 3 and gave him the story of the moment. His buddy stared at him, amazed and horror stricken.

"Don't do it," he said. "I mean it, don't fucking do it."

"I think something's wrong Henry."

"Maybe. But why is it your problem? Tell the Adjutant, he'll give it to the Snowdrops, and you can skedaddle back to the city."

"It's not that simple."

"Of course it fucking is."

Exasperated, he grabbed Grover's sleeve. Dragged him out of VMB 3 and led him towards the airport perimeter track. A couple of hundred yards from the nearest pair of ears, he began to lay down the law.

"Listen… Dawn this am. A C-54 Skymaster lifted off bound for Reykjavik. By now, it will have re-fuelled. And

209

Bradley Parsons, along with the last planeload of the only guys you've known for the past seven years – apart from me and a bunch of mechanics – will be halfway between Iceland and McGuire New Jersey. Home. Remember it?"

Grover could not cope with the fierce intent in Whelan's eyes. He looked away, along the perimeter road and into the distance. His buddy calmed down a little.

"Leave this where it is, Ed. Parsons has gone, along with all the miseries and memories. If you pursue this, the best you can expect is a one-way ticket to Leavenworth, and the worst... doesn't bear a moment's thought. Come on, I'll buy you a beer."

Grover shook his head.

"No thanks. I have to check in with Berger." He picked up the sudden look of alarm on Whelan's face. "Don't worry. I'll think about what you just said. He has to be briefed on what I'm doing officially at Filton. Catch up with you later."

He set off in the direction of the admin building. Whelan watched him go.

Two minutes later, Grover was sitting in the Adjutant's office, looking at him across the desk.

"They told me you were here on the base. Good to see you, Ed."

"And you, Sir." He peered at the Captain's flashes on Berger's collar and sleeves. "Congratulations."

Berger grinned at him. "Was up all night, sewing 'em on. He leaned back in his chair.

"So?..."

"I hear Parsons is on a plane home," Grover said.

Berger inspected his wrist watch.

"Just about there I reckon." He offered Grover an old-fashioned look. "You should be there too."

"We've been over this thing, Sir. I'm pleased to be where I am."

"Okay," Berger said. "Let me be frank with you. The army doesn't share your opinion. Yes, that's no more or less than you're expecting I know. But you've got to take it easy, Ed. Shelve this private investigator shit and stick with aero engines."

He paused, trying to assess Grover's reaction. He could not read it, so he went on.

"It's been decided that someone higher up the scale than a Sergeant Major should be heading up this liaison thing."

"So, you are going to relieve me of this job? Because if –"

"No," Berger said. "We're going to promote you. To full lieutenant. How'd you like them apples?"

Grover remembered his last promotion. In Berlin. He was getting up the army's ass at that time also. Berger knew what he was thinking about, and ploughed on.

"Hell, I know you don't give a shit about this. But it's a huge chunk of extra dollars a week. Just take it Ed. Accept this promotion in the spirit it's being offered. You deserve it." He stood up and extended his right arm across the desktop. "Welcome to the officer class."

Grover decided he would accept, regardless of what might happen down the line. He took Berger's hand.

"Thank you, Sir."

Berger added a final sentence, almost as an aside.

"I'm confident you will respect the rank you have now accepted, and the responsibilities that go with it."

He sat down again. Grover remained standing.

"Colonel Whitmore wants an update on the Filton situation. I'll tell him you're here."

He picked up the phone receiver.

In his office along the corridor, Whitmore was all smiles and bonhomie.

"Congratulations Lieutenant. Thoroughly deserved."

"Thank you, Sir."

"How is the Filton thing? Sit down, sit down."

Grover did so. 'Stick to the subject', he ordered his inner self.

"I like the whole gang. A very clever group of guys. I'm learning a lot about jet engines." Then his inner self countermanded, the order. "But also, about the city, and how it works."

Whitmore decided to let the last sentence pass. He shot a robust smile across the desk.

"Good. Just remember you're representing Uncle Sam. The greatest power in the world. With the greatest responsibility ever taken on in the name of humanity. And the one with all the aces."

Grover tried to look as cool as possible. Whitmore warmed to his subject.

"I'm sure Captain Berger has already given you the rundown on what we, what the country, expects from our ambassadors. After all, that's what you are. We all know and appreciate your track record since D Day, your commitment to help the building of peace in

Europe, and your feelings about this country we now work in."

Grover began to wonder how long Whitmore intended this bullshit to be. Clearly the CO had a little farther to go.

"You are a good man, Ed Grover…"

That again, although this time, not remotely sincere.

"And I know you will continue to do what we ask of you, to the best of your ability and in the traditions of the Service." He smiled once again. "Thank you, Lieutenant. Go and do what you do well."

Grover decided, at that moment, not to wonder what that was. Instead, he saluted, as smartly as he could. Wheeled through one hundred and eighty degrees, and left the office.

Henry Whelan was back in the Motor Pool.

"So that's what they think of you," he said. "Full Lieutenant." He raised his right hand in mock salute. "Sorry. Sir."

"I don't want the gig, Henry"

"Course you do. You deserve it."

"It comes with a set of -"

Whelan interrupted. "The job's a piece of piss. And a thousand times better than the alternative – getting shot at."

"Yeah well, I knew what I was doing when that was happening. Smash onwards and stay alive. A binary mission that."

"A what?"

"Never mind. Suffice it to say, the only thing that mattered each day, was getting through it."

Whelan completed the rationalisation.

"And then counting the number of men in Baker Company still alive at the end of it."

Grover looked at Whelan with some resolution.

"So, Henry, in the name of all that, I'm not taking this assault on my sensibilities lying down either."

"Then make your bed, because no one else will volunteer to do it for you."

"Okay," Grover said, "What's the simplest way to blow up a car?"

CHAPTER TWENTY-ONE

Detective Chief Inspector Bridge had been working on a similar idea. He made a call to the Army Ordnance Depot at Ridge Quarry near Corsham. The CO, Major Harrison, said he would be happy to talk with the constabulary about bombs and related stuff. Suggested Bridge and Goole pay a visit. The two detectives were being driven into Wiltshire by PC Grafton. Glancing back over his shoulder, he checked with Bridge.

"Is this the place which used to be called Tunnel Ridge Quarry? On the southern side of Box Tunnel?"

Bridge confirmed that it was.

"In which case, Sir, I can cut ten minutes off the journey across country. Providing the road's alright."

"Okay, give it a whirl."

Goole looked at his boss.

"Tunnel Bridge Quarry?"

"Old Bath Stone mine workings. Opened back in the early 1800s. Taken over by the army during the Great War to store TNT and cordite. Thousands of tons of it. Apparently, there are acres of storage space in there. A narrow-gauge railway connects the place with the GWR main line at Corsham. In '39, the place was handed to the RAF to store two hundred and fifty pound bombs. A year later they were all shipped to Cairo, and the quarry began taking in crates of light arms and ammunition from the US. This was when everybody was expecting Hitler to invade the next morning."

Goole was impressed with this lorry load of knowledge.

"Major Harrison told me all this, while you were having lunch in the canteen," Bridge said. "And the rest."

He looked out of the car window. Goole waited.

"Go on then."

"At one point during the Battle of Britain, the quarry stored five thousand hand grenades and close to one hundred thousand rounds of ammunition. When Hitler didn't arrive, it became the number one storage place for D Day. Which upped the ante a bit. The quarry was filled up with five hundred pound bombs, ready to be shipped to airfields."

"They were all used?"

"No, apparently. Thousands of them still there at the end of the war."

"What did they do with them?"

"Moved them eventually."

"And now?"

"Ah well, Detective Sergeant, that's something of a secret. 'A few thousand small arms' is the official word. Conventional armament. However, Major Harrison did say, that the place was running as part of the government 'cold war policy' – whatever that is."

"The mind boggles," Goole said. "Early warning systems, spy warfare, atomic bombs."

Bridge looked him.

"Over boggling there Tom, I think."

"You never know what these people are up to," Goole said.

There was silence between them for a while. The car slowed down and turned into a country lane with grass growing up the middle.

"The cross-country bit, Sir," Grafton said.

Goole came up with something else.

"My brother-in-law lives this side of Corsham," Goole said. "He mends tractors. Gets a lot of work among the farmers locally. I ought to pop in and see the family while we're here."

Bridge was thinking twice about that. Goole embellished a little.

"He makes demon cider. And we can always consider ourselves off duty when we've finished with Major erm…"

"Harrison."

"I'm sure Elwyn will be only too happy to open a bottle." He gave his boss an encouraging look. "You drink cider, don't you?"

"Maybe we could find some time to pop in," Bridge said. He leaned towards the driver and tapped him on the left shoulder. "You didn't hear any of that PC Grafton."

"Any of what, Sir?"

***

John Walton Harrison DSO and Bar, may not have been everybody's idea of a modern Major General, but Bridge and Goole thought he came close. Built straight and tall, clear and careful in speech, but with the joviality of Mr Fezziwig. He shook hands heartily with the detectives and gestured to the chairs in front of his desk.

"Tea gentlemen?" he asked.

Bridge and Goole accepted gracefully.

The major clicked a switch on the intercom box on his desk.

"Sir?..." a voice echoed back.

"Tea for all Martin, if you please."

"Sir." A click, and Martin was gone.

"Now then. How can we help you?"

Bridge gave the Major chapter and verse on the Bedminster car park explosion. The soldier listened intently, nodded his understanding at various points in the narrative, but did not speak until Bridge had finished the narrative. At which point, he brought his hands together across his waist and looked at each detective in turn.

"Hmm…"

On cue, tea for four arrived. Major Harrison introduced the waiter.

"Captain Martin Jackson. I'd like him to join us in this. However, tea first."

While this was being dispensed with due ceremony, the major summarised the story he had just been told for Jackson's benefit. He closed the narrative by looking at Bridge.

"Have I missed anything, Chief Inspector?"

Bridge was impressed. "No, Sir."

The major raised his cup and took his first sip of tea.

"Now Martin," he said. "You blew things up during the war. Thinking cap on."

Captain Jackson took a huge swallow of tea and fell to rationalising.

"Bombs. Tricky buggers," he said. "TNT, dynamite, detonators, complicated bits of wiring, primers, timing devices. A lot to think about. No job for an amateur. Not a last-minute thing either. Can't rehearse this kind of stuff without endangering yourself and everybody around you." He looked Bridge. "You said on the phone you had photographs."

"I've got them," Goole said.

He reached down beside his chair, picked up the small soft leather briefcase he had brought with him, unfastened the strap buckles and fished around inside it. Produced a ten by eight envelope and passed it across the desk to Jackson.

The Captain opened the envelope, scanned the half a dozen pictures one by one. 'Hmm', 'Ahh', 'Right', 'Oh yes', he offered in sequence. Major Harrison nodded confidently at the policemen as this went on. Finally, Jackson put down the pictures. The others waited for him.

"Definitely not a bomb," he pronounced.

He turned the pictures around and spread them over the desk in front of the detectives. Pointed at them.

"First… Black scorched oval on the concrete under the car and around it. Second… No hole in the ground, means the device was detonated inside the car chassis. Three… Pieces of the car – the frame, axles, heavy stuff blackened by flames but not blown up. Four… tiny pieces of debris spread over a small area. Five… No apparent collateral damage elsewhere in the car park."

He paused and smiled at the others. Only to be prodded by the Major.

"Come on Martin, no grandstanding please."

"The weapon used here, gentlemen," Jackson said, "was a grenade."

"You are sure?" the Major said.

"Absolutely."

Goole was almost moved to raise his hand, as if he was in school.

"You have a question sergeant?" Jackson asked.

"No, not at all. I'm just fascinated by the deduction."

Jackson picked up his cup and drained it of tea. Put the cup down again

"As I said, the device was most certainly detonated in the car. Probably the engine compartment. A bomb small enough to handle, and do the damage inflicted here would be a very tricky thing to construct. A clever, one time only, bespoke job with some special timing device. And from the time scale you have suggested – the bombing happening less than twenty-four hours after the decision was made to show the photographs around – it had to be done at the last minute. It is very unlikely somebody would have something like that on a shelf. Unless…"

He paused for a moment, as if not wishing to be impolite. The detectives waited. He finished what he meant to say.

"Unless… you have a well organised crime syndicate in the city."

"With guns and bombs," Bridge said. "No."

"Then a grenade it is."

Goole was lost in fascination now.

"How would that work?"

"A grenade contains around two ounces of TNT. The body is made of iron, designed to fragment, to shatter in tiny pieces, causing damage to everything in the blast radius. They are intended to be lobbed at things of course, but they could do just as much damage sitting somewhere."

"Under a car bonnet for example?"

"Yes," the Captain said. "Better than placed somewhere inside the car itself, where it might be found. Motorists don't usually check under the bonnet before moving out of a car park. They just get in, switch the engine on and drive away."

He paused. Waited for more reaction. Bridge responded this time.

"Two things," he said. "What sort of grenade do you mean? The traditional British Mills Bomb?"

"Probably not. The American 'pineapple' would be best for this. It is slimmer than the Mills Bomb, more cylindrical than round, smaller and easier to hold."

"Okay," Bridge said. "But as we know, this wasn't lobbed at the car."

"Then I should have said, more easily attached to something because of its shape. And the second thing?"

"How do you get the grenade to work, without somebody pulling the pin out?"

Captain Jackson smiled and bowed his head in acknowledgement of the question.

"That I cannot answer, Chief Inspector. Your department, not mine."

***

Grover and Whelan were back in VMB 3. Thirty-five feet square, with two service pits, two engine hoists and benches on three sides. The smallest VMB, the workshop for jeeps and staff cars. The place in which Sergeants Grover and Whelan Frankenstein had built Salome.

They had spent six weeks doing it. Using a collection of jeeps in pieces and destined for scrap. They began by choosing the best of the bunch. The chassis floor had a substantial hole in it, but it was still attached to the front axle and the gearbox. Grover found a back axle with a broken differential. Whelan found a working diff. Grover prised a clutch from Leading Mechanic Stokowski, handing over the four bottles of Jack Daniels he had exchanged for a German Luger with the Able Company Quartermaster. The engine re-build took two weeks; fitting the clutch and the gear box, two days. Whelan welded a new sub frame into the chassis. Grover stripped another dead jeep of its seats, and the two men had the final bits of their new creation. The lady made her debut, speeding around the air base perimeter road.

Whelan was taking time arranging his props. Grover watched every move with fascination.

"You can't be surprised, surely, that I can do this kind of thing." Whelan said. He waved his arm at the dozen or so pickups, jeeps and cars behind him. "Years of re-building these vehicles teaches you how to take them apart. But also, how to blow 'em up."

He grinned at his friend. Moved to a midnight blue Ford V8 Pilot, sitting with the bonnet open.

"The Brass have started using these Brit Fords as staff cars. Cheaper to buy over here than ship metal all the way from Dearborn Michigan. And the bonus is, they're right hand drive. Have a look under the hood. Sorry, bonnet."

He stuck his head into the engine space, Grover alongside him.

"See the throttle cable, way back to the left. It comes through the bulkhead behind the accelerator pedal in the car. The outer casing is made from metal and rubber, as far forward as this bracket here." He pointed to the spot where the throttle casing was bolted to the engine block. "This is where the business end starts. The interior wire runs out of the casing and towards the throttle body to your right. There's a foot of it exposed. Now keep your eye on it, while I turn the engine over."

He ducked out of the way, moved to the driver's door, slid into the seat and turned on the ignition. He pressed the accelerator and the cable pulled out from the throttle body a couple of inches. Whelan reduced the engine revs and shouted from the car.

"Did you get that?"

Grover yelled back. "Yeah."

Whelan demonstrated once again, for good measure. Grover pulled his head out from under the bonnet and waved. Whelan lifted his foot from the accelerator and switched off the engine. He climbed out of the car.

"You see?"

"Yeah. The throttle cable moved a couple of inches."

"A bit less, actually." Whelan said. "But just enough."

"To do what?"

Whelan grinned. "Pull the pin out of a grenade."

Grover was truly impressed. "How the hell did you come up with that?"

"I blew up a Mercedes staff car in the Nordhreinland, back in '45. The cheapest, simplest, and – this is the best bit – safest way of doing it. All you need, is a roll of duct tape and a short length of wire."

He walked over to a box on a work bench. Took a 'pineapple' out of it and tossed it to Grover. His knee jerk reaction was to catch it.

"Well held," Whelan said.

Grover looked down at the grenade in his hands. "Jesus Christ."

"It's not primed," Whelan assured him. "Let me show you what I mean."

He picked up a short length of thin wire from the bench, moved to Grover and held out his right hand.

"The grenade."

Grover handed it to him. Whelan, connected one end of the wire to the pin. Twisted the wire to make sure it would not slip.

"Okay Lieutenant, pay attention." He held the grenade in a horizontal position. "The grenade is attached to the throttle cable with duct tape, wrapped around tight. That's important. We don't want it to move."

He looped the other wire around his left forefinger and pulled it horizontal.

"Straight and true," he said. "Now then, this finger represents the point at which the throttle casing is bolted to the engine. We attach the wire from the grenade pin

224

to it, with no slack. That's important also. And when the accelerator is pressed, the cable wire, moves as you saw, and pulls the throttle open. Like this."

Whelan pulled sharply to the left with his finger. The pin slid out of the grenade.

"Boom."

Grover jumped in shock. Whelan chuckled.

"Always gets a laugh," he said. "Still frightening, even though you know the grenade isn't primed."

"That's your theory is it," Grover muttered, as he began to recover.

"Anybody who has handled a grenade can do this," Whelan said. "No bomb making expertise required. All he has to do is make sure there's no slack in the wire from the grenade pin to the throttle bracket."

"And you do need access to a grenade of course," Grover pointed out.

"Of course," Whelan said. "But they're much easier to get hold of than bomb making ingredients, or other army ordnance. Easy to hide too. You can wander round town with grenades in your pockets."

"So, somebody's doing this?"

"Hell, I don't know. Like you said, it's a theory."

CHAPTER TWENTY-TWO

A *Prides Rides* taxi cab pulled into the side of the road a few yards ahead of Donald Abey, who was walking back to *Eaves Night* with his lunch – a chicken mayonnaise sandwich and a bottle of Fentiman's ginger beer. The front passenger door opened and a man in a fifty bob suit slid out of the car. The unsuspecting Abey walked into him. Taller and several inches wider than the bookkeeper, the man wrapped his arms around Abey and lifted him off his feet. The kerbside rear passenger door was opened from inside the car. The big man swung Abey around the door and heaved him into the car. Another big man, also on the rear seat, hauled Abey upright. The outside man slammed the door. The inside man put his left arm around Abey's shoulders and tapped his cheek a couple of times with his right hand.

"Just a friendly ride, Donald" he said.

In the company garage on the Avon Trading Estate, he was dumped onto the seat of the wooden chair. Rodney Pride hitched at his trousers, bent his knees and looked straight into Abey's eyes.

"Is that all clear then?" he asked.

Abey nodded at him.

"Yes," he whispered.

"Sure?"

Abey nodded again.

"Because next time will be painful."

Abey's chair was in the middle of the floor, underneath a row of light bulbs with tin shades. His two hauliers were standing behind the chair. Rodney Pride straightened up.

High above the group, daylight filtered into the garage through barred skylights. Motes of dust, disturbed by the invasion of the place, danced in the air. The people on the floor were alternately highlighted and silhouetted by the light and shade.

Abey, in a courageous but brief moment, had attempted to reason with Pride. Pointing out that thirty pounds a week was more than his boss could afford to pay for protection; considering that the man who was supposedly providing it, was dishing out the threats and violence in the first place. A perfectly reasonable attitude to take, under ordered circumstances. But not to be considered when the orders were coming from a devoted sinner like Rodney Pride.

"Fuck the protection bollocks," he said. "Right now, I want to know what happened to the Benzedrine."

Abey swallowed. Cleared his throat.

"There isn't any more," he said. Then he managed another sentence. "The source dried up."

"What do you mean?"

Abey swallowed again.

"Well, actually… erm…," he muttered.

Pride swung his right leg and kicked the chair out from under Abey, who was tipped over onto the floor. One of the hauliers move forwards. Pride snarled at him.

"Leave him. Just fucking leave him."

He stepped to Abey and looked down at him. A voice echoed across the garage.

"Bradley Parsons is dead."

Sandy Eaves was standing just inside the wicket gate in the bottom corner of the left-hand door.

"Leave him alone gentlemen."

She moved across the floor. Stopped a couple of yards short of Pride. Looked down at Abey.

"Alright Donald?"

Abey nodded, and to prove the same, he got to his feet. Sandy returned her attention to Pride.

"It's all dead and gone Rodney," she said. "All of it. Parsons was knocked down by a car, would you believe?" She surveyed the room. "Get rid of these arseholes. No better still, get one of them to take Donald back to the club. We have to talk. You and me."

"In the office," Pride suggested.

Sandy shook her head. "Here will do."

Pride took a moment to think about that. He nodded at one of the hauliers.

"Do as she says."

The other haulier asked him if he should stay.

"You do as she says also."

Abey looked anxiously at his boss. She assured him she would be all right. Pride's employees escorted Abey to the wicket door and let him step outside into the afternoon sunshine.

Pride found another chair, set it facing the one Abey had vacated. He gestured at Sandy. She sat, he followed. Waited for her to begin whatever this was to be. She sat still. Pride snorted,

"It amazes me when I remember you used to have a thing for me."

"As I recall, it was the other way around," she said. "You're not the most attractive man in the city, by a country mile. I was pissed out of my mind when we did whatever it was we did, I can't remember."

For a second or two, Pride considered whether that insult was actionable. Then the frustration slipped from his eyes. He enquired how she knew his employees had picked up Donald Abey.

"Somebody I know saw it happen. Not exactly a subtle move, was it? Sweeping him up on a busy street in broad daylight. But then subtlety of the simplest kind was never your forté was it."

"My what?"

"Never mind."

Bur Pride could not leave the old times alone.

"Maybe, back in the day… Well there were moments on my mind… Maybe that's why I decided to help you distribute the bennies. Let's say it was for old times' sake."

"Let's say it was for the money," Sandy said. "And don't look so outraged; that never really works for you."

"Are you ever going to run out of insults?"

"And sulking doesn't suit you either."

"Look, don't imagine you can come in here and -"

"Oh, for fuck's sake…"

Pride got to his feet.

"That's enough," he yelled. "Just piss off. Back to that street end cellar you call a place of entertainment. We'll consider our short collaboration a mistake."

Eyes blazing, Sandy Eaves stood up too.

"If it's the last thing on God's earth I do -" she began.

Pride interrupted. Offered a body language that left his anger and hate only too visible.

"Just fuck off," he said.

Sandy left as swiftly as possible.

As she disappeared through the wicket gate, Pride picked up the chair he had been sitting on and hurled it across the floor. It bounced off the door, the tubular legs bending, the plastic seat splitting in half.

He looked up to the rafters and yelled, "Fucking bitch."

***

"Lieutenant Grover?" Mel bounced up and down. "That's amazing."

She stepped into Grover's arms. He picked her up, swung her through 360 degrees and dropped her back onto her feet. She leaned into him, smiling. Grover kissed her. She opened her mouth, her tongue found his, and it all started to work.

Then Mel pulled away from him.

"Not in the hall surely," she said. "I'm prepared to disrobe as swiftly as possible, but not out here."

Grover fumbled the flat key out of his pocket, gave it to Mel, lifted her off her feet and side stepped to the door. Mel unlocked it. He carried her into the hall. She asked him if this was a symbolic proposal. He replied by suggesting they talk about it later.

And they did.

Their bodies close together, Mel's head on Grover's shoulder.

"You will have to marry me now," she said. "You carried me over the threshold."

"Without so much as a 'by your leave'," Grover said. "Will you stay here tonight?"

"That was the plan."

"You had a plan?"

"More of a scheme." She raised her head and looked into his eyes. "I fear I could fall in love with you, Ed Grover."

"Would that be the wrong thing to do?"

"Only if you were not of the same mind."

"I don't think it was my mind that was working back there. It was all about what I was feeling. You have captured my heart Melanie Davis".

She took a moment. "That's good," she said.

"Do you think it's sensible?" he asked.

"Does it have to be?"

Grover pondered for a moment or two.

"I don't think it's in my nature to be sensible," he said. "All the momentous decisions in my life came as surprises."

Mel dropped her head back onto her pillow. She rolled onto her back and stared up at the ceiling.

"I don't know anything about your life," she said.

"Okay. What do you want to know?"

"Let's begin with how old you are."

"I'll be 29 next month" he said."

Mel, turned and propped herself onto on elbow.

"Are you looking forward to it?"

"Birthday's haven't meant much for a while."

"Really?"

"At least, not since my twenty-third. June the 4th, 1944. That one I'll always remember. It would have been twenty-four hours before Overlord, but a storm blew up. Eisenhauer postponed the invasion until the 6th. So, I was allowed a small celebration – just a gathering of buddies around a couple of tables in the bar. Three glasses of beer allowed to each of us. We were all on standby. And about to make history, we were told. We drank a toast to ourselves, the twelve of us, in the stuff that made Milwaukee famous, and tried not to think about what was coming." He paused, locked into the remembrance. "I was the only one who made it off the beach."

Mel read the moment and remained silent. Grover took a deep breath.

"The worst thing wasn't what you'd expect – the bullets and the dying. It was the sea sickness. 120 men packed shoulder to shoulder in the landing craft, throwing up from midnight to dawn. I've never felt as miserable at any other time in my life."

"May I ask you something else?" Mel said.

"Sure. Since I carried you over the threshold, my life has been an open book."

"What did you do before you came to England?"

"I was a cop. I left school at seventeen and joined the Tomah PD. Spent my time as a rookie in a prowl car with a huge black guy called Carlin. Nobody knew the town like he did. Streetwise and hard as nails, he taught me a hell of a lot in just a few weeks. And the work became important."

"Would you still be a cop if you hadn't gone to war?"

"I guess so," Grover said. "Although I got a rough lesson early. I'd been on the Tomah PD about three months when I came across my first case involving a black family. A white store owner, calling himself a patriot, was arrested for raping a black woman. She had a husband and two kids. No one in the family had ever been in trouble. The store owner was released on bail. Somebody went round to his place later that night and blew a hole in him with a shotgun."

"And a black person got the blame?"

"Her husband. Davis, his name was. Same as yours. He was arrested, held for a couple of days then sent home. Lack of evidence. But it was an open and shut case to some. Carlin and I were given the job of keeping an eye on the family. We spent three days, each of us on 12-hour shifts, parked outside their front door. Until the family and the Precinct Commander agreed we were wasting our time. And that same night, half a dozen Klansmen drove up from Missouri. Found the house and set fire to it."

Melanie absorbed that in silence.

"Carlin and me, we should have been there," Grover said. "We could have stopped it."

Melanie found her voice. "So, you fell out of love with the job."

"No. That was never going to happen. It just got harder to do. Then I got interested in the practice of the law - how it was supposed to work, not just enforcing it. I was about to do a law degree in Chicago, when the war arrived and got in the way."

"Do you have any family?"

"My father was killed by a drunk driver when I was six. My mother died while I was in Germany, trying to get to Berlin before the Russians. I didn't get the news until two weeks after her funeral. I have a brother, Arnold. He's in Detroit. Married with two kids. Builds gearboxes for Chrysler. We get on well enough. Or we did. I haven't seen the Michigan Grovers for almost ten years."

"Why don't you want to go home?"

"Zoe asked me that, the first day we met."

"What did you tell her?"

"The land of the free and the home of the brave, looks very different from half a world away. We Americans are an acquired taste. The US is very big. With big motor cars and big shopping malls and freeways that run for hundreds of miles. Where some very frightening people are working around the clock building atomic bombs. And mortuary plots are sold on billboards next to the freeway."

"That's not much of a recommendation," Mel suggested.

"I've been away too long. There's not much to go back for."

"A law degree perhaps."

"A lot of water under the bridge since 1940. I'd been out of Wisconsin twice by the age of nineteen. I'd seen nothing. Since then, I've been to hell and back. Which changes everything." He looked deep into Mel's eyes. "Besides, I like it here. Especially right here, right now."

Mel smiled at him. Affected her best down-home apple pie accent.

"Gee Lootenant, you do say the purtiest thaings."

She rolled onto his body, letting him take her weight. Giving him no alternative other than to respond. Neither of them heard the sound of the fire engine hurtling along Cumberland Road.

CHAPTER TWENTY-THREE

The *Western Daily Press* went to bed too early to scoop the story. The banner headline on the front page of the following lunchtime edition of the *Bristol Evening Post* grabbed it instead.

ARSON IN CLUBLAND – BODIES IN WRECKAGE

The copy underneath was just as lurid.

The night club once owned by notorious city playboy Ronnie Eaves who was shot to death four months ago, was put to the torch in the early hours of this morning. "Eaves Night" went up in flames after the blaze began near the office of current owner-operator Sandy Eaves, widow of the small-time crook. Fire and police officers have already called this a case of arson, and have confirmed the presence of two charred bodies inside the building.

"You can still smell the paraffin in there," the Fire Chief said.

He was standing in *Stage Door Lane* with Bridge and Goole, staring into the smoke blackened wreckage.

"A door from the lounge leads to a store room. Full of liquor, or at least it was. The storeroom door opens into a short corridor, six yards long and not much more than three feet wide. It leads to the office, where we found the bodies. Tailor made to funnel flames quickly."

"How quickly?" Goole asked.

"Seconds probably. By the time we got the call, the blaze was well established. I have a theory if you'd like to hear it?"

"Of course," Bridge said.

"Whoever did this, knew the layout of the place. But was probably working on the assumption that it was empty. He started the fire in the store room. It burned in two directions – into the lounge and along the corridor into the office."

"How much noise would this person make? Why wasn't whatever he was doing heard in the office?"

"Through two doors separated by a corridor? You know as well as I, Chief Inspector, that anybody up to no good at dead of night, goes about his business quietly. And setting fire to places is a noiseless activity mainly, unless you move furniture around. No need to in this case, the props were all there. Whoever did this, spread a few rags around, poured the paraffin and lit his match. And in the few seconds still available to him, opened the door into the corridor then left the store room. The people in the office would not have been aware of the fire until it was too late. The store would have been a small inferno. And opening the office door would have sucked the flames along the corridor towards them."

"So, the man and the woman were actually burnt to death," Goole said.

"Sadly, yes."

The two detectives pondered.

"Is there anything else you need to know at this time?"

"No," Bridge said. "Thank you Chief."

The officer walked away along *Stage Door Lane* to his car.

"Bombing and arson within seventy-two hours," Goole said. "And three deaths. It's the proverbial crime wave boss."

"You may be right," DCI Bridge acknowledged. "But let's face it, this place is no loss to the community."

A uniformed constable shouted from the patrol car ten yards away.

"Chief Inspector… Call for you."

Bridge walked to the car, picked up the receiver sitting on the driver's seat, and put it to his right ear.

"DCI Bridge."

"Sir," the Despatcher's voice said. "We have not been able to trace the whereabouts of the night club owner, Mrs Sandra Eaves. And the forensic pathologist wishes you to call at your earliest convenience."

***

Walter Pilkington, Professor of Pathology at Bristol University, was one of the cleverest in the trade. Well into his 60s and built like Oliver Hardy, there was little he did not know about the human body. Especially when deceased. He had been married four times. He had seven children and thirteen grandchildren. The eldest of which, had been given to suggesting he should retire. Which indeed he could afford to do. But the stipend Bristol Constabulary paid him, guaranteed enough pocket money for good wine, fancy coronas, and admission to the city's best restaurants. The one blot on his otherwise contented landscape was the miserable operating room he had to work in – an asbestos clad, corrugated iron roofed cavern, behind the abattoir on the Bath Road Industrial Estate.

Bridge and Goole answered his summons.

Pilkington waved at the two bodies.

"Slightly more to work on, than the bits I was presented with three days ago." he pronounced. "A man and a woman. The latter mid 40s I would say. The former older. Late 50s perhaps."

He smiled at the two detectives.

"Is that it?" Goole asked.

"So far," Pilkington said. "How much do you two know?"

Bridge relayed the conversation with the Fire Chief.

"I think you can take his words as gospel," the professor said. He gestured at the two bodies covered in sheets. "Do you want to see?"

"Not really," Bridge said.

"Nonetheless…"

Pilkington moved to the operating tables. Pulled back the sheet covering the man, exposing his head and shoulder. The head was little more than a skull, the flesh burned down to the smoke blackened bone. Bridge looked down at the floor and swallowed the bile which was rising. Goole turned away.

"The rest of the body, and the woman's, is the same," the professor explained. "With small pieces of scorched clothing attached to the carcase."

He pulled the sheet back over the man's face, some reverence in his touch.

239

"Identification won't be easy," he continued. "The woman was wearing a bracelet. But not a particularly significant one." He moved to a bench and a couple of trinkets, black and misshapen. "That's the man's ring, a simple gold band. From the third finger of his left hand."

"He was married then?" Goole said.

"Once upon a time, at least," Bridge said.

Pilkington pointed at the scorched bracelet. "It's gold, but as I said, there's nothing bespoke about it. Seems a run of the mill piece to me."

"That's all? No brooches or rings?"

Pilkington shook his head. "Afraid not. A dentist may be your only hope with this. Presuming he and she visited one."

"Bloody hell," Goole said. "How many dentists are there in the city?"

"And in Bath," the professor said. "In Swindon, and all places in between."

"We do know that the owner of the club is missing," Bridge offered. "The man may be her bookkeeper Donald Abey. He is, was, in his late 50s."

"Over to you then, gents," Pilkington said. "I'll let you know what else I find."

***

"Congratulations Lieutenant. We shall have to get you a better chair and a bigger office."

Turnbull and Grover had met for their mini weekly de-brief. The boffin set about handing over notes with timetables, rosters and work schedules.

"Officially you have to be across the bones of this stuff," he said. "The technical details and the figures may mean nothing to you. And if it baffles, I can take you through it all."

"I'll look at everything." Grover said. "It's likely to go way over my head. But I guess it's better to find out what I don't understand, than to remain in ignorance of all of it."

There was a polite knock on the office door. Grover asked whoever it was, to enter. The door opened. RAF Flight Lieutenant Lewis Mills from 501 Squadron, stepped into the room. He nodded to Turnbull and introduced himself to Grover. Grover stood up and shook hands across his desk.

"I hear you'd like to go for a stooge around. We've kicked the trainer Spit into life."

"Sure." Grover beamed like a kid under the tree on Christmas Day. "Now?"

"Absolutely, old boy. No time like the present."

Grover checked with Turnbull. "Have we finished?"

Turnbull nodded. "Go and enjoy yourself."

He stood by the engine cowling of the Spitfire, as Mills cleared the necessary paperwork in the flight office. 'You could be three fields away,' Grover told himself, 'facing the wind, with all the noise in the world at your back, but you would never fail to recognise the deep throated rumbling of a Rolls Royce Merlin engine.' This was the first time he had been close to the 'ballerina of the sky' since the autumn of 1943. There had never been such grace and beauty fused together in any object, let alone a fighting machine. Capable of diving at 450 miles per hour without tearing the wings off. Able to cruise, super cool, above the clouds. This time he wasn't going to be working a fourteen-hour shift, slumping exhausted into bed as dawn rose over the Norfolk coast; after tearing off bent and scarred metal, re-building a broken engine, or prising bullets out of the fuselage. This time he was going to fly. Lost in the expectation of it all, he barely noticed Mills arriving with his flight suit.

The engine checks took five minutes. Two minutes later they had taxied to the head of the runway. Sitting in the rear cockpit, Grover put on his head set and plugged into the dashboard. The intercom clicked into life.

"All right back there, old boy" Mills asked.

Drenched in emotion, Grover managed to croak out, "Yes".

And he scrolled back down the years. There were over 20,000 Spitfires built during the war, but back in 1940 there were so few. Still, they outnumbered the pilots, who somehow manged to turn up, screw their courage to the sticking place, climb in and take off. Some of them came back, but never all of them.

"Then, chocks away," Mills said.

The beautiful machine tore down the runway and was airborne within seconds. Grover's pulse rate rose by fifty beats. He felt the G Forces drawing blood from his heart, his eyes glued to the altimeter as the plane climbed and then levelled out at 1,500 feet.

His heart rate slowed, the knots in his stomach untightened, and he began to smile. The biggest, broadest smile ever. Speechless, he looked around him, into a world of shining blue serenity.

Mills talked to him again.

"You know what they say Ed. 'You don't fly a Spitfire'…"

Grover completed the mantra. "You put it on and wear it."

"I hear you joined the Eagle Squadron in '41," Mills said, in a voice full of respect.

"Yes. I wanted to be a flier."

"What happened?"

"I had something wrong with my sinuses, so they wouldn't let me fly. But I knew about chassis and engines, so I became Aircraftsman Ed Grover."

"Just as important," Mills said. "I mean that. I couldn't have dragged myself into the cockpit at dawn, without knowing that every screw, cog and rivet was in the right place. I presume you've been told this before, but I'll say it again. 'Thank you, Ed'."

Grover, his throat dry, mumbled something in response. Mills knew it was meant to be thanks in return. He changed the tempo.

"Okay old boy. Let's see what this lady will do."

The vibrations, increased momentarily as he poured on the boost. Then dropped as the spitfire soared up, away, over, back and down. All of Grover's senses came alive in those few seconds. He heard every change in engine note, he could smell the heady cockpit mix of aviation fuel, oil and leather. Level once more, Mills dipped the left wing gently, and then executed a perfect barrel roll through 360 degrees.

Suddenly Grover was back in the present, relaxed, cocooned in this incredibly well balanced, beautiful machine. He abandoned himself to pure joy.

"Do you want to take her, Ed?" he heard Mills say.

Instead of panicking he simply said. "Yes."

"I'll pilot from here. If anything goes wrong just give her back to me."

"Okay."

"Roger that. Take hold of the stick and hold it steady. Nothing else."

Mills released control. The tail dipped and he took control again."

"Although you didn't know it," he said, "you were pulling the stick back. Hold it again. Feel it. Don't drive, you have no need to. Ready?"

"Roger that," Grover said.

"I'll take my hands away slowly… Okay, she's all yours… Good. That's it… Comfortable?"

Grover breathed in and out. "Yes."

"Right, Ed. In front of you, slightly to the left is the pitch meter. See it?"

"Yes."

"When I say 'go', gently ease the stick forward. The nose will dip, the speed will increase and we will lose height. I'll count five seconds. Then you will pull the stick back, even more gently than you pushed it forwards, and we shall rise again. Any questions?"

Grover swallowed. "No."

"Stand by then… Countdown from three to 'go'. Three, two, one, go."

Watching the pitch meter, Grover eased the stick forwards. The nose of the Spitfire dropped instantly and the airspeed increased by 30 miles per hour. Then to twice that, as Mills counted through the seconds. On five, Grover pulled the stick back. A little too fiercely. The Spitfire bottomed out, rose, levelled and kept on climbing.

"I've got it," Mills said.

Grover realised he had not breathed throughout that manoeuvre. He blew out his cheeks and took his hands off the stick.

"Try going up this time," Mills said. "Take the stick… That's better. This time, gently back to rise. Then, all being well I'll count to nine and you will level on 'ten'. Countdown from three again. Three, two, one, go."

Eyes glued to the pitch meter, Grover pulled the stick back. The Spitfire started to climb. He dared to look to his right and saw the camouflage on the wing as it seemed to rise above the cockpit.

"Seven, eight, nine, ten," Mills said.

Grover levelled out and breathed again. Mills took the controls.

"That was terrifying," Grover said. "But maybe, the best moment of my life."

"We'll stooge around for another fifteen minutes or so, before we return to base."

No more heroics. Just some soaring, a full throttle belt across the sky and a huge wide banking turn to get onto course for home. The Spitfire touched down with a gentle sigh, as the front wheel hydraulics compressed and took the weight. Mills taxied to a stop.

Grover pushed back the canopy, unlocked the seat harness, climbed out of the cockpit onto the wing, and dropped to the ground.

Mills joined him. Shook his hand. Grinned.

"When I get stressed, can I join you again?" Grover asked.

"Any time, old boy." He looked at his watch. "Almost sixteen hundred hours. Just about time for a pink gin."

Grover had never had a pink gin in his life. In fact, he was not sure what it was. But right now, with the adrenalin still surging through his veins, he was liable to agree with anything, short of violence or pain."

"At your disposal Flight Lieutenant," he said.

CHAPTER TWENTY-FOUR

He returned to his office on a high. Turnbull asked him how it went. Grover gave him a second by second account of his twenty minutes in the air; the words tumbling out with all the excitement of a young football fan who has just watched his team win the FA Cup. Turnbull could not help but smile along with him.

At his desk however, Grover fell back to terra ferma with something of a jolt.

As part of his job, in order to keep abreast of the doings of the city, he had the two Bristol newspapers delivered to his desk every day. The afternoon edition of the *Post* was waiting for him, the front-page headline no less lurid than the lunchtime version.

THE SCORCHED CORPSES – WHO ARE THEY?
And underneath…

The identity of the two corpses found in the smoke blackened ruins of city nightclub 'Eaves Night' is still shrouded in mystery. It is known however, that the club owner, Sandy Eaves, and her bookkeeper Donald Abey, cannot be found. Absolute identification is impossible at this moment and it may be some days before speculation becomes fact.

Grover marvelled at the irony. Speculation was all he had at his disposal too. He considered the chain of events which had led him to this hour in this day in history.

He had been given this liaison job because he did not want to go home. Whereupon, the music of the spheres had descended into discord.

Less than hours after arriving in the city he had witnessed an accident. Private Bradley Parsons, absent without leave, had been run down by a car. Close friends had become involved. The hospital doctor who had operated on the soldier was nowhere to be found. A club owner, had in all probability, perished in the burning ruins of her night club. He added the other ingredients to the recipe; Benzedrine tablets, Parsons' missing girlfriend, the exploding car, his employers reading him the riot act, the head of the Special Crimes Team doing the same. He was left wondering why he had not taken his seat on the plane to Reykjavik.

The developing relationship with Mel was a bonus, so long as it didn't end in tears. He calculated the odds on it not doing that were long indeed. He wasn't a betting man. But he came to the conclusion that a dollar on the nose might make him rich, as the chance it might all work out was not exceedingly low. At which point he chastised himself for being ridiculous. He and Mel would work or they wouldn't. And reducing serious contemplation to the whims of the betting track was not the way to enjoy the developing relationship.

Back to sensible questions.

So, what was the main racket going on here? Certainly not pockets full of Benzedrine tablets.

Still, there was a group of bad guys who wanted the problem, whatever it was, to go away. Although his employer was satisfied that all was done and dusted. The bennies had dissolved with the death of Bradley Parsons and the swift repatriation of his body home. It was all over too for Sandy Eaves and Donald Abey, if speculation was correct. Nothing more for them to worry about. The sun continued to shine down on the garden of the city's criminal head honcho. And Daniel Zampa had assured him he was an award-winning gardener.

Meanwhile the good guys were getting nowhere. The lawyers were engaged in a damage limitation exercise and the cops were struggling to find motive, means and opportunity in any of this. Lauren Mason was missing. And somebody had blown up Rita Caton, as a result of his embarkation on a mission to find Hanna Gunther. Somehow, he had to atone for that by tracing her himself. To do so, he needed to clear an inside track.

The conclusion he came to, was to go back to the Gardener himself. As he was contemplating how dangerous that might prove to be, the phone on his desk rang.

"I need to talk with you," Doctor Mason said.

Grover was stunned for a moment.

"Ed?..."

"I'm here, I'm here," he managed. "Where are you?"

"At home."

"I'm on my way."

He grabbed his jacket from the bentwood stand by the door and left the office. *Salome* took fifteen minutes to get from Filton to Morland Road. No two people were ever so delighted to see each other. Grover asked her where the hell she had been. Lauren poured two large measures of whisky and they sat down in the armchairs either side of the fireplace. Then she proceeded to astound Grover with her next sentence.

"I don't know where I've been" she said.

"What?"

"Honestly, Ed. I have no idea. I was blindfolded as soon as we cleared the street. The journey took twenty minutes or so. I can't be more precise." She nodded towards the mantelpiece. "I looked at that clock when the doorbell rang. 5 past 8 it said. I looked at my watch when they took the blindfold off. It was almost 8.30."

"Mrs Maitland said she saw you leave with some men."

"On the ball as usual then," Lauren said. "There were two men actually. In matching, tailored light grey suits. Both six feet tall. They looked rather like a top of the bill singing duo. Not twins exactly, but brothers perhaps. And there was a driver in the car. One of the brothers put a sack, or something like that, over my head, as soon as I was in the back seat."

Grover asked what make of car it was.

"It was a Humber. You know, the big graceful one. Long bonnet, huge engine. It was light brown, very stylish."

"Can't be too many of those around."

"I've not seen one in this neck of the woods before."

"And when the sack came off?..."

"I was in a sitting room in a rather splendid house. A huge marble fireplace. Tall double windows, looking out into the garden I suppose. With William Morris curtains pulled across them. It was too early in the evening to be dark outside. The room was lit by sideboard and table lamps."

"And?..."

"Extreme politeness all round. The driver went off to get supper ready. One of the brothers asked if I would like a drink. He dispensed a gin and tonic."

"Did they drink?"

"No. They talked to me. Apologised for the evacuation from my home. Said I was in absolutely no danger. Merely a guest for forty-eight hours. Then two other men arrived and the brothers left. There was no menace. No threats."

"What happened during the time you were there?"

"I was locked into a bedroom at the back of the house, on the first floor. Almost as big as the living room. A four-poster bed with a very comfortable mattress. Its own bathroom with sky blue tiles and fluffy white towels. Oh yes, and back in the bedroom, a tapestry no less, lit with art gallery spotlights. I'm no expert on wall art, but it looked and felt like the real thing."

"Could you see anything out of the windows?"

Lauren shook her head. "A corner of the garden. A high stone wall, yew trees and a section of lawn."

Grover was marvelling at her composure.

"Did they ask you anything?"

"Nothing. No menace whatsoever. They obviously had someone stationed outside the bedroom all the time. They brought me meals, a box of books from the library, a radio. Checked regularly on my welfare. There was no harm intended. I was… a guest. Only with restricted access to the rest of the building."

"They wanted you away from the Coroner," Grover said.

"That's what I imagined. What did he come up with?"

"An open verdict."

"Ah… Which means the United States Army got their man back."

"Yeah," Grover said. "By now, Bradley Parsons will be lying under the green grass of home."

"Mysterious, eh?"

"Actually, it's getting clearer. Have you heard of a man called Daniel Zampa?"

"Yes, I have. He runs a club called erm… something Spanish."

"The *El Paradiso*."

Grover wound back a couple of months. And recalled his five minutes sitting on the rear seat of a light brown Humber Super Snipe; the brand new four litre version, styled for 'the money no object' clientele. At his elbow, Daniel Zampa, who had offered him a job. The whole encounter was dramatically staged, with James and Jonathan in attendance – chauffeurs and executive assistants. Close shaved, great haircuts, the best, light grey bespoke suits Neville Reed could provide. Both men were ex-commandoes and had worked for Zampa since the end of the war. They were the real deal. Unlike Rodney Pride's second-string enforcers and the broken noses who worked at *Eaves Night*.

"Zampa didn't want any investigation into the matter of Parsons death either. So, he offered my employers a deal, swooped you up and imposed a couple of days hospitality."

He downed the rest of his whisky. Doctor Mason asked what he had been up to during her house arrest.

"I've discovered who Parsons' girlfriend is," he said. "Her name is Hanna Gunther. She's a Berliner with a US Passport. Parsons got her out of the city on a USAF mercy flight. And she's here, somewhere in the shire, well over four months pregnant."

He regaled her with the whole back story. She was amazed and impressed. In return, Grover asked another question.

"I'm a bit low on knowledge in this area. But I assume that four months is too late for a termination?"

"It's very dangerous for both parties. If Hanna had wanted to get rid of the baby, she would have done so weeks ago."

"Then she is going to have it?" Grover said

"The way you told the tale, it would seem her doctor thought so."

"But no one has seen her for almost three weeks."

"If she is alive and well, somebody has." Lauren said.

"If…" Grover echoed.

There was a pause while they both considered the implications. Then Grover moved things along.

"Where would Hanna go to find an abortionist?"

Lauren stared at him.

"You do realise you are asking this question of a legally authorised medical practitioner?"

Grover pondered for a second or two.

"Then, as Perry Mason says, 'I will re-phrase the question Your Honour'. Supposing Hanna decided she wanted an abortion, where might she start looking?"

Lauren mused.

"I have no contacts, personal or non-personal.

Although I'm sure if I asked around, I would come across a doctor or a nurse somewhere who had been approached at some time."

"But you haven't?"

Lauren took a moment.

"I have, in a way. I suppose I can tell you this now, as the person involved is dead and there are no official records." She sipped her whisky and stared into the fireplace. "I am attached to the South Gloucester Prison Emergency Medical Unit. I've been called to deal with wounds after fights, collapses, breakages, that sort of thing. I've even taken out someone's appendix in the prison hospital ward. I did once deal with the results of a miscarriage." She sipped again from her glass and looked back at Grover. "Do you know anything about the Ruby Willis story?"

"The murderess, yes. Made the news all over the country."

"Ruby was pregnant when she was sentenced. Nobody knew. Not even Ruby. She was probably two months along the way when she ended up in her condemned cell."

"Surely pregnant women don't get hanged?"

"No, they don't. But by the time she found out, Ruby was way beyond reasoning. She had been sentenced to hang for murdering the man who sent her to an abortionist eighteen months earlier. Which had worked – in the violent and bloody way these things do. But it broke her heart and her spirit. And her health. She was very unlikely to conceive again. Or so she thought."

"But she did?"

"The afternoon before she shot him. During an hour of threats and beatings and rape. Oh, she may have agreed to it in the end; because she couldn't stop him from doing it anyway. That's how most of these encounters work. She told me she cried all the way through the indignity. He put his prick back in his trousers and went off to the pub. She found the gun, loaded it, and went after him. She realised she was pregnant nine or ten weeks later."

"And she spoke to the prison governor, yes?"

"Not immediately. She thought for a while. Deep down in her bones she knew she had no hope of looking after a child once she was back in the world. But she did realise, giving birth could save her life. It was likely she would be made to give the baby away. But under a case review, with the child clearly the result of sexual congress on the day she was arrested, her sentence would be commuted to life imprisonment at least. In the end she told the prison doctor."

She stopped talking. Shook her head as if in disbelief. Grover waited

"Nothing went as it should, of course," Lauren continued. "But then that was Ruby's misfortune throughout her whole life. She miscarried. I was called in. And we talked. In the end she said, 'It was all for the best.' She decided that no life, was better than a life in prison. She accepted what the law had decreed and resigned herself to the gallows."

"Jesus…" Grover whispered.

"I saw her again, a week later. And once again, a few days before she was hanged. And... I think, by then, she had found a kind of peace that she was comfortable with."

"That's one hell of a story. And there are no records?"

"Just a note in the prison hospital about a miscarriage," Lauren said. "Ruby Willis wasn't born bad. She just lived in desperation. Part of an underclass nobody considers, until the *News of the World* runs the headline. Then they come out of the woodwork, the 'holier than thou' people, bent on retribution. Ruby was never going to make old bones."

They both fell into silence. Until Lauren asked Grover if he wanted another drink. He said no thank you and levered himself out of the armchair. Doctor Mason stood up too.

"So, where to now?" she asked.

"I'm going to beard the lion in his den."

***

Across the city, Xavier and the band were rehearsing a couple of the night's numbers. *I'm Beginning to See the Light*, featured Rachel's smoky contralto, improvising with the rhythm and finding the offbeat with an instinctive lazy control. Neither singer nor band noticed Winston moving swiftly across the lounge in his dress suit trousers and shirt, without bow tie or jacket. He launched himself into the office without knocking.

"Ah Leroy," Zampa said. "Thanks for reacting so swiftly. Allow me to introduce a couple of degenerates. Gilbert and Irving. Members of the local branch of the *The Empire League*. Heard of them? No? Well they don't like foreigners very much. And they believe you should be sent back to where you came from. They want to hang on to the Empire and keep Britain great. But they would rather do that without the Empire, that is to say you, actually being here, in this country. In other words, exploit you from thousands of miles away, rather than have you living next door."

Gilbert attempted to protest.

"Mr Zampa, I er…"

"They don't care much for your music either, Leroy"

Irving tried to step in.

"I think you have displayed little interest in what we have to say."

"Little?" Zampa said. "No no. None what so fucking ever."

"What would you like me to do, sir?" Winston asked.

"Throw the bastards out on their arses."

Gilbert headed for the office door. Winston reached him before he could get there. Grabbed the lapels of his jacket and pulled him close. Nose to nose.

"Say a polite 'goodbye', Sir," Winston said. He turned and glared at a now terrified Irving. "Both of you. Together."

Gilbert and Irving produced an out of sync chorus of 'goodbyes'. Winston put his left arm around Gilbert's shoulders his right around Irving's.

"Time to leave, Sirs," he said.

Out in the street, Grover was three steps away from the front door, when Irving was hurled out of the club. A flailing elbow hit Grover in the face. There was a bit of a commotion in the doorway as Gilbert was carted out by Winston. Irving got to his feet, yelling blue murder.

"Ed," Leroy called out. "Hold him while I fix this one."

The action was over in moments. With a mighty heave, Winston lifted his cargo clear of the ground and hurled him in the direction of his associate. Grover neatly sidestepped as Irving flew past him and ploughed into Gilbert. Yells of protest and surprise morphed into cries of pain as the empire loyalists fell on top of one another onto the cobbles.

Winston nodded to Grover, bowed slightly and waved him into the club.

"Who the hell were they?" Grover asked as they arrived in the lobby.

"Ask the boss," Winston said. "He seems to know about them."

"What sort of mood is he in?"

"He enjoyed that little bit of business," Winston said. "Do you want me to announce you?"

"No, I need to surprise him. Don't want him ordering you to throw me out."

In the lounge, Xavier was listening to a chord sequence from the piano player. Rachel was humming the melody to *Take My Heart*. The base player was improvising. Grover made his way around the room. Rachel saw him and waved. His knock on the office door was received with a cheerful 'Enter'. Zampa was revelling in the bum's rush he had given to his previous guests. So much so, he welcomed Grover's intrusion.

"Who were those two guys?" Grover asked.

"Imperialists."

"And what do they do?"

"They hate, mainly."

"Who do they hate?"

"Bolsheviks, Jews, the Chinese, the Japanese, black people. They don't like what's happening in India. Handing the country back to the poor sods they've raped, robbed and slaughtered down the years, is to be opposed. Actually, they don't like Americans either. They believe your countrymen are supporting a Jewish led conspiracy to break up the British Empire."

"Why would we do that?" Grover asked.

Zampa picked up a leaflet on his desk. Handed it to Grover.

"Here...The two Imperialists insisted I read it. You take a look. I've no desire to read a fucking word."

Grover looked at the first paragraph.

"This is mostly about what they don't like," he said.

"The lazy way to pretend you have a cause worth supporting."

"Anti-Communism, anti-Semitism, anti-immigration..."

"And all the other right-wing antis you can come up with."

Grover dropped the leaflet back onto Zampa's desk.

"You're Maltese. They can't like you, surely."

"They don't," Zampa said. "But Malta's part of the Empire. They came in here to ask me to help finance their cause for Christ's sake."

Grover decided, given Zampa's jovial mood, that he'd seize the day.

"I need to ask you something."

Zampa waved him to a seat.

"Fire away."

Grover subsided into the huge sofa again.

"Actually, it's er… regarding a friend of mine."

He paused, not convinced that he had spent enough time rehearsing his approach to this. Zampa knew exactly what was on Grover's mind and decided to ease the conversation along.

"Yes. I did a favour for the US Army. That's what you want to know, right?"

Grover stared at him.

"Don't look so shocked. No villainy involved. The people you work for were only too pleased when I offered to help. I understood that nothing short of five-star hospitality was required for a couple of days, for an associate. I was also given to understand that the guest readily accepted."

"You kidnapped her."

"Hardly that. I had no hand whatsoever in the er…" he searched for the word, "re-location… Apparently, two very cultured gentlemen, picked her up in a beautiful car, drove her a few miles to a large country house offering bed, breakfast and evening meal."

"The police won't see it that way."

Zampa snorted.

"Such a touching belief in the guardians of laws and order." He got to the point. "I was the only one who could make it work, Ed. After all, the US Army couldn't leave itself open to charges of conspiracy and breaking the law. Surely we don't want valued friends and allies to be seen behaving like those two bastards we just threw out of here."

Grover stood up.

"Leaving so soon?" Zampa asked.

Grover considered the reception he might get, then thought 'what the hell'… "Well, there is one more thing."

"Fire away."

"The Maddox Zampa axis," Grover said. "Is it going to be a long-term thing, or was it just a one off?"

Zampa rose to his feet and moved towards the office door. He stretched out his left arm to collect Grover on the way.

"Who knows, Lieutenant?" He looked at the expression on Grover's face. "You're surprised I know about your promotion. This is my garden remember."

Grover decided to risk another question.

"The torching of *Eaves Night*," he said. "Was that sanctioned by you?"

Zampa's mateyness evaporated.

"There are three practicing arsonists in this city. One is in prison. I had James and Jonathan bring in the other two for a chat. Neither were connected in any capacity with the *Eaves Night* business."

"Are you sure of that?"

The expression on Zampa's face said 'Do you really have to ask that question?' He opened the office door.

"Do come back soon."

Rachel and the band had disappeared. Leroy Winston and the Maitre D' were engaged in preparations for opening the club. Grover crossed the lounge, nodded in the direction of the cloakroom lady and stepped out into the dusk coated street. There was no wind, the late spring evening was warm. He walked the two hundred years to *Salome*, climbed into the jeep and stared ahead through the windscreen. Once again, he had blown it with Zampa. How many lives did he have left?

He thumped the steering wheel in frustration.

CHAPTER TWENTY-FIVE

Another man whose temper was a little short, was Rodney Pride. He was sitting in the taxi office on the garage mezzanine floor. Sparsely furnished from a warehouse still retailing stock from bombed out buildings. There was one phone on the desk in front of him, and two others on a long trestle table across the room – this the base for another lucrative operation as a loan shark and weekend bookie.

Pride was glaring down at the Accounts Owing ledger on the desk.

"Some of these buggers owe us a small fortune," he growled.

He looked up at Water Scardale and his associate enforcer Louis Lennon, both standing a respectful distance from the desk.

This blue-collar trio would have been a huge disappointment to any halfway decent tailor. The employees were attempting to look like Robert Mitcham in *Build My Gallows High*, but the whole languid, laid back style was way beyond them. Pride looked as if he had got dressed in the dark. The pink shirt appeared ready to vomit out from under the brown sports jacket. The white tie was a wide, kippered style article. Even Scardale and Lennon knew the ensemble was a disaster, but had the boss asked 'what do you think?' both would have applauded. No one criticised Rodney Pride's dress sense.

"Landers will pay on time this week," Scardale said.

"So will Upton," Lennon added.

"Pay them a visit, to remind them. And Mr Flynn?"

Scardale thought about that. Then lifted his right hand and rotated his wrist.

"Send him some flowers," the boss said. "Lilies."

Scardale and Lennon grinned on cue. Pride closed the ledger, swung the swivel chair through 90 degrees, stood up and moved to the trestle table. He opened the top draw of the filing cabinet next to it, took out the Loans Book and settled himself in another chair. Scardale and Lennon stepped towards him. Pride placed the book on his knees and opened it.

"This isn't much of a read either," he said. "The last entry was a week ago."

"It's due to be updated tomorrow morning," Lennon volunteered.

"And what's this?... Paddy Halloran is way behind in his payments."

"He's been losing heavily at the track," Scardale said. "Greyhounds."

"No excuse," Pride said.

He rose from the chair, holding the book out to Scardale.

"Put that back and we'll take a ride."

Down on the garage floor he chose the least ostentatious piece of metal in his personal fleet – the Chevrolet Bel Air. This was the enforcer's workhorse. The midnight blue Buick Jetback, with its sawtooth engine grill, was meant to intimidate. His favourite, the Pontiac Chieftain Coupé designed to impress.

Twenty minutes later, Patsy Halloran was just plain scared stiff. He was sitting on the edge of *Albion Gym* boxing ring, close to a panic attack. Pride and Scardale stood in front of him.

"Tell him how much he owes us Mr Scardale."

"Two hundred and seventy-five pounds Boss."

Halloran begin to shake his head.

"No no, that's not right. It's a straight two hundred."

"No. Now it's that, plus two week's interest at fifteen percent," Pride said. "And from this moment, a further five percent each day. The bill is mounting Patsy."

Halloran was too overwhelmed to reply. He swallowed and choked and looked as if was about to throw up. Pride made him an offer.

"However, there is one way we can improve matters. Help you out of the situation you're in."

He paused to invest as much tension in the moment as possible. Halloran swallowed some more bile, and waited.

"Your young fighter, Leroy Winston," he said. "He has his first bout the day after tomorrow."

Halloran nodded. "At Trinity Hall in Old Market."

"The place is sold out."

"Yes, oh yes. Leroy is the best prospect in town."

"And he's going to win."

"Oh yes, yes he is."

"There's no doubt of that?"

"No. Just look at the betting odds."

"Oh, I have Patsy," Pride said. "The best I'm offering

is 6 to 4 on. Nobody's going to win much. Unless, Winston loses and some fortunate person has a lot of money on Euros Jenkins at 14 to 1."

Pride was spraying clues as to his proposal all over the gym. And suddenly Halloran got the message. He began shaking his head again.

"Leroy won't… no no no… he won't lose…" His voice tailed away. "Jesus Christ."

"Yes, he will. You will tell him so. In the strictest confidence. The two hundred and whatever it is pounds by the weekend, will be stricken from the ledger. The alternative, Patsy, is… Well you don't want to think about that. Does he Mr Scardale?"

The enforcer shook his head. Took a shiny knuckle duster out of a jacket pocket. Slid it onto his right hand. Pride dug into the trainer's conscience.

"You can make this work. I'm not suggesting a knockout in the second round. The fight can play through a bit. If Leroy goes down in seven, or doesn't come out for eight… Job done. Debt paid."

"And in the process, you'll come out ahead too," Halloran mumbled.

He stood up and faced Pride. They were the same height and looked into the other's eyes.

"No," the trainer said. "I can't ask Leroy to throw his first fight."

Scardale took a step towards him. Pride raised his right arm.

"Not yet." He stepped into the space between Scardale and Halloran. "Patsy. Take this on board seriously. A debt you have no chance of paying on time.

266

The slate wiped clean. And best of all, you still in one piece."

Halloran stood still, his face a mask now. Pride knew he did not own the situation yet.

"Then I guess we need to take this to more neutral ground," he said.

A door banged in the corridor. Roly Bevan yelled, "Patsy".

"In the gym boss," Halloran shouted back.

Bevan pushed open the double gym doors and stepped through the doorway. The doors swung away behind him, then forwards again hitting the heels of his shoes. Scardale stuck the dustered hand into his jacket pocket and reversed a couple of paces. Pride swung to face Bevan. Who was the first to speak.

"What the hell are you doing here?"

Pride summoned up as much charm as he possessed. Not exactly a pocketful, but it was enough to disarm Bevan a little.

"I've been watching the odds on your boy Winston," he said.

"Really. Because?"

"He appears to be the favourite. And er... for old times' sake, I wondered if I could call in and see him working. Check out how true to form the odds are."

"He's not training today."

"Yes. That's clear."

"And his training sessions are not open to visitors."

Pride pasted a smile on his face.

"In which case, Roly, Mr Scardale and I will leave." He looked at Halloran. "And thank you for your time

Patsy. I'm sure the outcome of the fight will be good for us all."

Scardale followed Pride across the floor. Bevan hauled open the right-hand door, stepped back a pace and allowed the visitors to move into the corridor. He let go of the door and it swung closed.

"What did he mean by that, Patsy?"

Halloran improvised.

"You know he runs a book?"

"Yes."

"He came to say he's offering 6 to 4 on for Leroy. He's made him the clear favourite."

"And why would he like us to know that?"

"Er… I don't know. We didn't get round to it. You came in."

Bevan wondered for a moment if that was true.

"I was just going to put the kettle on Boss. And we've got china tea in the office."

Bevan smiled at him.

"Break out the jammy dodgers too."

***

DCI Bridge, his hat on his head, his coat over his left arm, was reaching for the office door handle, when the phone rang on his desk. He looked at the clock on the wall. 7.05.

He opened the door.

"Shit."

He closed it again, moved back to his desk, dropped his coat onto it and picked up the phone receiver.

"Bridge," he grumbled. "And this had better be good."

"Sorry Boss," Goole said. "But it's important. I'm with the army munitions bloke we asked for. He's looked at Rita Caton's car and his team have done their own sweep of the car park. He confirms the incident was definitely the result of a grenade explosion. A US 'pineapple'. He found enough pieces of the iron casing to be certain."

Bridge let all that sink in. In the end, all he had to say was, "See you in the morning, Tom."

He put the phone receiver back in its cradle and stared at it malevolently.

"Shit…"

CHAPTER TWENTY-SIX

Winston was working out with the heavy bag at 9 o'clock the following morning. Halloran arrived at the gym ten minutes later. He stood in the doorway watching the best two-handed fighter he had seen in a long while. The boy was light on his feet, his upper body strong, but balanced and graceful. Qualities disposed on him by the boxing gods; not something Halloran or any trainer could have taught him.

"That's enough Leroy," he called out.

Winston threw a final right cross at the bag and stepped back a pace. Halloran moved across the floor.

"You don't need to do any of this stuff today. You're ready. No point risking a sprained wrist. We both know you can out box the Welshman. Even at his best, which is not where he is now. Give me your hands."

Winston stretched his arms. The trainer undid the laces of his gloves and pulled them off Winston's hands.

"The only reason for this fight is to show you off. It's your first, and that's why Roly has set up one you can win. When you do, we'll match you with a middleweight contender. And when you've dealt with him, the rest will come banging on this door. You got that?"

"Yes Patsy."

"Do some skipping, if you must. But stop before you start to sweat. You can do a couple of laps of the

270

recreation ground, come back and shower. Then we'll talk the fight through round by round."

He walked to the gym office, took a ring of keys out of his pocket, chose one of them and unlocked the door. Inside the office, he closed the door behind him and leaned against it.

"Oh Christ," he murmured. "The boy's too good."

***

"We need a grenade end user," Goole said. "A front line soldier."

He was elaborating on his message from the evening before, while eating breakfast in the canteen. His boss was watching him. Bridge had begun the day at home a couple of hours earlier with tea and scrambled eggs on toast; followed by more tea, and a none too successful hour of reflection. Grenades on the manor was frightening at best. At worst, the whole business was likely to end up a Scotland Yard or Special Branch problem. And the last thing any provincial detective worth his salary needed, was a squad of Metropolitan smart buggers lording it over the locals. Goole speared the last piece of bacon onto his fork, jabbed it into the remains of the fried bread, and conveyed all to his mouth. Put down the knife and fork, swallowed, wiped his mouth with a napkin and sat back in his chair.

"From who's army?" Bridge asked

"Preferably the United States," Goole said. "After all, it was their grenade."

"And how are we to handle that with intelligence and tact?"

271

"We'll have to be sneaky."

Bridge was fed up with the cavorting around and got to the point.

"You mean we should call in Ed Grover."

"Why not? The US Army could sub-let him to us, without actually having to be informed. Grover is a liaison officer, after all."

Bridge was having difficulty with the proposal. He looked across the room. Goole persisted.

"Neither of us did active service during the late conflict. Grover was in the thick of it. He must have lobbed a few grenades while crossing northern Europe."

Bridge was thinking. Goole re-doubled his efforts.

"We know him boss. We can trust him."

"It will have to be a secret," Bridge said. "And I hate secrets. They always come back to bite you on the arse. If we cock it up, we'll do more than rock the boat, we'll sink it. And more than likely go down with it."

Goole grinned. "Are we downhearted?"

Bridge grimaced. "Close to it. But you're right. Grover's a dead ringer for this. Find him."

***

"What's the matter Patsy? Not worried surely. Leroy's in great shape."

Bevan sat down in the chair facing Halloran's office desk. The two man had known each other since VE Day. There had never been secrets between them.

"Come on. Out with it."

Halloran was sitting with his elbows on the desk, forearms raised, forming a triangle with the desktop, his right hand enclosing his left balled fist, his chin resting on his thumbs. Bevan leaned forward, dropped his right shoulder, sank lower in the chair and manoeuvred his eyes into line with Halloran's. The trainer looked away. That was enough for Bevan. He sharpened his voice.

"If this is work, I want to know."

"It's personal really," Patsy said.

"That's just as important."

"Well it started that way. Now it's to do with work."

"Stop buggering about Patsy, let's have it."

Patsy unlocked his hands, brushed them through what was left of his thinning hair, then looked straight at his boss.

"I borrowed some money. I can't pay it back."

Bevan asked him who he had borrowed from. Patsy did not respond. Bevan asked him again, pushing for an answer. Eventually he got it.

"Rodney Pride".

Gobsmacked, Bevan stared at him. Silence enveloped the office. Bevan rose to his feet, moved to the office door, opened it and walked out into the gym. Halloran looked across the space his boss had just occupied. He sat stock still for some time, then closed his eyes and leaned back in his chair. He heard the sound of feet stepping into the office. He opened his eyes. His boss was back, standing in the centre of the room.

"Why didn't you ask me for the money Patsy?"

"You bailed me out the last time I got into trouble – three years ago. You told me never again. Threatened to sack me if I did."

"How much did you borrow?"

"A hundred and fifty pounds."

"And what do you owe?"

"Two hundred and seventy-five."

Bevan just about manged to keep the exasperation out of his voice.

"Why the hell did you let this happen? Again."

"I just… did. It adds up."

"Of course it fucking does Patsy." Bevan was all but yelling now. "What were you going to do? Eh?"

"I wasn't going to pay him. I can't."

"You were just going to let one of his heavies beat the shit out of you?"

Patsy shrugged. "He offered me a deal."

"And what was that."

"Get Leroy to throw the fight while he bet on the Welshman at 14 to 1."

Bevan was glaring at him. Halloran jumped to his feet.

"But I didn't, I mean I told him I wouldn't, I was never going to ask Leroy -"

"You stupid old bastard," Bevan yelled. "You should still have come to me. You should still have come to me. Oh for Christ's sake…"

He ran out of anger and emotion. Looked at Halloran again.

"I'll be at the fight tomorrow. In the dressing room and in a front row seat. Leroy will never get to hear of this. I'll deal with Rodney Pride. But you will live on bread and dripping whatever the outcome. No betting, no drinking, no leaving the bloody house. If I have to lock you in I will… You getting this?"

Patsy nodded. "Yes boss. Yes I am…"

Bevan raised his arms, locked his fingers and placed them behind his head. Raised it and stretched the muscles in his neck. He grunted and exhaled. Unlocked his fingers and dropped his arms.

"Where is Leroy?"

"Jogging round the rec."

"Okay. The best, the very best of care until he gets into the ring."

"Sure boss."

Bevan shook his head, sighed and walked out of the office.

***

The atmosphere was not much better at the Bridewell. At least, not in the office of Detective Chief Superintendent Edwin Holmes.

"I was worried that you wouldn't like the idea, Sir," Bridge said.

"I don't. I hate it. But the Commissioner says it's okay. However, if it goes tits up…"

"I understand, Sir."

"Just get this bloody scheme right, Bob. For all our sakes."

Bridge spent the time it took to get back to his office wishing he kept a bottle of brandy in the bottom drawer of the filing cabinet. Goole on the other hand was massively encouraged by the development.

"Sherlock said it was alright, did he?"

He rubbed his fingers in something approaching glee. Bridge could not help but feel his sergeant was doing a passable imitation of King Canute.

"All the way through this," Bridge said, "I'm going to remember it was your bloody idea."

"I got Grover in his office," Goole said. "He suggested we call on him at Filton."

"That's better than here. Although we should actually do this unwitnessed, in the middle of nowhere."

Bridge decided to make the journey without PC Grafton. Goole took the wheel. Half an hour later, a large man with a handle-bar moustache, wide shoulders and a straight back was inspecting their police ID.

"That will do, Sirs," he said with the voice of a retired drill sergeant. He pointed to a space beyond the barrier. "You will park there, on the left. Lieutenant Grover, will come and fetch you." He stepped back a pace and nodded in the direction of his associate in the cabin, who pressed a switch alongside the PBX in front of him. The barrier rose. Goole piloted the Wolseley to the appointed parking space.

Grover arrived in *Salome* a couple of minutes later.

"Would you like the grand tour gentlemen?"

"We need to go somewhere away from prying eyes," Bridge said.

"Climb in."

With Bridge sitting next to him and Goole in the seat behind, Grover swung *Salome* round, took a left between two rainbow shaped Nissen huts, gunned the motor and headed for the airfield perimeter. Goole hunkered down in the back seat, hanging on to his hat.

Grover pulled up in the lee of an empty aircraft hangar.

"Will this do?" he asked Bridge.

Bridge nodded. "Yes, this is fine."

Grover swung to his right. Goole moved along the back seat so that Grover could get a two shot of him and his boss. Bridge began the story.

"It's been established that Rita's car was blown up by a grenade," he said.

Grover nodded. Waited for the rest of the information.

"US Army issue," Bridge went on. "A 'pineapple'."

Grover stared at him. Anticipating where this was leading.

"So, we have a problem. I'm sure you'd agree."

Grover continued to say nothing. Goole tried to help out.

"This a little tricky, Ed. Normally we wouldn't share this kind of knowledge with anyone outside of the SCT. But er…"

He paused. Glanced at his boss. Bridge was waiting for a response from Grover; who took his time over this.

"I see the 'problem'," he said. "Of course I do. Blowing up an English woman with a US grenade, begs all sorts of questions. Not the least of which is, where did that particular piece of ordnance come from?"

"There are two places on the list," Bridge said. "The British Army Munitions Depot at Corsham, or…"

He paused. Grover ignored the alternative for the meantime and asked the DCI where Corsham was. He had not heard of the place, and a concern for munitions was not part of his brief. Bridge accepted that and explained.

"East of Bath. Tunnel Bridge Quarry was used during the war, and still is to some extent, to store small arms and ammunition, both British and American. It's run by the British Army Ordnance Corps. It's a difficult place for outsiders, even allies, to penetrate."

Grover gave in.

"Okay. And place number two, is here."

"Yes."

"And I take it you haven't spoken to the CO, or Maddox, about this?"

"That's correct."

"Because any finger you pointed in this direction, even in idle speculation, would cause the biggest crisis since the Boston Tea Party."

"In a nutshell," Bridge said. "And as we – you and Tom and I – have worked together in the recent past…"

The meaningful pause gave Grover all the time in the world to jump in.

"Which you stipulated at that time, was never to occur again."

Bridge threw in the towel.

"We're in a bind here, Ed."

"Aren't we just."

"No one in the cast is going to appreciate what happens next," Bridge said. "And as much as I hate to say this, Tom here says the only alternative is to be sneaky."

Grover turned in the driving seat and climbed out of *Salome*. He straightened his back. Walked around the front of the jeep. Stared across the airfield perimeter, for a while. Bridge and Goole waited patiently. Then Grover turned to face them.

"I don't have a problem with sneaky," he said. "But we do have, you and me, a pyramid of bosses. Anyone of them could come down on us like a fifty storey lift. We could be responsible for ruining the 'Special Relationship', three handed. We'd be kicked out on our collective ass, or buried somewhere in a corner office, filing bits of paper. I don't know about your line of work, but the US Army produces crates of the stuff."

Goole spoke up.

"We know what a hot potato this is," he said.

"Third degree burns at least," Grover suggested.

"So, we need to help each other out."

Grover did some more thinking, Bridge and Goole some more waiting. Then Grover nodded.

"Okay detectives. Do we have a plan?"

Bridge's explanation did not take long. There was no way they could avoid updating the US Army. A move which would clearly put the SCT investigation at risk. No one in the trio could imagine the JAG lawyer Maddox giving a team of British policemen the okay to operate as they wished in matters which concerned the military. So, the simple plan was to tell the army everything and, basically, improvise thereafter. With Grover acting as a double agent.

Maddox was with Colonel Whitmore when the call came in from Filton. Grover began his rehearsed story. The CO stopped him.

"Wait a minute."

At his end, Grover heard the phone line click a couple of times and then the voice of Maddox.

"Lieutenant…"

With Bridge and Goole alongside him in the office, Grover revealed all about the grenade. Suggesting that where there was one grenade, there were in all probability more. Maddox and Whitmore said stuff like 'yes', 'right', 'okay' then asked if the cops had any plan of action. Grover said he believed they were clueless, raising his eyebrows in apology to Bridge and Goole. Maddox ended up telling Grover to give nothing away at his end and rescinded his previous order. Now he was stay as close as possible to the police investigation.

"We'll get back to you," the lawyer said, and ended the call.

In Filton, Grover blew out his cheeks and placed the receiver back in its cradle.

"And?..." Bridge asked.

"They said I should stick to you like glue, only be subtle about it."

CHAPTER TWENTY-SEVEN

The senior representatives of the US Army in Gloucestershire, spent the rest of the day in controlled panic. Maddox issued a page full of orders to Whitmore who passed it on to the Adjutant. Who then roped in a man he hoped he could trust – Captain Eugene Kreel, OIC Ordnance. No one a rank lower, no assistant to an assistant, was to be drafted into the exercise. Not even the meanest task was to be devolved to any clerical secretary. All the peering into accounts and files, all reading, checking and investigation was to be done by Kreel and Berger.

Ordnance personnel were told there was to be a snap inspection within the hour and were liberated from their duties for the rest of the day. Left alone, Kreel and Berger began to read and list all ordnance processing for the last fourteen days.

The lists were short but comprehensive. There was a place for everything and, apparently, everything was in its place. Preparations for the transfer to a Korean theatre of war were confined to lectures and to boosting fitness. Nobody was firing at, or blowing up, anything.

Armed with the accomplished book work and the keys to 21st ORD 1 and 2, Kreel and Berger began counting. The contents of ORD 1 matched, line by line, in the lists the captains had made, down to the last box of .38 bullets and the last packet of trigger springs. The result in ORD 2 was the same – lists, guns, grenades and ammunition in total alignment.

"That's it then," Kreel said.

"That," Berger suggested, "is only the half of it."

Kreel was not sure what he meant. Berger explained.

"Okay. Every bit of hardware in the ledgers is accounted for. Of course, it is. Thieving is easy. All you need…" He held up a key ring, shook his wrist and allowed the keys to jangle, "is the wherewithal to break in. The clever bit is to ensure that no one discovers that anything has been stolen."

"But the paperwork matches," Kreel said. "The books are clean. Two boxes of grenades listed, equals two boxes of grenades in here. The same with single shot carbines, semi-automatic assault rifles, machine guns, colt 45 automatics, Smith & Wesson revolvers." He held up his paperwork. "All of it listed here, and on the shelf there."

"And so it should be."

"I still don't know what you're driving at."

"Right. Let's assume we're not on a wild turkey chase. And that stuff from in here has been getting out of the base."

Kreel nodded in agreement. "Okay…"

"The guy we should be looking for isn't the thief, it's the bookkeeper. Not the guy who broke in. The guy who made it look right. Sure, you've got twelve ammunition belts per box on your list, and the same on that shelf. But suppose there ought to be fifteen boxes here, not twelve; fifteen boxes listed in the books, not twelve."

He paused, waiting for a reaction. Kreel took a deep breath, opened his mouth, then closed it again.

"We have to go back further. Look at the stuff which came in, not the stuff which has gone out."

"For Christ's sake Steve," Kreel said. "That'll take the rest of the day."

"And probably all night, Eugene. So, where does it all come from?"

"Everything is stored in a bunch of old stone quarries in the next county. By the main railway line from London. The Brits run the operation."

"Alright, get onto them. Tell them we're on the way down. How long will it take us to drive there?"

"Hell I don't know. Two hours, maybe. I'll find out."

"No don't. I'll get a jeep from the Motor Pool. Nobody's going to query that, I do it all the time. Meet me outside my office in twenty minutes."

***

Just after 5 o'clock, DCI Bridge received the call he was expecting. Major Harrison rang him from Tunnel Ridge Quarry. Bridge replaced the receiver as Goole stepped into the office.

"Sergeant," he said. "I think this department of the Bristol Constabulary is now, unofficially, at war with the Unites States."

Goole grinned at him. "They took the bait then."

"Major Harrison just called. He says the 21st Infantry Adjutant and Captain Kreel, OIC Ordnance, have been to see him. They gave him a load of hoopla about some mislaid files and took away copies of all ordnance deliveries to Fairford over the past six months."

"Which means, what their bookkeeping says worries them."

"Either they have decided it's wrong," Bridge said. "Or it's so correct it must be wrong."

"And how does that help us?"

"It may give us an edge. Because, if there is something wrong at their end, and they believe stuff is being smuggled out of the base, they will have to treat us, you and me Tom, with a little more caution and respect."

"And the more questions we ask them about 'pineapples', the more jumpy they will become."

"That's the theory," Bridge said. "However, the bottom line – isn't that what the Americans say? – is where it's going. And that's our case to close. We still have to find the buggers who are using it. Without the help of Private Parsons who is dead, and his girlfriend who has disappeared. We can't congratulate ourselves on anything yet."

"What about Ed Grover? Where does he sit in all this?"

***

At that moment, he was having tea and crumpets in Flat 2, 5 Blenheim Villas, with Rachel, Mel and Neil Adkins. The quartet was nervous about the evening ahead. Rachel most of all.

"I could have hosted this downstairs you know," Grover said.

Rachel shook her head. "I'm so frightened, I need something to do. I don't even know what happens at a boxing match, other than... Oh we're missing the jam."

She went back into the kitchen. Mel looked at Grover.

"I've never been to a boxing match either. All I hear about the game seems far too brutal."

"There is a kind of poetry to it," Grover said.

"Really?"

Adkins asked Grover if he had ever boxed.

"When I was a cop. The six Tomah precincts had boxing teams. And the top guy of the year represented the town in interstate championships."

"Did you?"

"I was about to, before I decided to go to war."

***

Kreel and Berger had come to the conclusion they were in a similar position.

"How long is the list?" he asked.

"Long enough to be worried," Berger said. "Time to talk with Maddox and the CO."

Berger handed Whitmore the list. There was a box of grenades missing, a dozen Colt .45 automatics, along with one hundred clips of ammunition.

"Some fucker's about to start a small war," Whitmore said. "With US Army weapons."

"Questions?" Maddox asked.

"Just four," Berger said. "How did it get out of the base? Who managed to make that work? Where did it go? And who has it?"

"And there's a fifth," Whitmore said. He looked at Maddox. "How do we find the answers to those questions?"

Maddox took his time. He had the complete and undivided attention of the others.

"Maybe we don't need to be concerned," he said.

"What do you mean?" asked Whitmore, irritated now. "Stay quiet until some cop knocks on the door?"

"Sometimes no action is the best action," Kreel suggested.

"Until somewhere down the line somebody stumbles over the truth. And we have to concoct a story to cover our collective ass."

"It buys us time Colonel," Maddox said. "We are the only people on the inside. And if we -"

Whitmore lifted his right hand and called for silence. Looked in the direction of his Adjutant.

"Steve. You've been with this outfit since '43. Is this the sort of game we should play?"

Captain Berger was probably the brightest and the most pragmatic man in the room. He had helped steer the 21st Infantry through battles, successes, reversals and the desperate days in West Berlin; in the belief that everything ought to be the best in the best of all possible worlds. He knew that was never so, but he had always tried to balance the moments, one against the other. Sometimes he had been wrong, and on occasions overruled. He chose his words carefully.

"The answer here Colonel, should major on the 21st, its record and its relationships."

Maddox opened his mouth to say something. Berger looked at him directly.

"Just a moment, Sir… Our service to the army has been commended on a number of occasions. We have always looked good, even during crises. But whichever way we work this, the result will be a problem. We need a few home truths and a PR exercise to sort this, not an act of expediency. Covering up now will not help us later. In all probability it will make matters worse."

Maddox was shaking his head.

"We need to keep this in house."

"We can't," Berger insisted. "A British citizen has been murdered. We know this was facilitated by the US Army."

"No, we don't," Maddox said. "We are not part of that investigation. It's a matter for a bunch of British detectives. And until they produce evidence that the murder weapon was ours and we handed it over, before the fact, to some Brit who then blew up someone up with it, we are not involved. And that must remain the legal position."

Berger could not respond to that. He looked at his CO and shrugged.

"So, gentlemen, what do we do? Whitmore asked.

"We get Lieutenant Grover to work some magic," Maddox said.

"You want him to pull a rabbit out of the hat?"

Maddox looked around him.

"Don't over-complicate this, guys. Not until the police knock on this door. Just let Grover loose at his end."

"Leaving him exposed," Berger said. "He might be left with only one course of action, if the cops cotton on."

"Grover's a tough guy," Maddox said. "And straight arrow enough to know where his loyalties lie."

***

Trinity Hall in Old Market, was once the Church of the Holy Trinity; a Baptist Chapel gradually deserted by its congregation in the years between the two World Wars. Overnight, during the blitz of January 3rd 1941, some enterprising persons successfully stripped the building of all its pews. Police, emergency services and residents were too busy to notice. And only a handful of others cared. The sawn up pews graced many an otherwise cold fireplace during that winter and somebody made a bob or two in the process.

Roly Bevan bought the place in 1948, and a year later set about transforming it. Contractors began work inside the building nine years to the day on which the pews disappeared, and by the end of April he had the finished article – a 450 seat auditorium with everything the best dressed boxing venue could boast of. Throughout the restoration he had considered how the place should open. As he watched Patsy Halloran develop Leroy Winston into a promising middleweight, he began to think this was the opportunity. And when he saw the boy's ring craft and the ease, grace and confidence he displayed sparring with the ex-champions Patsy hired, he began to believe. He knew he was in possession of the gold needed for Trinity Hall's opening night.

The purse was small. The Welsh ex-champion needed the fight to prove his career was not on the slide.

Leroy Winston was costing Bevan nothing. Other than the promotion of the handsome, graceful, strong, 'best for a generation' local boy embarking on the road to a world middleweight title. To ramp up the excitement, Bevan had packed the front rows with fellow promoters, national guests, journalists, local and Welsh worthies, all on freebies. Every other seat was taken, Bristol boxing fans paying minimum prices. The hall was bursting at the seams.

Daniel Zampa had a bottle of champagne and twenty-four red roses delivered to the dressing room, with a note saying *We believe in you, Leroy. No good luck wishes required.* Sam Nicholson, leader of the City Council and posing on this night as the champion of civic and social re-birth, was sitting in the front row. Three seats away from Mel and Neil Adkins.

The only man in town who had not been sent, or sold, a ticket was Rodney Pride. He eventually got over seething at the insult and menaced a back row seat from one of his 'clients', the owner of the *Broken Gate* pub in Bedminster. He sent a bouquet of carnations to the dressing room, accompanied by a note *Here's to a great result*, took up his G37 seat and, looking around him, began seething all over again.

The Star Dressing Room was a comparatively calm place in the midst of all the excitement. Patsy Halloran usually a master of pre bout atmosphere, was a little nervous. He was endeavouring not to let it show. Roly Bevan, dumped Pride's carnations in the bin reserved for used hand bandages, cotton wool, Elastoplast pull offs and bloody towels. Grover, acting for the evening as Winston's second corner man, felt as tense he had been since the bridge at Remagen. Leroy Winston was the coolest man in the room, lying on the bench, breathing gently.

Rachel was at the *El Paradis*, singing with the band and thinking about her man between numbers.

At 8.55, a portion of the crowd rose to its feet and applauded as Euros Jenkins appeared and made his way to the ring. He climbed through the ropes, raised his arms above his head, circled the ring and sat down in the red corner. The rest of the crowd, roared into life as Winston made his entrance. Looking every inch a contender in the making, he took the stool in the blue corner. The MC introduced the Referee, the PA system drowned out by thunderous applause as the two fighters moved to the centre of the ring to hear a few words from the man in charge of the bout.

They returned to their corners. Jenkins banged his gloves together. Began dancing on the spot, loosening up and exercising his shoulders. Winston stood quietly, breathing gently.

The bell rang for round one. Jenkins was out first, a man anxious to get on with it. In contrast, Winston strolled out of his corner. The two fighters touched gloves then stepped back. Jenkins waded into the fray, Winston and his cool taken by surprise. The Welshman threw a lot of punches, the Jamaican dodging and retreating, taking a couple of jabs as the line of least resistance. Jenkins scored points and clearly won round one. He did the same in round two.

In the blue corner, Grover took out Winston's mouth guard and held his water bottle as he drank; then towelled his face, as Halloran issued instructions.

"He's offered all he has. There's nothing else in his repertoire. You can out box him, you're lighter on your feet going forwards and backwards. And you can out punch him. Just find the jabs and the crosses. You're also fitter than he is. He can't stay out of your range and he knows that, but he's slow to come in. Then he hangs on. That's because he's already tired. Take the fight to him. Get it done."

Winston knocked Jenkins down in the first minute of round three. The Welshman took a mandatory count in the second minute of round four. Thirty-five seconds into the fifth, he was down again. On his face, with blood from his nose leaking onto the canvas. The referee was counting. Jenkins got on to all fours by 6. Onto his knees by 8. He swayed sideways, shook his head and sprayed blood in an arc across the ring. The referee stopped the fight. Jenkins sank onto his heels and lifted his glazed eyes to his corner in mute apology. Trainer Matty Green, climbed into the ring and moved to him. He tried to staunch the blood from Jenkins broken nose. Jenkins buried his face into Green's chest and cried, in pain and humiliation.

Winston raised his arms and took a tour around the ring. By the time he got back to his corner, Jenkins was on his feet. Winston moved to him, and the two men embraced, in the centre of a wall of noise.

On the back row, in seat G37, Rodney Pride was speechless with rage.

In the dressing room, Bevan opened the champagne to rousing cheers and the team toasted their new star and prospects for the future. Sam Nicholson, all hearty congratulations and beaming smiles, joined them in time to catch the last drops from the bottle. Halloran left the dressing room for the phone in the hall. He called Zampa and gave him a message to pass on to Rachel.

"Is our man okay?" Zampa asked.

"Fine. Only a few cuts and bruises. He'll be back at work tomorrow."

"Hell no," Zampa said. Tell Leroy to rest up for a couple of days. We'll celebrate here when he's ready."

It wasn't until he ended the call, that Halloran noticed Walter Scardale standing in the half-light by the 'exit' door. He froze, his heartrate climbing up the scale. Scardale touched the brim of his hat in mock salute, then turned and walked out of the door.

CHAPTER TWENTY-EIGHT

Rodney Pride was now the angriest man in Angryville.

At 6 to 4 on, the book had not lost much money on the fight, but he was truly pissed off at not making a killing on Jenkins, whose odds had lengthened to 16 to 1. He spent the night raging at the injustice of it all, slept exceedingly badly and woke with a headache – this mainly due to an excess of whisky during the early hours.

He snarled at his reflection in the mirror above the bathroom washbasin. "Some fucker will have to pay for this."

He drove across the city feeding his resentment and by the time he got to his office he was close to boiling point. He found an envelope on the doormat containing two hundred and seventy-five pounds in cash. Far from assuaging the violent notions in his head, the money simply increased his fever. Which surged close to delirium when he read the note the money was wrapped in. *Thanks for the Carnations*.

***

Roly Bevan, meanwhile, was on cloud nine.

Wrapped in a red and matching colours, paisley patterned, silk dressing gown, he was standing in the living room of his three storey regency house on Sion Hill, looking out at the suspension bridge. Drenched in equanimity and love for the world – save perhaps for the part of it in which Rodney Pride was allowed to flourish.

The view towards and beyond the bridge was always satisfying; constantly reinforcing that his organised, safe and sound life was blessed. Especially here in this house, which he had paid huge sums to have re-designed. The basement, actually hewn out of the cliff-side rock under the house was divided into two rooms. One of them a substantial wine cellar. The other a home cinema, graced by armchairs with red crushed velvet upholstery, a 16mm film projector and a screen which was, effectively, the fourth wall of the room. There were three guest bedrooms on the ground floor above. The first floor in which he was standing, was a kind of *grande salle*. A laundry and kitchen, accessed directly from the stairwell, flowed into a dining area. Which seamlessly dissolved into a living area, dominated by two Eames aluminium framed chesterfield sofas, looking at each other across a matching coffee table. There were floor to ceiling bookshelves along one wall, stacked with books Bevan had not read and was never likely too, but the collection looked impressive. His own bedroom and en-suite bathroom boasted the best views, and along with his dressing room and office, completed the top floor facilities. The whole house was neat and reverentially tidy. Nothing out of place.

In the kitchen, Mrs Maltravers was arranging his breakfast

"Tea or coffee Mr B?" she asked.

On the sofa, Bevan turned to face the kitchen.

"Oh, tea Mrs M, I think."

"Indian, Ceylon, China?" she asked. "Earl Grey perhaps? Or just plain ordinary grocer's tea?"

"I think the young man who stayed overnight is a grocer's tea person."

Mrs M did not so much as bat an eyelid. She picked up the new chrome electric kettle, filled it from the tap and plugged it into a point on one of the expensively tiled walls. The toast popped up in the Sunbeam SuperToaster as she arrived at the fluffy serving moment of the scrambled eggs. She arranged the toast and eggs on a big white oval plate with a red rose design in the centre. The kettle boiled and Mrs M poured the water into a white teapot with an elegant curved spout and the same red rose on each side of the bowl. She took a bottle of milk out of the enormous American *Prestcold* fridge and decanted some into a matching milk jug. She collected a silver-plated tray from a cupboard, arranged the toast, the teapot and the milk jug neatly, creating the appropriate space for two cups, two saucers and two breakfast plates. Bevan gave the tray the once over.

"You are a treasure Mrs M."

"Thank you Mr B. Shall I begin cleaning downstairs?"

"A very good idea, thank you."

She was sure the place would need no more than a swish of a duster, but she would find something to do, in order to leave Mr B and his young man alone. She was, naturally, more than a little curious about Mr B's friends, but she felt that speculating about such was the last thing the hired help should indulge in, and a gentleman's life was his own to carry on as he chose.

A slim blonde in his early 20s, arrived at the foot of the stairs from above.

"Good morning Michael," Bevan said.

"Morning Roly."

Michael crossed the room, bent down and kissed his host on the forehead.

"I hope you slept as well as I did." He sat down at the dining table. "Scrambled eggs a la Mrs M," he said.

"Small luxuries I know," Bevan said. "But in times of austerity…"

Bevan poured milk and tea into a cup and checked the contents of the matching sugar bowl.

"I forget," he said. "Do you take sugar?"

Michael gave him an old-fashioned look.

"I apologise," Bevan said. "But there are other things about you which I really do not forget."

Michael smiled. "No, I don't take sugar."

They ate breakfast in polite silence. Roly had a way of doing things and Michael knew how to behave.

***

The same could not be claimed by putative gangster in waiting, Rodney Pride. Scardale was giving his boss a précis of his handling of Patsy Halloran.

"I left him in the alleyway behind his flat, in a half-loaded skip. The blokes doing the landlord's building work should have found him by now. Louis is going to ring when he's checked."

Pride was a little pissed off that this rudimentary exercise in brutality had proved unnecessary.

"Still, it will be a warning to others to stay in line," his employee suggested.

Pride glared at him.

"If and when I need advice on strategy, Walter, you'll be the last person I call. So, stick to obeying orders and doing what you do best."

The desk phone rang. Pride nodded at Scardale, who picked up the receiver.

"Pride's Rides… Yes Louis."

He listened to the narrative Lennon had to impart.

"Right… Yeah, later."

He replaced the receiver and delivered the message to Pride.

"From Louis at the BRI. Halloran is out of Casualty and onto a ward. He's lost two teeth, has bruising all over his face and three cracked ribs." He grinned. "Otherwise, he's alright."

On the hospital ward, Halloran was insisting to the copper at his bedside that he had no idea who had reduced him to this state.

"A total stranger Detective Constable," he resolutely maintained.

***

On Sion Hill, PC Grafton reversed the Wolseley into the only remaining parking space in front of Roly Bevan's regency pile. He shifted the gear stick into neutral and switched off the ignition. From the rear seat, Goole opened the nearside passenger door and slid out onto the pavement. Bridge got out road side and looked across the roof of the Wolseley, towards the beautifully glossed blue door of number 23.

"How many times have we knocked on that bloody door, Tom?"

"Can't recall."

"Have we ever been rewarded?"

"No."

"We'll get him one day. Meanwhile, let's ask him to put the kettle on."

Mrs Maltravers answered the door, a little alarmed at being introduced to a brace of detectives. She asked Bridge and Goole if they wouldn't mind waiting in the hall and set off upstairs, calling out for 'Mr Bevan'. He arrived a couple of minutes later and posed on the first-floor landing above. He smiled. He was getting tapped up again. And he knew enough of DCI Bridge to play whatever was coming with care.

"To what do I owe the pleasure this time?"

"It's a case of aggravated bodily harm Roly."

The pose and the bonhomie dropped.

"And you bring these tidings to me because?..."

"May we come up?" Bridge asked.

"Yes of course, Chief Inspector, please do."

He bade the policemen follow him upstairs to the first floor. Pointed them in the direction of the sofas and moved into the kitchen.

"I can only offer you tea or coffee I'm afraid," he said. "I believe your last visit coincided with one of Mrs Maltravers baking days. But she has yet to exercise her culinary skills this week."

Already irritated beyond measure, Goole opened his mouth to say something. Bridge raised his right hand to stop him.

"Tea for two," he said. "Thank you."

"Then I shall make that so," Bevan said.

Bridge looked down at the coffee table, at a selection of books, carefully arranged to display their covers. In pride of place was a glossy furniture catalogue, and a photo book about the Hawaiian Islands. A pictorial history of the first half of the century, sitting under a couple of Raymond Chandler novels. Bridge picked up *The Big Sleep* and began to leaf through it.

Bevan called across from the kitchen.

"Are you a fan?"

"As long as we stay within the realms of fiction, yes."

Bevan smiled. Bridge waited until the host arrived at the table with a tray and positioned himself on the sofa opposite the two detectives, before he spoke again. Bevan poured milk into Goole's cup, and then transferred the jug to the cup and saucer in front of Bridge.

"Well?..."

"Two hours ago, Patsy Halloran was found, beaten up, in a skip behind his flat."

Bevan's hand shook and milk spilled into the saucer. He put the jug down, looked into Bridge's eyes, then sank back against the sofa cushions.

There was a long silence. Bevan spoke first.

"Do you know who did this?"

Bridge shook his head. "It's too early in the investigation."

Bevan looked at Goole. "Sergeant?"

"At the moment we have no leads," Goole said.

Bevan returned his attention to Bridge.

"I'm glad you took the time to tell me in person, Chief Inspector."

"The least we could do."

Bevan shuffled into another position on the sofa. Stared down at his knees. Goole attempted to move the conversation along.

"We need to ask you the same question you just asked us," Goole said. "Is there anyone you can think of who would do this?"

Bevan breathed in and out.

"No." He stood up. "So, if that is it, I would rather you left."

"I rather think we have more to -" Goole began.

Bridge got to his feet too.

"We can return to this later, Tom," he said.

Goole looked at him astonished. Bridge ignored his sergeant and stepped away from the table.

"It is important however."

Bevan nodded. "Of course."

He moved past Bridge and guided the two detectives across the room. He watched them go down the stairs, turn the right-hand corner at the ground floor, and listened as they stepped to the front door.

He heard the door open and close.

Out in the street, Detective Sergeant Goole had no idea what his boss was up to.

"Why did we leave it there?"

"I'll tell you why sergeant. Roly Bevan is churning

inside. He knows who beat the shite out of his main man. And he is going to do something about it. So, put a tail on him and watch where he goes."

He slid into the rear seat of the Wolseley. Goole got into the front passenger seat and picked up the radio handset.

Inside the house, Bevan had not moved an inch.

To his left, he heard Michael approach. He extended his right arm and waited until Michael took hold of his hand.

"Bad news?"

Bevan dropped his head. Michael waited for a response. Bevan raised his head and bellowed across the stairwell.

"Rodney Pride. Rodney fucking Pride!"

CHAPTER TWENTY-NINE

The aforementioned, was in his counting house, counting out his money. His mood had improved substantially since earlier in the day. Scardale knocked on the office door, opened it a foot or so and stuck his head around it.

"Sorry to intrude Boss, but Sam Nich -"

Nicholson kicked the door open and barged in.

"Is coming in nonetheless," he shouted.

Scardale tried to grab him and missed. Nicholson steamed as far as the desk before the enforcer caught hold of him.

"Sit down Sam," Pride yelled.

Scardale let go of the intruder. Grabbed a guest chair, placed it behind Nicholson's calves, plonked him down onto it and held onto his shoulders. Physically restricted, but not verbally.

Pride bellowed at him again.

"For Christ's sake Sam, shut up!"

For good measure, Scardale heaved Nicholson into a half nelson and held him still. The intruder choked into silence.

"Thank you," Pride said. "I think he's calmed down enough, Walter. You can let him go."

He did. Nicholson slumped back into his seat. Pride proceeded to complete the conversation with Scardale as if his visitor wasn't there.

"Not as bad as it might have been Walter. We made just over three hundred quid from the deluded arseholes who thought Jenkins had enough in him to get a result. We lost a bit less than that to the favourite, so we'll just have to wear it."

He folded the notes and dropped them into the open cashbox on his desk. Held it against the side of the desk with his right hand, swept up the pile of coins and guided them into the box. He opened a desk drawer, dug out a key ring, stood up and crossed to the safe, unlocked it, stashed the box, closed the door and re-locked it.

Then he looked in Scardale's direction.

"Go on. I don't think Sam is going to be any trouble."

Scardale left the office. Sam sulked. Pride took ages to move things along. Nicholson shuffled in his seat. Eventually, satisfied he had control over the situation, Pride conjured up his best indulgent face and looked at Nicholson.

"Now, what's all this about?"

"Roly Bevan isn't going to take this lying down," Nicholson said.

"It's a pity his fighter didn't."

"What the hell are you trying to do? Draw attention to us all."

"Roly's not in a position to do anything," Pride said. "He's outgunned for a start."

Nicholson thought about that for a moment. Hoped to hell the words 'out gunned' were just a colourful simile.

"If you see what I mean," Pride said.

Nicholson was by no means sure that he did.

Pride looked at the miserable expression on his associate's face. Leaned down to his right and opened the drawer at the bottom of the desk pedestal. He straightened up, a.38 revolver in his hand. It took a moment for Nicholson to believe his eyes. Whereupon he stared at the gun in terror.

"It's not loaded." He looked down to his right. "Bullets in there though."

Nicholson found his voice.

"Put the thing away for Christ's sake."

Pride grinned. "Frightens you does it?"

"Of course it fucking does."

Pride unlocked the chamber. It fell open. Nicholson flinched. Pride put the gun onto the desk and got down to business.

"The thing with you bastards who didn't fight one day of the last war, is you have no sense of what it takes. I carried a machine gun and this .38 across North Africa, Sicily, then most of the length of pissing Italy. A real saga of blood and brutality that was. Monte Cassino, Christ. A monastery on top of a hill, just over a mile high. We ended up there just after Christmas 1943. We didn't take it until May '44. Months of fucking misery and freezing rain. Thousands of men stumbling over the dead bodies of the poor bastards who had been ordered up the hill the day before and the day before that. For what? One hill, which the fucking generals had decreed was the way to Rome… Meanwhile, you sat at home on your arse. Roly Bevan made a fortune and lived the life of Reilly." He paused dramatically, then ended with a huge dollop of menace. "So now, I'm going to take it all away from him."

The diatribe was so direct that Nicholson caught up. His mouth was dry and the confession so disturbing he could not find the wherewithal to respond. Pride added the tin lid.

"And you're going to help me. That is, if you wish to remain City Council Leader, with your reputation intact."

"You're crazy," Nicholson said. "Stark staring fucking crazy."

Pride grinned from ear to ear.

"And I don't give a toss."

Nicholson was shaking his head.

"No no… That's it. I'm finished."

Pride got to his feet, walked round the desk and stood glaring down at Nicholson, now terrified and glued to his seat.

"Only when I say so. And only if you don't want your wheeling and dealing, fencing of stolen goods, bending the rules, abusing your position in the council chamber, and making money out of our hospital operation, to hit the headlines." He wound up the sermon. "There are people in this town who owe me. And I intend to collect. I've waited a long time for this. But I'm on a roll now, Sam, and you are along for the ride."

For a moment or two Nicholson was immobile. Imprisoned in the hideous prospect. Pride stared at him.

"Something else?"

Nicholson came back to the present.

"I can go then?"

Pride simply opened his arms wide, question marks in his eyes. Nicholson stood up, did a swift about turn and fled.

On cue, the phone rang.

"I have something to tell you," Doctor Havers said. "Er… a complication here."

***

DS Goole walked into his boss's office.

"We just had a call from the unmarked car that followed Roly Bevan after he left home."

"And?..."

"He went to see Daniel Zampa."

Bridge stared at him. Goole went on.

"At least we are assuming so, in that he paid a visit to the *El Paradis*."

"And we know why don't we?"

"An educated guess," Goole said, "would suggest that he needs help in some action he wants to take against Rodney Pride. Zampa being the only man in town who can sanction that without war breaking out."

Bridge pondered. "We hope…"

Goole shook his head. "No. Pride won't go up against Zampa, surely?"

"He might, "Bridge said. "He's angry and stupid enough."

Goole brightened up. "Then perhaps we should just let them get on with it. Pick up the pieces afterwards."

"That's not a bad idea Detective Sergeant. In the best of otherwise well-ordered worlds, it would be exceedingly useful to allow natural selection to solve the problems of police keeping. Unfortunately, we are here, and this is now."

He rose to his feet, stepped to the window and looked out over Broadmead. Goole recognised this as a familiar thinking routine. He waited. Eventually, Bridge turned and looked at his sergeant.

"Send another car full of detectives round to the club. Follow whoever comes out, Zampa and or Bevan, on foot if necessary. And another car to find Pride and keep tabs on him."

"That's a hell a lot of manpower," Goole said.

"Give Inspector Rankin my compliments and borrow from Robbery. Same with Inspector whatsisname in Vice."

"Gerrard," Goole offered.

"Take some PCs out of uniform if you have to. Let's throw a blanket over this whole bloody triangle of sin and see what happens. Get across town to a spare desk in traffic. Co-ordinate everything from there. Open a direct line to every car. Zero phone calls, unless they are made from police boxes. Radio communication only. Maybe, just maybe, this is the moment to get these buggers off the streets once and for all."

Goole smiled. Finally, something he had been banging on about for ages was going to happen.

"On my way Boss," he said, and was out of the office in seconds.

Bridge breathed in and out.

"Okay gents," he murmured. "Let's see the colour of your money."

***

Daniel Zampa was up to speed also. Coming to the end of a conversation with James and Jonathan.

"And you're sure it's a police car out there?"

"Absolutely," James said. "Two blokes sitting inside it. Another two in the street. All of them in cheap suits. One lounging by the Colston Hall stage door, the other outside the drinking den at the top of Christmas Steps. We don't know how clued up they all are."

Bevan was watching and listening from the other side of the desk, trying to be patient. Zampa asked James who was in the building. To be told that the cleaners had finished and gone. And apart from the people in this office, only the bar manager and Sidney were around.

Jonathan chipped in.

"Leroy is expected however."

"Why?"

"Just wanted to show his face, I think. Negotiate his return to work."

Zampa added that to the computations in his head. He began with directions to Bevan.

"Leave this with us Roly. Go home, or to the *Albion*, and behave as if nothing untoward has happened. Do not go anywhere else and don't dawdle between either place. This will be over within hours. We'll catch up later."

Jonathan ushered Bevan out of the office. Zampa waited until he closed the door, then talked to him first.

"You stay here. Watch for Leroy. Scoop him up when he arrives. Tell him I'm out, which I shall indeed be, buy him a drink and be sociable."

Then he gave orders to James.

"Get two cars ready. You will drive me in one, until we lose the police car outside. At which point we'll find a phone and call Jonathan. He will pick up the second car and join us. And in the process, if necessary, convey Leroy home. Clear so far?"

James and Jonathan signified it was.

"The final task will be to pick up Rodney Pride, wherever he is, and take him to a secluded spot for a meaningful conversation."

**

The Mayor was out visiting a group of people lobbying for fewer prefabs and an extended programme of new council housing. Sam Nicholson was alone in the office, shaking from head to foot in anger and terror, and measurably the worse for drink. He had no motivation to work and even less desire to go home. He was just plain out of sorts, out of reason, at the mercy of Rodney Pride and without allies. He could not go to the police. He had already made up his mind that all the ambition of the last twenty years, his step by step campaign to improve his lot and make his future secure, was the one thing he had to honour and cherish. To have that all taken away, along with the bonus of a prison sentence, did not bear thinking about. He had used Rodney Pride to help make his money and now he could either pay the price or go along with whatever the egregious bastard was set to do next.

Maybe Roly Bevan might help. He and Nicholson had, after all, joined forces on small endeavours in the past. And Pride was still smarting from the fallout over the business with a previous member of Roly's stable, middleweight contender Robbie McAllister. A very conflicted man, with a chip on his shoulder and a head full of demons. McAllister was also homosexual. Nicholson had let this slip to Pride; an act of stupidity he immediately had cause to regret. Pride had used this knowledge to take all the advantage he could.

Despite having the best cover available – he was in the butchest of professions, no nancy boys in the ring – McAllister was vulnerable. He had promise as a boxer. Patsy Halloran believed in him, but McAllister could not control his temper, could not focus when he needed to. He was always broke. Roly and Sam lent him a few pounds here and there. But they lost patience after the boxer bought a new Triumph Mayflower; spending five hundred and twenty-five pounds, because it was sold as *The Small Car with the Up-market Image*. He could not afford cash, so he was paying on the never-never with a couple of years to go.

In desperation he went to Pride, who locked McAllister into payments he could not make, bled him dry, and then sold him the bullets he shot himself with. McAllister drove up to the end of a track above the Avon Gorge in Leigh Woods. He was found by a couple walking their dog. Sitting in the driving seat of the Mayflower, a huge bloody hole in the left-hand side of his head, his left arm across the passenger seat, the gun gripped by reflex, still in his hand.

Bevan discovered that Pride was the means and set out to 'bury the bastard'. Daniel Zampa, found out.

James and Jonathan got to him before he could do anything beyond minimal damage. Bevan was reminded of the order of things. A deeply resentful Rodney Pride was returned to his basket, left to sulk and to plan revenge.

Nicholson stared at the phone on his desk for ages. Eventually he decided he did not have all the time in the world for this, and picked up the receiver. He called Bevan at *The Mighty Albion*, to be told by whoever answered the phone that he wasn't there. He got the same response from Halloran at the *Albion Gym*. He phoned the house on Sion Hill. No one answered the call.

Suddenly alone, like a man self-isolating from the plague without having worked out why, he panicked. Casting about desperately for a solution, he came up with the one man he had no reason to disrespect. A man, who unlike his business partner, had survived the war with compassion and purpose and might actually be in a position to help him.

Perhaps.

He knew that Ed Grover was different from all others on his radar. He had no idea what the soldier would say to any proposition he might suggest, but he decided the risk was worth it. At worst, he reasoned, however amused by the proposal Grover was, he was unlikely to beat a path to the nearest police station.

Possibly.

And knowing that Grover had crossed swords with Pride in the recent past, had refused to be intimidated, and had proved his ability to hand it out as well as take it, he might at least lend an ear.

Hopefully.

Armed with this triptych of optimism, he picked up the phone receiver and called Filton. Turnbull apologised for Ed Grover's absence. Nicholson spun a yarn about this being important city council business and asked for Grover's personal phone number. Turnbull believed him and gave it to him.

The phone in the hall at 5 Blenheim Villas rang unanswered.

***

Grover was in Doctor Mason's office at the General Hospital. Lauren had been thinking about Hanna Gunther.

"Yesterday I talked with her GP. He elaborated a little on the stuff he told you. She was supposed to confirm the next regular check-up she had scheduled in three days' time. He's worried that Hanna has dropped completely from his radar. His judgment, although he hates to consider it, is that following the death of her boyfriend, she has decided on some drastic action."

"Which she might not have survived," Grover said.

"If she is still alive, somebody has to find her. I've checked with colleagues all over the hospital. A couple of them have come into contact with the police over abortion issues. There is a detective at the Bridewell, in Vice, who deals with this kind of thing. A sort of spin off from the department. He's happy to work with a senior medical practitioner in confidence, and he's doing some digging for me. Says he may turn up a name, which may lead to another, and that contact might…" Lauren did not complete the sentence. "The best he can do he says."

Grover nodded. "Yeah. Thanks anyway. Thinking caps stay on, I guess. May I use your phone before I go. I ought to check in with Filton."

"Of course."

Grover called the aero engines switchboard and asked for Turnbull's office.

"Did you get a call from Sam Nicholson?" Turnbull asked. "You remember, the bloke we met at the Grand Hotel bash."

"Yes I do."

"He wanted to talk with you. Said it was about something you were working on together. I gave him your home phone number. He was a bit insistent. I hope I did the right thing."

Grover told him that was fine. Turnbull asked if he planned to come back to the office later.

"Not unless I need to."

"That's fine. See you tomorrow."

Holding on to the receiver, Grover depressed the phone cradle with his left hand. Looked at Doctor Mason.

"May I make another call?"

"Of course."

Sam Nicholson was pacing his office like a caged lion. Out of sorts and almost out of control. He stared at the phone as it began ringing, then decided it might be best if he answered the call.

"You have been looking for me," Grover said.

"Christ yes. I have something to tell you."

"Go on."

"No not here, on an open line. Do you know your way around Southville?"

"Just about."

"Do you know where the Imperial Tobacco Factory is?"

"Hang on a second."

He took the receiver away from his ear, covered the mouthpiece with his left hand. Looked at Doctor Mason.

"The Tobacco Factory. Where is it?"

"Erm... Near Ashton Gate. At the eastern end of North Street. Do you know where that is?"

Grover nodded and put the receiver back against his ear.

"Yes, I do."

"There is a cul de sac opposite. Baynton Close. At the end, on the left, is a garage with an office above it. No name, but you will recognise it for what it is. Meet me there as soon as you can. Don't park that jeep of yours outside it though. Best not to attract attention."

"What's this about?" Grover asked.

"Later," Nicholson said and ended the call.

***

Bridge and Goole missed Rodney Pride by seconds. As the police Wolseley pulled onto the site in Albert Vale, the unmarked Morris Oxford taxi was a couple of hundred yards away, turning onto the Feeder Road.

Ten minutes later Pride had crossed the city centre and was driving along Hotwell Road, the floating harbour to his left. Within another three minutes he was over the Cumberland Basin and on the A370 heading in the direction of Weston Super Mare. With his foot to the floor and the road clear of traffic he made the next twelve miles in the same number of minutes. One mile later, approaching Cleeve village, Pride went down through the gears, slowed the car and turned left onto the road which skirted Brockley Wood and Wrington Warren. He checked the rear-view mirror for the umpteenth time A two tone grey Austin A70 appeared behind him. He cut his speed slightly. The Austin closed. There was a long slow right hand bend ahead. Unable to overtake, the driver cut his speed also.

Pride drove another hundred yards, located the bus stop he was looking for, and fifty yards later he picked out the gate leading to the track through the wood. He swung the Morris into the layby beyond and stopped. The Austin accelerated, drove past him and disappeared into the distance. Pride checked his watch. Waited for a desperate five minutes, breathing deeply. Then he slid out of the driver's seat, locked the car and walked back towards the gate.

After one final look round, he opened the gate and stepped onto the hospital grounds.

Half a mile away, Zampa and James were in *The Woodsman* pub. The Austin was sitting in the car park. The boss was in the lounge, looking out of the window, cradling a gin and tonic. James was at the phone box in the corridor outside the Gents.

"Pride's got something going at the old Scarlett Fever Hospital in Brockley Woods. There's an entrance gate in

315

the hedgerow on the Wrington Warren side of the hospital grounds. Get a pencil, I'll give you directions to the pub. You can be here in twenty-five minutes if you don't get lost. We'll wait for you."

***

In Baynton Close, Ed Grover was looking at Hanna Gunther's statistics.

"You think that's her?" Sam Nicholson asked.

"I'm sure of it."

He looked around the office.

"How long has this been going on?"

Nicholson sketched out the enterprise. Ended up by insisting he had nothing to do with it, beyond providing the office and a bit of finance here and there.

"I haven't visited the place. At least not since it's been up and running."

Grover took time to assess what he thought of the man in front of him. Not a great deal, and the moment was over swiftly

"Okay," Grover said. "I'll drive."

Nicholson began shaking his head.

"No. I'm not… No no no."

Grover stepped to Nicholson, grabbed him by the lapels of his jacket, raised him on his tip toes until their eyes were locked together.

"Sam, you are a miserable excuse for a human being. But you are all I've got. We are taking a look at this place. You will give directions and a guided tour. Any questions?"

Nicholson was unable to speak.

"Good. Let's go."

***

On the estate, Pride stepped into the clearing behind the hospital wards. There was a brazier burning, long yellow flames licking upwards. The smell from whatever was fuelling it was truly unpleasant. He moved on, into what now constituted the hospital entrance foyer. The single room to his immediate left was a store and laundry, stacked with sheets and towels and featuring two new Bendix automatic washing machines. Not easy to come by, Pride reflected. But as he had an electrical store owner's neck in a headlock…

Both machines were in business. One chugging through the initial wash; the second whirring away, its laundry barrel spinning. Sitting on top of this machine, was a plastic laundry basket filled with blood-stained sheets and towels.

Pride knew little short of nothing about being pregnant, but he could recognise when something was wrong. He turned around. Dr Havers came out of the birthing room. Pride looked at him, question marks in his eyes. Havers stopped in his tracks.

"Mr Pride…"

"What's happened?"

"Er… We have had an emergency."

"What sort of emergency?"

"One of the ladies… er…"

Havers faltered. Pride waited. The doctor looked at Pride's chin rather than into his eyes.

"There was a miscarriage."

Pride did not know much about those things either. But he was bloody swift at recognising a crisis. He elbowed Havers out of his way and stepped into the birthing room. The place was empty, the bed was stripped and there was an ugly dark red stain in the centre of the mattress, with smudged lines stretching out from it like points of a compass. No need to ask what that was all about. Behind him, Havers cleared his throat.

"We have not finished clearing up," Pride heard him say.

The lingering smell of blood made even Pride's cast iron stomach heave. He backed out of the room. Havers moved to one side, let him pass and shadowed him into the lobby. Pride looked at him, dead centre.

"So, there's no baby?"

"I'm afraid not."

"But there was?"

"Yes."

"What have you done with it?"

"We have incinerated it."

Pride flashed back to a picture of the brazier outside.

"What?" He breathed in and choked. "Out there? Oh for fuck's sake…"

"Well that's er…" Havers cleared his throat again. "More or less what happens at a crematorium."

Pride stared at him.

"Yes. But with a few relatives gathered in reverence, some flowers, a priest and a few prayers. Jesus Christ."

"We were prepared for this. We knew it might happen."

"Oh great… So that's some consolation then."

Pride looked past Havers in the direction of the ward doors. Havers shepherded him away towards the other end of the lobby. Pride shook himself loose.

"So, how's the mother?"

Havers look at him, surprised. "Well she's dead too, Mr Pride."

There was a long silence. Pride stared at him. No respect or pity, simply repressed anger.

"Where is she?" she asked. "Incinerated too."

Havers gestured along the corridor towards the exit to the woods.

"She is in a box outside the door."

"Christ," Pride muttered. "And I thought I was supposed to be a cold-hearted bastard."

CHAPTER THIRTY

Grover pulled *Salome* into the layby behind the Morris Oxford. Nicholson began to shake.

"Christ he's here?"

"Who is?" Grover asked.

Nicholson began blathering.

"Oh Jesus Christ. No no. No…"

Grover put two and two together.

"Is that one of Pride's cars."

Nicholson swallowed and choked and swallowed again. Then he opened the door and scrambled out. It seemed he was about to throw up. Grover joined him. Nicholson looked up at him. He began pleading.

"I can't go in there. Don't make me. I can't. If only…"

His words segued into incoherent mumbling again. Grover opened the palm of his right hand and swung a hook that would have matched one of Leroy Winston's. It spun Nicholson's head through ninety degrees. He would have fallen over but for the grasp Grover had on his left arm. Nicholson yelled in pain, then fell silent.

"Right Sam. We are going in there together. You are going to point me in the right direction and show me where everything is."

Nicholson was too physically and emotionally weak to protest further. Merely swallowed again and nodded.

He worked hard on his geographical recall. Fifty paces or so from the gate, the path flattened and widened slightly; thanks to the hefty agricultural work from the Pride employees now on their sabbatical. Within a couple of minutes, the two men were approaching the new hospital doors.

Grover noticed the brazier, still alight but no longer burning. Seeping from it, was a smell he could place instantly. An odour he last smelled after stumbling over the burnt corpse of a German soldier. It brought him up with a jolt. Suddenly he was back on the bank of the Saar River, watching a Tiger tank in flames and the unconscious soldier leaning against the broken wheel tracks, burning to death.

He realised that a man had stepped out of the door ahead of him.

"That's Doctor Havers," Nicholson hissed in a stage whisper.

"Mr Nicholson…" Havers managed to say. "May I ask what you are doing here?"

He switched his attention to Grover

"Who are you?"

"Ed Grover. I'm looking for Mr Pride. Where is he?"

Havers looked uncomfortable. "I don't think erm… It will not do -"

"Where is he Havers?" Nicholson said. A sudden low menace that frightened the doctor and even impressed Grover. "Where the fuck is he?

He squared up to the doctor. Havers out matched him by a couple of inches, but somehow Nicholson was giving the impression he was prepared to kick the shit out of him.

Grover stepped in. His body language friendly, his voice the soul of reason.

"Doctor Havers," he said. "Answer the man. Where is Mr Pride?"

"Mr Pride is in the wood." He took a deep breath and pointed beyond Grover. "In a straight line, that way."

"Thank you. You have an office I suppose."

Havers nodded.

"We will talk in there if we may?"

He turned to Nicholson, who answered the question before Grover asked it.

"I'll stay here. Give you warning if Rodney comes back."

Havers and Grover stepped into the hospital entrance. Smart and clean and now smelling strongly of disinfectant.

"I gather you know all," Havers said and pointed in the direction of his office door. "I would be pleased if you'd keep your visit low key, Mr Grover. We have patients to consider."

He opened the door. "Please do go in."

Grover was amazed at the man's courtesy and obvious professionalism. The absurdity of the situation, and the fact that the whole operation was unlicensed, un-monitored, and illegally financed seemed to be of no consequence. This man was in effect running his own private hospital and enjoying it no end.

"It is actually a potential patient that I'm calling about."

Havers grasped the wrong end of the stick.

"Ah well," he said. "You must do all business with the office. All clients are admitted via the administration department. And I have nothing whatsoever to do with that. We are medical professionals here. Dedicated to caring, in the best way possible, for the ladies in residence."

All flannel aside, the caring thing was probably true. And thinking about it, Havers probably had no idea that the administration department personnel consisted solely of a secretary, with part time assistance from a malicious shakedown artist and his enforcers.

"I don't want to disturb anything you've got going here. Not my concern. I'm simply looking for a missing woman. If she's here and well and I can talk with her, I'll be out of your way in ten minutes."

The expression on Havers' face brightened a little.

"You're an American," he said. The question 'Why are you here?' implicit.

"I'm a soldier. A liaison officer at the Bristol Aero Engine Company."

"Important work I suppose…"

Havers tailed off. He had offered all he had to say. Grover cut to the chase.

"Hanna Gunther," he said.

The shock on Havers' face could not have been more clearly etched. The doctor fell into a bruising silence. Grover gave him a second or two.

"I take it, she is here."

Havers began to shake his head.

"No," he said. Then looked straight into Grover's eyes. "I'm afraid she's not".

"She's gone?"

"Erm…"

Grover's patience was being tested. But this was no time for threats. He simply waited. Havers grew more and more uncomfortable. In the end, he said all he could say.

"Hanna Gunther is dead. So is her child. There was a miscarriage."

Suddenly defeated, he collapsed into his chair, as though someone had let all the air out of his body. Grover had only one question.

"And Rodney Pride is out in the woods?"

The doctor nodded. Grover left the office and headed for the front door. Sam Nicholson was nowhere to be seen. Grover did not waste time wondering where he had gone. He set off in the direction Havers had pointed out earlier.

Nicholson had done that too. He was five minutes ahead.

Pride was standing inside a patch of ground shaped like a small circus ring. It had been cleared some time in the past, and was now stubbled with tree stumps and carpeted with moss. Walter Scardale and Louis Lennon, were thigh deep in soil. Their jackets and Scardale's shoulder holster were draped over the handle of a spade, speared into the ground a couple of yards from the grave they were digging. A body, wrapped up and roped in a green tarpaulin, lay on the moss alongside.

To the left of the grave, Pride lit a cigar. He didn't like them much but he thought they upped his class rating a notch or two. A couple of feet below him, Lennon stopped digging, stretched his back and looked up.

"Deep enough now," he suggested.

Pride blew cigar smoke in Lennon's direction. "No. Keep digging."

Behind him he heard a stomping of twigs and ferns and the laboured snorting of a man out of breath. He swung round to face Nicholson.

"Well well well. Couldn't keep away in the end."

Nicholson had no response. He had run only two hundred yards through the undergrowth, but that was enough. He bent forward, placed his hands on his knees and gulped in air.

Scardale looked at Pride again, 'what shall we do with you?' etched on his face. Pride raised his left hand and gestured to his employees to carry on. He moved towards Nicholson, looked down at the top of his head and waited for him to control his breathing. Eventually Nicholson straightened up and found some words to say.

"You stupid, uncaring, evil bastard…"

Pride grinned at him. "Oh right. So, we have a conscience now. Where was it a month ago when we started taking people's money?" He gestured at the tarpaulin. "There were complications. She bled to death. But don't worry, we're already making arrangements to re-fill the bed space."

He grabbed Nicholson by the elbow and steered him towards the dig. Sam swung at Pride, who body-swerved, grabbed hold of his partner and dumped him into the grave. Nicholson dropped on to Lennon, rolled off his shoulder and landed on the edge of Scardale's spade. It was not sharp enough to cut through Nicholson's jacket, but it managed to crack a rib. Groaning in pain, he was heaved into one corner of the grave by Pride's employees and propped upright. They climbed out and stood next to the wrapped-up body.

Pride knelt beside the grave, looked at Nicholson and asked a question.

"Do you think it's deep enough?"

"Fuck off," Nicholson spat at him.

Pride grinned and stood up again.

Nicholson could not manage to get to his feet. Pride moved to Lennon and gestured towards his shovel. Lennon handed it to him. Pride dug into the pile of soil by the graveside, lifted it, and sprayed the contents downwards over Nicholson's head. Sam yelled in terror.

A hundred or so yards away, Grover was moving in what he hoped was a straight line. He knew that such a thing was an impossibility on terrain which doesn't vary and has no landmarks. He had seen pictures of footprints in the desert which simply went around in circles; all sense of direction lost, because the soldier had no idea where he was going. Grover had his own version of this problem. He did not want to crash straight forwards and give away his position. He had to travel slowly and move around obstacles. A degree to the right or the left could send him anywhere.

Then he heard Sam Nicolson scream. He stopped, located what he thought was the direction it came from. He confirmed it was so, when he heard the second scream. He began moving again.

In the yard behind *The Woodsman*, Jonathan changed cars. He climbed into the front passenger seat of the Austin, James gunned the motor and the car surged out onto the road. Less than a minute later, he was braking and swinging the car into the layby.

"A popular spot today," Jonathan muttered.

"The jeep is Grover's," Zampa said. "What the hell is he doing here?"

James slid out of the Austin and moved to the boot. He lifted the lid. Reached inside and unclipped the lid of a wooden box, three feet long and ten inches square. There were two .357 lightweight rifles inside it. He handed a Winchester lever action to Jonathan.

"Ten rounds loaded," he said.

He picked up the second rifle. A pump action Remington with a custom-made stock and a short barrel.

"I'll take this."

He pumped a bullet into the chamber.

CHAPTER THIRTY-ONE

At the burial site, Pride finally took pity on his sometime associate and hauled Nicholson out of the grave. Sam's ribs moved and he yelled out again. Scardale and Lennon returned to digging. Standing upright, Nicholson shifted his weight from one hip to the other, attempting to get comfortable. The courage, summoned up earlier, had evaporated. He made one last attempt at washing his hands of this project.

"I don't want to be involved in this Rod," he said. "I mean..." He looked down at the tarpaulin. "This is..."

He gave up. Pride stepped up to him. They stood toe to toe. Neither of them said anything for a second or two. Nicholson blinked first. Shrugged his shoulders in apology.

"It's just that... I mean, you don't need me, really. I'll just go and... And forget about it all."

Pride stepped back a pace. Nicholson waited for the onslaught. Pride's eyes never left his.

"Okay," he said. No emphasis, no menace.

Nicholson found his voice again.

"Oh good. Right..."

"But breathe one word, just one word, and the whole fucking city will get to know this idea was yours."

Nicholson swallowed. And then the menace arrived. Pride leaned forward into his partner's face. Their foreheads touched. Nicholson held his breath.

"I can make that stick," Pride said quietly.

Nicholson swallowed a second time.

"You know I can," Pride went on, his voice now barely a whisper. "Along with everything else. Remember, it's a hell of a list. Wheeling and dealing, backhanders, all expenses paid weekends in posh hotels, handing out sweetheart deals, fencing stolen property... So, fuck off out of here,"

Nicholson turned to walk away. Then Pride grabbed an arm and swung him round again.

"On second thoughts," he said. "In a minute."

He turned and nodded at the grave. Lennon stopped digging, stabbed his spade into the ground and looked up.

"That'll do," Pride said.

Nicholson watched transfixed, as Scardale and Lennon climbed out, grabbed at the ropes wrapped around the tarpaulin, and lifted the body. Nicholson stepped back, turned away, tripped over a tree stump and pitched onto his face. Pride grinned, then waved Scardale and Lennon on.

The sound of a gunshot roared through the air.

Scardale and Lennon froze. Nicholson looked up from his position on the ground. Pride stared across the clearing. Towards Grover standing at the tree line, a US army issue Colt.45 semi-automatic pistol in his right hand, pointing at the sky.

"Put that tarpaulin down," he said. "Gently. Bend your knees."

Scardale and Lennon were never likely to do anything but. Both had been on the receiving end of

Grover's efficiency before. They deposited Hanna as gently as they could.

"Get into the grave."

The two men looked at each other, as if not understanding the order. Grover raised the .45 and pointed it straight at Lennon.

"Now," Grover said.

Lennon jumped into the grave. Scardale, believing that even a trained soldier did not have the capacity to see in two directions at once, managed two steps towards his holster. Grover re-sighted and pulled the trigger. The .45 bullet hit Scardale in the shoulder, spinning him through ninety degrees. He dropped to his knees, grunting in pain. Grover turned to look at Pride who had not moved a muscle. Then waved the .45 in Scardale's direction.

"Help him."

Pride moved to his lieutenant and hauled him to his feet. Grover walked across the clearing. He looked down at Nicholson.

"Alright?"

Nicholson nodded and manoeuvred himself into a sitting position. Grover surveyed the scene.

"Okay Rodney. Into the grave with Louis."

Pride and Scardale did as they were ordered. Grover moved to a tree stump five paces from the grave.

"Now gents, let's have a little talk."

"About what?" Pride asked. With too much of a snarl.

Grover fired across Pride's shoulder, inches from his right ear. In shock, Pride staggered back against the wall of the grave.

"Politely, Rodney. No sneering."

He sat down on the tree stump.

"Mr Scardale, I suggest you sit down next to Mr Lennon. Rodney, you stay on your feet." He waited until the shuffling in the grave was over, then continued. "Okay, let's talk."

"Nothing to talk about," Pride snorted.

Grover's next shot almost parted Pride's hair. He bellowed in fear and dropped to his knees. Which left his head poking over the parapet of the grave.

"Gentlemen," Grover said. "I don't know how many shots you have counted. Actually, it was four. There are five more in the magazine clip and one up the spout. So just accept that the odds on any of you surviving the next attempt to improve the shining hour are truly fantastical. And we'll get this over as quickly as possible." He called over his shoulder. "Sam, can you hear all this? Because if you can't, I will happily ask Mr Pride to speak up."

"I can hear."

"Fine. Then we shall begin." Grover glanced to his right, pointed at the tarpaulin. "Do you know who that is, all wrapped up?"

"How the hell should I know that? None of my business."

Grover called to Nicholson again.

"We need your help Sam." He pointed at the tarpaulin again. "Will you undo the ropes please. That's all. No more."

Not over excited by the task, Nicholson got to his feet and moved slowly. Grover took up his conversation with Pride again.

"Meanwhile Rodney, we shall move things along."

"Where to?" he complained. Just a little short of surly this time.

"About Bradley Parsons and Benzedrine," Grover continued.

Pride segued from surly to smug.

"Oh, that started as a thing between him and Sandy Eaves. He was trying to make a few quid, to entertain his girl on weekends."

"How did you get involved?"

"Parsons realised I was a bigger fish. So, he switched to me."

"And at that point, the lady got annoyed."

"Yes. She became a nuisance."

"And you had somebody torch the night club?"

"I didn't know she was inside."

"Would it have made any difference if you'd known she was?"

"Probably not. She was an infuriating bitch. Getting in the way. Ideas above her station."

Sam Nicholson reacted to that remark. He dropped the ropes in his hands and stood up as straight as he could.

"That's bloody rich coming from you Rodney."

Pride couldn't help himself. He bellowed at Nicholson.

"And you have no fucking ambition Sam. I have plans. And I'll do what it -"

Grover interrupted the sparring.

"You won't do anything Rodney. The glory days are over."

Pride fell to sulking now. Grover glanced at Nicholson.

"Anywhere near ready Sam?"

Nicholson heaved on a long length of rope, pulled it clear of the eyelets in the tarpaulin and stepped back. Grover pointed the .45 at Pride once more.

"Don't move a muscle." He looked to his right. "Sam, come over here and keep an eye on him."

The two men switched positions. Grover moved to the tarpaulin. Pulled the closed edges apart. And looked down at Hanna Gunther.

Twenty-two years old, dark haired and dark eyed. Her skin pale, her young life over. The first dead body Grover had seen since his days in West Berlin. The difference was, the people he tried to help then had nothing to live for. One day ago, Hanna had a whole new world ahead of her. Taken away by a medical emergency, sure. But in death, wrapped up in a soiled tarpaulin and destined for a muddy grave in the woods. Un-mourned and disposed of. Forgotten to death. Those who died in West Berlin while he and his buddies were there, were given funerals with at least a handful of people who cared standing at the graveside.

He walked back towards Pride. Nicholson moved out of his way.

"Do you know who that girl is Rodney?"

Pride shook his head.

"It is Bradley Parsons' girl. Hanna."

"Hell, she's just a Kraut, "Pride said. "You know all about them. Fuck 'em. You probably killed as many as I did."

Grover raised the .45 and sighted it on the space above the bridge of Pride's nose. And in that moment, Pride believed Grover meant to kill him. He stood rooted to the spot.

Daniel Zampa yelled across the clearing. "Don't do it Ed."

Grover and the gun did not move.

"You don't have to," Zampa went on. "He's not worth the risk. Neither the cops nor the US Army will empathise. Court Martial or an English Judge, you will end up with the death penalty… Ed. Listen to me."

Zampa was flanked by James and Jonathan, pointing rifles across the clearing. He upped the ante.

"Rodney Pride is pond scum. He deserves to be shot where he is and the soil shovelled over him. His mates too. But please, leave me to administer the justice."

Sam Nicholson joined in.

"He's right Ed. He's the Boss. It's his job, not yours."

"Actually, it's a job for the police. But in their absence… it needs Wyatt Earp. And that's me."

He stopped talking. Waited, with all the patience in the world. The Colt pointed unwavering at Pride's head.

Pride closed his eyes and pissed himself.

Grover clicked on the safety catch, lowered the gun and stepped back a couple of paces. Pride opened his eyes again. Zampa began to move across the clearing. James and Jonathan fanned left and right.

At the graveside, Zampa looked down at Pride.

"Climb out."

Pride made several attempts and failed. Zampa cast a look at Lennon.

"Help him."

Lennon got to his feet and heaved his boss out of the grave.

"Sit on that tree stump." Zampa said.

Pride crawled over to it and did so. Jonathan pointed the Winchester at him. James offered Scardale and Lennon a close up view of the Remington.

"Rodney," Zampa said. "Now tell me this. Where are the grenades the guns and the ammunition?"

Pride offered a grade A wrong response.

"What are you talking about?"

Zampa nodded at Jonathan. He aimed at the tree stump and despatched a bullet into it, inches from Pride's crotch. Pride leapt to his feet and began stamping around as if they were on fire.

"Christ no. Christ. I mean for God's sake…"

Zampa stepped forward grabbed Pride and pushed him back down onto the tree stump. He overbalanced and fell backwards onto the ground.

Sam Nicholson was astonished. Grover was transfixed.

Pride sat up. Zampa nodded at Jonathan; who took a couple of steps forward and raised the Winchester again.

"Let's try once more Rodney," Zampa said.

Grover watched, as in slow motion, Zampa's face froze into a mask. If he or Rodney Pride had doubted Zampa's claim to know everything about everything, they had no cause to do so now. For the first time in their relationship, Grover experienced real menace aimed at the bad guy. Powerful, implacable, no quarter given. Like on Omaha Beach.

The pulse in Pride's temple would not stop pounding. Satisfied that his message had been received and understood, Zampa allowed the mask to slip.

"Now. Who killed Rita Caton?"

Pride made one more attempt at foolishness. He began shaking his head. This time the bullet from the Winchester tore through the flesh of his left arm. He screamed, grabbed at his arm, bending his head, rocking back and forth in pain. He steadied himself enough to study the blood seeping between his fingers. Looked up at, Zampa, beseeching him to stop.

"This is all so unnecessary Rodney. It will take moments to answer a few questions. After which, James and Jonathan will conduct you in the direction of Doctor Havers."

He paused for what seemed an eternity, then wound up.

"The alternative, need I say, is to die right where you are. So, for the last time, who killed Rita Caton?"

"Somebody I hired. A bloke I was in the army with."

"And the grenade came from where?"

"Same place as the guns and the ammo." He nodded in Grover's direction. "His mob."

"And why were you stockpiling US Army ordnance?"

Pride said nothing.

Zampa repeated the question.

Jonathan re-sighted the Winchester. Pride, his face the colour of parchment, leaned forward and threw up in front of him.

Zampa looked down pitilessly.

"Ambition get the better of your sense. Going to start a war, were you?"

He changed tack, swung around and looked into the grave.

"Was it to be that Walter? A coup?"

Walter looked puzzled. He wasn't sure what a coup was. Zampa simplified the question.

"I had no idea that your boss, and you and Louis there, had such an imagination. Take over from me? The whole idea is pure fantasy. And you screwed everything up. Blackmail, threats, arson, the grenade business… All bargain basement stuff. Did you really imagine you could take my place?"

Walter looked at Pride, pleading for some help with this. Zampa continued.

"Where is the stuff Walter?"

To his left, James sighted the Remington. Walter caved.

"Underneath the floor of the shed by the new hospital entrance."

Zampa offered the field to Grover.

"Your witness, Ed."

Grover took a couple of steps forward.

"How did the stuff get here?"

"It arrived in a truck," Scardale said. "I don't know how Parsons made it work."

"Who delivered it?"

"I don't know."

Zampa nodded at James. Who shifted the Remington a couple of degrees. Fired between the two men in the grave. Pumped another bullet into the chamber and re-sighted on Scardale's forehead. He panicked. He looked to his boss for guidance. Got nothing. Turned back to James.

"Honest," he said. "Swear to God. I don't know his name."

"Was he American?" Grover asked.

Scardale began nodding his head like an over-wound motorised toy.

"Describe him."

Scardale took a moment to collect his thoughts.

"Tall. Strong looking. An accent. Like in the westerns. He's a mechanic. He knew all about the car Louis and me drive. The Chevy."

Grover's stomach began to churn.

"Anything else?"

"He was a black man."

In that moment, Grover felt his heart break. He dropped his head and turned away from the grave.

Zampa watched him. Picked up the vibe. Realised Grover was in trouble.

He motioned to James and Jonathan. Pride was hauled to his feet. Scardale and Lennon were extricated from the grave and ordered to lead the way. Sam Nicholson chose to remain where he was.

Zampa moved to Grover's shoulder.

"How long have you known about this?" Grover asked.

"The maternity ward caper? A week or two. They were never going to keep it secret. Not from me. Actually, I've come to like the idea. Legally set up as a private hospital, it might actually work. With somebody other than the sexual and social deviant in charge. I'll take a look at the set up in a minute."

Daniel Zampa the philanthropist. Grover did not have the strength to consider the morality of all that. Zampa directed his attention to Hanna's body.

"You do realise the burial will have to go ahead. Here. In this place."

Grover nodded silently. One more unmarked grave in his register ought to make no impression at all.

"All this has to stay the way it is now," Zampa said. "You do understand?"

Grover spoke. "Yes."

"I promise you, I will make sure the burial is done with all due solemnity and respect. James and Jonathan will be at the graveside."

"Thank you."

"And we shall come back from this, you and I."

"I doubt that," Grover said.

It was Zampa's turn to mull things over. Grover moved to Hanna. Looked down once more at the girl who had come such a long way, only to end up in Brockley Woods.

"The arms delivery man is a friend of friend of yours I take it," Zampa said.

"Yes."

"A close friend."

"I saved his life. He saved mine in return. And you know what they say about that. We have care of each other's souls for the rest of our time."

"And now, you will do what you have to do."

Grover breathed deeply. Turned and looked deep into Zampa's eyes.

"Yes."

CHAPTER THIRTY-TWO

Grover and *Salome* ate up the miles on the A420. Alternating between bouts of roaring speed and solemn driving, as his concentration swung between one purpose and the next.

There was no sign of Henry Whelan at Fairford. He was not in the Motor Pool. Or the workshop, his barrack block, the refectory, the bar. He was off duty and appeared to be nowhere on the base at all. Back in the workshop, Grover managed to locate Corporal Anstey.

"Henry didn't just go out for a walk," Grover said. "He must have left in a vehicle."

"Guess so," Anstey said, not exactly up to speed on the issue.

"I need to talk with him Corporal. Can you demonstrate a little more interest?"

Anstey slid off the workbench stool and stood up.

"Yes, Sir. Let's take a look."

A small Dodge Truck was out somewhere. Weighing three quarters of a ton, it was essentially a pick up with a hood over the back of it.

"Doesn't take a big load," Anstey said. "He's probably just out for a drive around the Cotswolds. Maybe he's found himself a girl."

That was not beyond the bounds of possibility. And for a moment, Grover hoped it was plausible, and real enough to believe. There were black guys all over the place. Three of them in the Motor Pool. But of that trio, one was short, one was bald, and the third had a Bronx accent you could cut salt beef with. No one remotely close to six feet plus, with the lazy Texan drawl that was Henry's alone.

Grover drove back to the base entrance. A Snowdrop he knew was on duty. Sergeant Nick Angelo opened the exit ledger.

"He booked out at 10 o'clock this morning, on a twelve-hour pass. He ought to be back within four hours. Something wrong?"

"No no," Grover said. "I had a couple of questions to ask him. But he's not here and I've got to get back to Bristol. So, it'll have to wait."

"How you enjoying things in the big city?"

"It's… different. Thanks again."

Grover U-turned *Salome*, drove out on to the perimeter road. He parked and looked at his watch, yet again. 6 o'clock. At best, he had no longer than three hours and something minutes to decide what to do. He came to the conclusion he needed to talk with the Adjutant.

Welcomed into Berger's office, he decided not to beat around the bush.

"I know what Bradley Parsons did on his weekends off," he said. "I know where the missing ordnance is. And I think I know how it got there."

Berger reached for the phone on his desk. Grover stopped him making the call.

"Not yet. Hear me out before you talk with Whitmore and Maddox."

Berger paused, the receiver in his left hand.

"Trust me, for the moment," Grover said.

Berger put the receiver back in place. Grover relayed the whole saga from day one. The Adjutant listened without interrupting. Although by the end, he was speechless. Finally, he dredged up the 64,000 dollar question.

"And you want time with Whelan before anyone moves in?"

"Yes. Wherever he is. Wherever I find him."

"Has he gone out for the day, or has he gone forever?"

"As far as I know, Henry believes he has nothing to worry about. Unless he put in a call to Bristol late last night or early this morning. You can check that. Calls to and from NCOs go through the switchboard."

The Adjutant did. Whelan had not called anyone.

"What if he called from a public phone off base?" Berger said

"He didn't leave until 10 o'clock. By then, Rodney Pride was out of his office and otherwise engaged."

"Whelan's on a date then."

"It's a fair bet. Evens at least."

"So, we wait for him to return," Berger said. He looked at his watch. "He has three hours at most."

Grover came up with a proposal.

"Does a Captain have enough clout to act unilaterally?"

"Only in retrospect, as long as the scheme he conjures up works out."

"If I can get Henry into the Motor Pool workshop and you ring it with Snowdrops, will that do it?"

"To a degree. He certainly won't get out of there."

Grover took a moment or two.

"Okay. All this stays in house for the duration, right?"

"Yes."

"May I use the phone?"

Berger nodded and gestured 'go ahead'.

Grover called Nick Angelo.

"I'm here for a while after all," he said. "Watch out for Henry Whelan. Tell him I'm waiting in the Motor Pool workshop to spend a few minutes with him before I go back to Bristol. Then call me as soon as he drives away from the gate… Thanks."

"It will take Whelan barely forty-five seconds to make that journey," Berger suggested.

"Time enough, as long as Angelo is on the ball."

Berger looked at his watch. Asked Grover what time he had. Grover told him. The Adjutant counted down to the top of the next minute.

"19.05 now," he said. "Got it?"

Grover breathed in and out. "Got it."

"I'll organise the MPs. We'll surround the Motor Pool but keep in the shadows until Whelan joins you. Then give you time with him before we bust in."

Grover said nothing. Berger wound things up.

"You better get over there. Whelan might be early." He opened the bottom drawer in the right pedestal of his desk and produced a half bottle of brandy. "And you might need this."

Grover spent the next hour and forty-three minutes sitting on a stool adjacent to the workshop phone. An ugly black instrument on the wall, grimy with use. The waiting was no hardship. Unlike the dark nights he had spent, immobile and silent, in dugouts, ditches and the cellars of ruined buildings; waiting for the next moment of fury, the next surge of violence, to be doled out. This was a short shift on watch, but he hated it. The penultimate scene to a melodrama of anger and disappointment. His best buddy on the hook for deeds way beyond anything Grover would have dreamed him capable of. Henry Whelan was the most enterprising guy he knew, especially in war time, but he was no gun runner. Not on this day in history. The more he tried to rationalise the more his imagination ran riot. 'Maybes' grew more and more grotesque, until he told himself to stop speculating and just wait.

He could hear nothing outside. The Snowdrops were going about their business without a sound.

Just wait.

He drank once from the brandy bottle. Decided he'd better not drink a second or third time. He needed to stay fully awake, to stay frightened. He lost count of the times he looked at his watch, as the light grew darker outside. The luminous dial was reading 8 minutes to 10 when the wall phone rang, shattering the silence. Grover grabbed the receiver.

"On his way," Nick Angelo said.

Grover started counting. Opened the brandy bottle and took his second drink. Continued counting. '29 28 27 26 25…' He moved away from the phone, positioned himself in direct line of sight to the door. '16 15 14 13'… He heard the familiar growl of a Dodge Truck engine as it decelerated and pulled up outside the door.

He stopped counting, his heart rate rising, and waited the last few seconds. The wicket gate door rattled. It opened. Henry Whelan stepped into the workshop.

"Ed" he smiled, and closed the door behind him.

"Henry…"

"So, to what do I owe the pleasure?"

What could Grover say but 'I want to talk with you'? He could have rehearsed it for weeks and it would never have come out right. It did not in that moment.

Henry knew something was wrong.

"It's late," he said. "How long have you been here?"

"I've been on the base four and a bit hours."

Henry walked in Grover's direction, then veered slightly towards his desk. Grover did a mirror movement. He stopped moving as his buddy opened a drawer and produced a Smith and Wesson .38 revolver.

"You're not going to use that, surely," Grover said.

"I might have to," Henry said. "How much do you know?"

"All of it. Except why. Two whys actually."

Whelan said nothing; the silence inviting Grover to go on.

"Why did you give me the 'how to blow up a car with a grenade' stuff? I might have put two and two together."

"I figured, as we were buddies, you wouldn't. And you didn't. You needed a theory. And it wasn't me who did the job."

"Alright," Grover said. "The other why. The big one?"

Whelan sighed.

"I'm sick of this goddam place. I want to go home."

"We all do."

"Not you Ed, clearly."

"It's not the same for me."

"For me either, old buddy. I've been told I'm destined for Korea. Supposed to ship out next week. I'm not going. I spent two months on Guadalcanal in '42. I have no intention of being sent to another fucking jungle swamp. No more guns and bullets and bombs and being scared shitless. I don't do war any more, Ed. Like you."

Grover had to concede that. No shortage of empathy in the workshop.

"Not one more fucking minute," Whelan said. "I can get myself a flight out of here. But it costs money. A lot of people to pay. So, I shipped stuff in the Dodge, for that fucking asshole Bradley Parsons."

"And who doctored the paperwork?"

Whelan shook his head.

"You don't get that from me."

"So where is the money?"

"Hidden in the truck outside. I picked it up earlier. A girl I know has been looking after it. She's in love with me. I don't want to leave her. Said I'd take her with me."

For a moment he was miles away. Grover filled the silence.

"But you are not going to."

Whelan shook his head.

"There's a Skymaster standing outside Hanger 7. It takes off at first light. By then I'll be inside, stashed among the bits of cargo. Taking the girl along is too big a risk." His eyes misted and he exhaled. "So…"

Grover took time over his response.

"This is tearing my guts out Henry."

Whelan took as much time to reply.

"Mine too."

"It could still work out."

"No bullshit Ed. There was never any of that between you and me. We did what we had to do, shoulder to shoulder."

"And we made it through."

"So we could go home," Henry said. "Not back to war." He was quiet for a moment. Then he yelled across the space between them. "Why do we have to fucking do it again? In some other God forsaken crap hole thousands of miles from home. Tell me why?"

Grover shook his head. "I can't."

"Yeah well… Some fucker should be doing so. I don't know any Koreans. I don't know how they live their lives. I still couldn't point out the fucking place on a map."

"So, let this be about us Henry. You and me. Forget about the politics – whatever the cause is. We survived. And we have to honour that, not waste it. Put the gun away."

Whelan shook his head.

"No going back now."

He looked at his buddy, dead centre

"Then I have to do something about that," Grover said. "Give me the gun, Henry. Berger has the place ringed with Snowdrops. You've nowhere to go."

Whelan absorbed that. Decided it was not true.

"Oh, but I have. So long, Ed."

He put the barrel of the .38 into his mouth and pulled the trigger.

EPILOGUE

The fall out was substantial.

It took most of the following day to organise the repatriation of Henry Whelan's body to the States. At 15.00 hours, the delayed Skymaster rose up into the afternoon sun and began the journey home. It took the rest of the day to prepare a statement about his death which would not disgrace either his name, or his history in the 21st Infantry. And another twenty-four hours to deal with questions from rank and file on the base.

Finally, Maddox read out a litany of nonsense to Grover, in the presence of his CO and the Adjutant. Grover was considering where to begin in response to this intention to shift the blame, when Whitmore interrupted proceedings.

"I'll take this Lieutenant…"

Maddox stared at Whitmore. Opened his mouth to say something. The CO raised his right hand.

"That's the biggest truckload of horseshit I've heard in a long time, Maddox." He gestured at Grover. "This man is a first-class officer, with a service record to match. He was killing the civilised world's enemies and upholding the honour of this regiment, when you were back in the Blue Ridge Mountains shooting grouse and eating them with the best Chablis you could buy. I have no doubt you are revered in JAG circles, but here, you are just another fucking asshole of a lawyer."

He swung to face Berger.

"Are you getting all this down Captain?"

"Yes, Sir," Berger said. "Every word, Sir."

Whitmore turned back to Maddox.

"And when he reads that back to me, I'll learn it off by heart and repeat every goddam word I've just said to the Grand Jury, to Congress, and any other bastard who is prepared to listen."

Maddox was too flabbergasted to reply. Whitmore finished the elegy.

"You are dismissed Captain Maddox. Haul your ass out of here."

Maddox left without bothering to salute. Whitmore's response was to sit upright in his chair, straighten his jacket sleeves and shoot his shirt cuffs.

"Never liked the smarmy sonovabitch," he said.

***

Grover phoned Fincher Reade and Holborne. Neil Adkins answered the call. Asked how he was. Hoped he had righted all the wrongs on his list. Said that Zoe and Mel were in court. In their absence, he had been deputised to invite luminaries to an exclusive gathering in the board room the following day.

"To celebrate," he said, "the one hundred and twenty-fifth anniversary of the founding of the firm."

"I qualify as a luminary?"

"Mel thinks so. In fact, she insists."

"Really?"

"Is there something going on between you two?"

349

"Luminaries don't give away secrets."

"So, I'll put you down to attend?"

"I'll be there with bell's on."

"A black tie will do. I can lend you one." He responded to a knock on his office door. "Hold on…"

Grover heard him call 'Come in'. Then he came back on the line again.

"Zoe's here," he said. "Handing you over…"

"Ed. How are you?"

"I'm good. And it's all over. We've solved the ordnance issue. The man responsible for shifting the stuff is… er…"

Suddenly, he could not finish the sentence. Zoe asked him if he was still there. Grover cleared his throat.

"Yes."

"The man responsible you were saying…"

"Yes. He's out of the way."

"That's good," Zoe said. "And the rest?"

"Rodney Pride was on the receiving end in Bristol. He ordered the grenade attack. And the torching of Sandy Eaves club."

"Have you told this to the police?"

Tricky this. He decided a portion of the truth was better than evasion.

"Actually no," he said. "I thought I would talk with you in confidence first. As an officer of the court, as long as your client has not misled -"

Zoe, up to speed, interrupted swiftly.

"And my client in this instance would be you?"

"If your client has played no criminal role in any of this business – other than not telling the police stuff they don't know he knows – is he able to disclose to his lawyer what he knows, without her being mandated to hand over that information?"

Zoe accepted the problem. "In other words, if you don't tell the police something they don't know you know, even though you know they would like to know, and you tell your lawyer instead, will this situation land you in trouble?"

"Yes."

"Well that's the answer. Yes. And if subsequently we don't tell the police what we both know, I'll be in trouble too."

"Then I can only tell the police what I have just told you and no more?"

"You can choose to do so, yes. As long as you give me no cause to ask you questions about what you have not disclosed to me."

In short, Grover decided, it was best not to do that. The other party involved – not in the commitment of crimes, but in the solution thereof – had to remain anonymous. Daniel Zampa had Rodney Pride somewhere and he could be trusted to deal with that situation.

"So, I need to tell the police what I know about Rodney Pride?"

"Yes. But be careful how you do so."

"I've got it worked out. And basically, it's true. Myself and the good old US Army discovered our suspicions about the grenade business during our own internal investigation into the doings of Bradley Parsons. Will that do?"

"Yes. And if the SCT want to take it further, they can do so, with your superiors."

"And good luck with that."

Zoe ended with the big question.

"And if the police do go after Pride," she asked. "Are they likely to find him?"

"I would think not."

There was a moment's silence. Grover listened to the line buzz.

"I'm handing you back to Neil," Zoe said.

"Ed… Report here tomorrow, 13.00 hours," he said."

***

Grover set out for Bristol after lunching with Berger. The Adjutant said an official recommendation would have to wait until the fuss had died down. But he would personally like to thank the Lieutenant for the way he had handled all that was thrown at him.

At Filton, Turnbull welcomed him back. Presented him with the end of month work summaries, and projections for the months to come. Grover sat down and read them. He actually enjoyed doing so.

He phoned Fincher Reade and Holborne again. Got Mel this time.

"I was told earlier today that I was a luminary," he said.

"Are you busy tonight?"

"I'm planning on being with somebody special, actually".

"Do I know this person?"

"Come around tonight and we'll get down to exploring exactly how well."

"Oh yes, Lieutenant. See you at 7.30."

Driving home from Filton he found roads crossing the A38 blocked by uniformed police officers. He parked *Salome* and made his way to a barrier in Stokes Croft. The Westcountry branch of the *Society Against Capital Punishment* was on the march down Gloucester Road. Hundreds of people blowing horns, banging drums, and carrying banners which read *Life For A Life? NO* and *Hanging is State Murder*. A woman passed by him with a placard which read *Do You Know What It's Like Waiting To Die?*

She looked at him and shouted, "Well do you?"

And then she was gone. Swallowed up by the surge and the noise.

THE END

Printed in Great Britain
by Amazon